ACROSS STATE LINES

A CITY OF FOUNTAINS NOVEL

C.J. JOHNSON

PRESS

To all those who have lived through nightmares and those who helped get them through.

CHAPTER
ONE

THE SOUND of the tires rolling across the pavement echoed in Heather's ears. She twisted her body but couldn't loosen the duct tape binding her hands and feet. She took slow, deep breaths, trying not to panic as the trunk walls close in around her.

Heather felt the car begin to slow down and eventually stop. She could feel her heart pounding in her chest. She listened to the muffled voices but couldn't quite make out what they were saying. The doors of the car creaked open, then slammed shut. She waited.

After what seemed like forever, Heather heard the doors of the car open again. The car shuddered as the engine turned over and roared to a start. Laughter echoed from the backseat as tears rolled down Heather's cheeks.

Heather felt the seat back move against her head, then the center console lower. A rush of cool air forced its way into the hot, cramped trunk. Heather gulped the fresh air and fought the urge to scream.

"Drink this."

Heather saw a straw sticking out of a white Styrofoam cup. She hesitated, afraid of what might be inside. Tentatively she sipped the amber liquid, sighing with relief at the familiar taste of cola. The cup was moved abruptly from her mouth causing the liquid to dribble down her chin.

Heather pleaded when the console started to close, "Please! Leave it open. It's so hot back here."

She heard the men chuckling in the backseat, but the console was left down.

"Where are you taking me?"

Heather lay there listening to the sounds of the radio, waiting for an answer to her question. She twisted her hands to loosen the tape, but her efforts were futile. If anything, the binds felt tighter.

"Let me out of here. Why are you doing this? Where are we going? Just let me go." Heather continued to ask questions, barely stopping long enough to take a breath.

Once again Heather felt the car slow. When it came to a stop, the radio went silent. The chatter within the car came to a lull and the car door creaked open. Heather heard steps thump on the pavement then come to a stop at the back of the car. The latch holding the trunk closed was released. The trunk opened to bright sunlight shielded by the hulking man who had shoved her inside. They appeared to be on the side of the road, but Heather did not know where they were. Heather wriggled her body and tried to sit up.

"Please let me out of here. I won't tell anyone if you just let me go."

Corey looked at her and laughed a deep, sinister laugh. "You aren't going anywhere." He grabbed a pillowcase from the trunk. He pulled Heather into a sitting position and started to put it over her head.

"Please don't! I promise, I'll be quiet! Please don't cover my head. I won't be able to breathe!"

Corey looked at Tubby and said, "Does your dad still have that fishing boat?"

Tubby started to shake his head no, then saw the look in Corey's eyes and said, "Yeah. He said I can use it any time I want."

"We should take this girl for a boat ride. Maybe at sunset? I hear girls like that," Corey chuckled. He looked back at Heather and said, "It will be the last sunset you see before I throw your dead body into the water."

Corey put the pillowcase over Heather's head and grabbed the duct tape. She continued to plead until he removed the fabric but took a strip of tape and covered her mouth. He hesitated before shoving her back into the trunk, dropping the roll of duct tape next to her body.

Heather twisted her body and moved her head from side to side, trying to get the tape off her mouth. But the more she twisted the more the tape pulled against her hair. She finally stopped moving and lay quietly wondering why someone she thought was her friend would do something like this to her.

CHAPTER
TWO

HEATHER DIDN'T KNOW how long they drove before the car once again came to a stop. Her eyes were sore from crying, and her chest hurt from the strain of trying to breathe inside the cramped space.

The car doors opened, and Heather could hear the muffled sounds of someone talking, but she couldn't make out what they were saying. Sweat trickled from her damp hair down her face and into her red eyes. Heather blinked, trying to clear her vision. Blood oozed from the wound on her cheek and mixed with the salt of her tears. Heather's body ached from being cramped inside the trunk. The fear of her fate echoed in her mind.

Corey knocked on the door and after a few moments the doorway filled with a dark, imposing figure.

"Hey Big Bruce."

"What do you want?"

"We need to stash a girl here while we use her car. Can we put her in your basement?"

Bruce looked through the doorway to the car. Not seeing anyone inside, he said, "Boy, quit messin' with me."

Bruce turned his back to Corey and let the door slam closed behind him.

Corey returned to the car and unlocked the trunk. The lid popped open, causing Heather to jump in surprise. Corey stood over her body with William and a man she only knew as Tubby.

Corey grabbed her by the shoulders, looked at Tubby, and said, "Get her feet."

The pair carried Heather to the back door of the small block house. She twisted her head and tried to catch a glimpse of the rundown neighborhood as William opened the back door. He stepped aside to give Corey and Tubby room to carry Heather into the kitchen.

Corey was moving towards the basement stairs when a man's voice boomed, "What the hell's going on in here?"

"Big Bruce, I told you we needed a place to hold this girl."

"What's wrong with you, boy. Don't take her down there," Bruce barked. "Go sit her on the couch."

Corey and Tubby carried Heather into the sparsely furnished living room and dropped her as directed. Heather suddenly wished the tape was off her mouth, so she did not have to breathe through her nose. The smell of rotting food and days-old garbage made her gag with each breath. Heather surveyed the room, and a motion out of the corner of her eye caused her to turn just as cockroaches scurried up the wall.

Big Bruce followed the men into the living room. He stood in front of Heather and looked down, towering over her with question in his eyes. She jerked her head backward in fear as he reached down with his bearlike hand and grabbed the tape's edge, then ripped it from her mouth. Heather gulped the air hungrily and then began to cough. She opened her mouth to speak, but the look in Corey's eyes caused her to stop.

Bruce walked into the kitchen, with William close behind. Tubby retrieved a brown vial from his pants pocket and poured a fine white powder onto a mirror lying on the coffee table. Using a razor, he divided the powder into lines. Tubby made a straw out of a twenty-dollar bill, placed it near the powder and inhaled. Corey took the makeshift straw and snorted the rest. Heather looked on in silence.

Snapping his head to the side, Corey said, "Damn man, that's good stuff. You aren't cooking with that shit, are you?"

"Naw, man, this is my personal stash."

Corey nodded then stood up to leave the room. Tubby's eyes bore through Heather. With her hands and feet still bound, she scooted her body as far back against the couch as she could. Sensing her fear, Tubby stood up and started to move towards her, a smirk forming on his mouth.

"Corey and William got theirs, now it's time for me to get mines."

Softly Heather asked, "What about Audrey? Won't she be mad?"

"Bitch don't own me. I do what I want. I'm my own man." Heather cowered as Tubby made his way to stand in front of her. He exposed himself, grabbed her hair, and said, "Suck it bitch."

She clenched her lips tightly.

Tubby twisted her hair and jerked, "Maybe you didn't hear what I said. I said, suck it."

Tears trickled down Heather's red cheeks as she complied with Tubby's orders. When he was finished, he shoved her back onto the couch, zipped his pants, and left the room.

CHAPTER
THREE

BIG BRUCE LED the men back into the living room and asked, "How long are you going to be gone?"

"A few hours. I got some business to handle," Corey answered.

"Why can't you take her with you?"

Corey looked at Heather, "I need the space in the trunk. Besides, she ain't going nowhere. Accept maybe the morgue. She won't be no problem for you."

Heather flinched as Tubby ran the side of his hand across her jaw and said, "I'm sure she'll take care of whatever needs you have. Won't you?"

Bruce hesitated before saying, "Leave her."

"Give me your phone number," Corey demanded.

Bruce looked from Heather to Corey, "741-1925."

"Okay. We'll call you when we're done. Don't let her out of your sight."

Bruce waited until the men left to ask Heather her name.

"Heather. Heather Whitaker."

"Where are you from?"

"South Kansas City. Grandview, actually."

"How'd you get mixed up with them boys?"

"Tubby's girlfriend, Audrey. She's my roommate at the women's shelter." Heather paused before quietly adding, "I thought Audrey was my friend."

Bruce gently placed his hand on Heather's knee. She instinctively jerked her knee away in fear. Realizing what she must have thought, Bruce lifted his hand and said, "I'm not going to do anything to you. You have got to be about my baby girl's age."

Heather didn't respond but her stomach began to rumble.

"Are you hungry?"

She nodded.

"Do you like chicken nuggets?"

Heather nodded.

"Alright. I'll go fix you some." Bruce clicked the power onto the television and went into the kitchen.

Heather could hear Bruce talking to someone, but the television masked what he said. She moved her body, trying to ease the pain in her wrists and shoulders. When Bruce finally returned with a plate of food, she softly asked, "Can you please undo my hands?"

Tears returned to Heather's eyes and her stomach sank with defeat when Bruce turned and left the room. She sat and stared at the food, silently wondering if he expected her to eat like a dog with her hands bound behind her back.

A few moments later, Bruce returned with a knife in his hand. Heather shrank into the sofa, jumping when a bug crawled across her leg.

"Can you stand up?"

She looked up with hesitation, then nodded her head slightly. She scooted towards the edge of the sofa, put her bound feet on the floor, and used her hands to push herself up. Bruce pulled her hands away from her body and sliced the tape.

"Oh my gosh, thank you!" Heather rubbed her shoulder and rolled her neck. "My arms were starting to go numb. Can I cut the tape on my feet too?"

Bruce paused, unsure if giving this woman a knife was a good idea.

Sensing his reluctance, Heather said, "I promise I won't do anything or try to go anywhere. I just want to undo the tape."

Bruce said, "Sit down."

Just as Heather thought he was going to leave her feet bound together, Bruce knelt and cut the tape.

Once her hands and feet were free, Heather hungrily ate the chicken pieces that had been laid before her. When she was almost finished, she asked, "Can I please have something to drink?"

Bruce went to the kitchen and returned with a glass of water. Sitting it on the table, he asked, "Where do you live?"

Heather took a long drink of water then said, "I've been staying at the women's shelter by the highway. I've only been there for a few weeks. I couldn't stay in my apartment anymore."

"Why not?"

"Bobby-that's my ex-boyfriend-he tried to kill me a few weeks ago, so the cops thought I'd be safer in a shelter. My caseworker said they'd help me transition into my own place again, but I need to find a job first. Do you know of anywhere I could work? I'm reliable. I have a car. Shoot, they're going to bring me my car back, right? I mean, I have to have the car. It's not even my car. It's my grandma's. She's going to be so mad if I don't get it back. Do you think they'll bring it back?"

Bruce tried to keep up with all of Heather's ramblings without answering her. He had no idea what these boys were capable of.

WHEN HEATHER finally stopped her barrage of questions to take a breath, Bruce said, "I thought they would be back with your car by now. Let me see if I can get them on the phone."

Bruce picked up the phone then realized Corey never gave him *his* number. They hadn't called him, and Bruce knew he was going to have to do something.

The sunlight coming through the window was starting to fade when he looked at Heather and said, "I can't keep you here. My lady friend will be coming by tonight and if she sees you here, there'll be a heap of trouble."

Tears welled in Heather's eyes. She blinked to keep them from falling down her cheeks. She was afraid to voice her thoughts but to herself she wondered, "*Is he going to kill me?*"

"Where do you want me to take you?" Bruce asked.

"Can you take me back to the shelter? I'm not sure where I am, so I don't think I can walk there. Or can you at least take me by it? I can walk some of the ways."

Bruce nodded and then asked, "Where's the shelter?"

Heather thought for a minute before saying, "I'm not supposed to tell anyone the address. Can you take me by Prospect? I can show you where to drop me off."

Heather noticed the tape Tubby had taken off her mouth lying on the couch. When Bruce looked away, she carefully grasped it in her hand. With a barely perceptible nod, Bruce led Heather to the back door.

Heather directed Bruce to the neighborhood near the shelter. Before they could see the gate that enclosed the property, she told him to let her out of the car, "I'll walk from here."

"Are you going to call the cops?"

Heather shook her head as she surreptitiously moved the tape that had been on her mouth from her hand to the back pocket of her pants.

Before she got out of the car Heather turned to Bruce and said, "Thank you, Big Bruce."

Bruce nodded.

Heather stepped out of the car and closed the door softly behind her. Tears streamed down her cheeks, but Heather held her head high as she walked away.

Once Bruce pulled away Heather walked to a bus stop a couple blocks from the shelter and sat on the bench to contemplate her options. She could go back to the shelter but wasn't sure she'd be safe there. Her roommate was how she met the men who kidnapped her. She could call the cops, but Corey said he'd kill her if she did. And she believed him.

Heather sat at the bus stop shelter until the sky started to turn gray and the first stars began to dot the sky. When she saw the drug dealers taking their positions on the corner, Heather started to get scared and walked back to the shelter.

CHAPTER
FIVE

NIGHT LAY like a heavy blanket on the City of Fountains. The police cars parked on either side of the road reflected the glow of the street-lamps and lights from the buildings surrounding them. Detective Francesca "Frankie" Thomas stood looking out her fourth-floor office window, not seeing the scene below. She couldn't shake the thoughts racing through her head. Or the images. The sound of the telephone ringing jolted Frankie from her thoughts, but she didn't turn away from the window, knowing her partner would answer.

"Sex Crimes, Detective Boden."

Frankie waited while Mia listened to the person on the phone.

"Okay. Where is she now?" Silence. "Do we know where this happened?"

Frankie turned and walked back to her desk.

"Okay. One of us will meet you at the hospital," Mia hung up the phone.

"Well?"

"Kidnap. Rape. Assault. Two jurisdictions. The other agency is en route and will meet us at County Hospital. Here I thought we were going to leave on time tonight."

"Is there a scene or anything?"

"No. Sounds like there were a couple of houses and a car, but the officer doesn't know the location of the houses, and the suspects still have her car. They have put a BOLO out for the car."

"Why don't you go on home. I'll get a preliminary statement, and we can follow up on the locations tomorrow."

"Are you sure?" Mia asked.

"Yeah. The kids are with Sophie, so I'm in no hurry to get home. You should go be with Erik. Besides, I'm on call anyway."

Mia smiled, "Okay. I'll gladly go spend some time with the hubs."

The detectives continued talking as they walked down the four flights of stairs to the garage exit and then said their good-byes.

"Thanks again, Frankie. Call me if you need any help."

Frankie smiled, knowing Mia was being genuine and would come back to work if she called. "I will. See you tomorrow!"

During the ten-minute drive to County Hospital, Frankie let her thoughts return to what she had seen earlier that evening. She and Mia had been at the county jail interviewing Tessa Kemp about her connection to another case. Frankie and Mia were responsible for the investigation that originally brought Tessa into custody a few months prior. Tessa and another woman, Hannah Reitzell, reported a physical assault and a rape during a lawsuit they had filed against their employer. Frankie and Mia discovered Tessa wasn't a victim but had collaborated with her friend Geoffrey Finnegan to facilitate the attack to increase the value of a civil settlement. Tessa and Finnegan were both in jail awaiting trial.

During an unrelated rape investigation, Frankie and Mia stumbled upon two dead women in a hotel, both of which had a rose tattoo on the inside of their wrists. The same tattoo Tessa had on her wrist. The same tattoo as another woman found in the trunk of a car in the West Bottoms over a year before. The Intelligence Unit and FBI had been called in to work the case, and since Frankie and Mia were familiar with Tessa, they were asked to talk to her and see if they could make a connection. Tessa had identified the dead women but had clammed up as soon as they asked about the tattoo.

When they left the jail to return to police headquarters, Frankie and Mia passed by the county courthouse. Frankie glanced over at the near-empty parking lot and watched the man she was dating, Derek Kensington, leaving in his car with a woman in the passenger seat. She couldn't be certain but thought it was his co-counsel, Jessica Moon. The woman he had been sleeping with and had told Frankie he would stop seeing.

Frankie wasn't sure what she should say or do with this information. She and Derek had a long history of being casual, but she had recently told him she wanted more. Derek had agreed to end his affair with Moon, which gave Frankie hope they would be taking things to the next level. Now it seemed like he might not have ended the affair after all.

As she pulled into the parking garage at the hospital, Frankie shook her head and said, "Get it together."

CHAPTER
SIX

FRANKIE WALKED through the doors of the hospital emergency department with the confidence of someone who had been there many times and knew exactly where to go. She nodded at the security guard and told the admissions desk she was going to the forensic examination room. She navigated the hallways and found the room designated for collecting evidence in what was often referred to as a rape kit.

Frankie knocked lightly, then opened the door. She was baffled by what she saw. The tiny room was full of people. The examination table was flanked by a police officer from Kansas City, Missouri, an officer and detective from the Wyandotte County Sheriff's office, and Alex, a victim advocate from the local rape crisis center. All were towering over the young girl seated on the examination table.

Frankie surveyed the young woman who looked to be about nineteen or twenty years old. Gray duct tape circled the pant legs of her torn blue jeans, and streaks of blood covered her white t-shirt. More duct tape cuffed the wrists of her hands which were clasped tightly in her lap. Frankie tried not to stare at the purple and black bruises forming around both her eyes or at the gash that dissected the left side of her face.

"Looks like I'm the last one to arrive," Frankie said, trying to make light of the overwhelming number of people in the room. Looking towards the young woman, she said, "I'm Detective Thomas. And you are?"

"Heather Whitaker."

Looking towards the uniformed officers, Frankie asked, "Do you guys have what you need to write your incident reports?"

Both officers nodded.

"Okay, why don't you leave Detective…" Frankie looked at the other detective with a look of question.

"Steel" was the gruff response.

"…Detective Steel and I to talk to Ms. Whitaker."

The officers quickly left the room.

"Now that's better. Would you mind if we sit down?"

"Sure."

Frankie pulled up a chair for Detective Steel and a stool for herself. Alex sat in the chair on the opposite side of the examination table. The tension in the room lessened slightly.

"Can you tell us what happened that made you come to the hospital tonight?" Frankie asked.

"I was…um…raped."

Frankie waited to see if Heather would elaborate. When it became clear she was not going to say anything additional, Frankie asked, "Can you tell us more about that?"

Heather took a deep breath, then exhaled. When she finally began to speak, the words came out quickly in clipped sentences with very little inflection.

"I was at this party with my friend Audrey, and she told me she wanted me to meet this guy she knew. We left and picked him up and then went back to the party. We picked up Audrey's boyfriend Tubby and when I think they somewhere together. Actually, there were two guys besides Tubby at the party. I wasn't really interested in William, even though he was pretty nice to me. There weren't many people at the party, but me and Corey, that was the guy that I picked up, we went out to my car. That's where he raped me the first time. I left after that and drove over to a friend's house.

"When I came back to the apartment, they put me in the trunk of my car and drove me around. Well, first they put duct tape on me and then they drove me around. I thought they were going to kill me. They finally took me to Big Bruce's house. That's what they called him, Big Bruce. Oh, and Corey raped me at the house when I got there this morning. At Bruce's house, Tubby made me give him head. Eventually, they left and took my car. Are you going to get my car back? I really need my car. Bruce took me to the shelter. He didn't take me all the way to the shelter, they have rules against that. He just took me to the bus stop. I finally went back to the shelter, and they brought me to the hospital."

Heather continued to share what happened to her with Frankie and Detective Steel. Her sentences were in rapid staccato. The storyline was anything but straight and made very little sense. Frankie looked at Detective Steel and saw disbelief written all over his face. She hoped Heather did not notice. When Heather paused, Frankie waited.

When she was sure Heather wasn't going to say anything additional, Frankie asked, "Detective Steel, can we talk out in the hallway?"

Steel followed Frankie into the hallway and said, "That girl is full of shit. There is no way things went down the way she said. She was all over the freaking place."

Frankie nodded in understanding and then said, "I hear what you're saying. Her story is far-fetched, but I can't get past the fact that she has duct tape on her ankles and wrists and has two black eyes. *Something* happened to her. Mind if I ask her a few more questions before we leave?"

"Go for it," disdain dripped from Steel's mouth.

CHAPTER
SEVEN

FRANKIE UNDERSTOOD the disorganization in Heather's statements could be a result of the trauma she experienced, but the combination of trauma and the impulsive behavior she described could also indicate something more.

"Heather has anyone ever told you they thought you might have a mental illness?"

"When I was in high school, they told me I had attention deficit disorder. But I didn't like the way the medicine made me feel so I wouldn't take it. My aunt, she's a psychologist, she told me she thinks I have bipolar disorder."

Frankie nodded, alarms sounding in her head. While on patrol she had been trained as a crisis intervention team member which involved an education on mental illness.

"Do you take any medication to treat the symptoms of bipolar?"

Heather shook her head.

"Do you take any medications at all?"

"Just birth control."

"Okay, can I ask you a few questions about what happened? We can get a full statement later, but I need to clarify a couple things now."

Heather nodded.

"Who is Audrey?"

"She is my roommate at the shelter. Or she was. I don't think I can be her roommate anymore. I've only been there for a couple weeks. I moved there after my boyfriend…anyway, I was moping around, and Audrey asked if I'd drive her to a party over in Kansas. She said there'd be cute guys there. She told me if I took her to get her boyfriend and drove them to the party, they'd give me money for gas."

"Where was the party?"

"I know it was in Kansas, but I'm not sure what the exact address is. I can ask Audrey, but I don't really want to talk to her. I mean, she didn't try to stop them or anything." Heather started to choke up, "I thought she was my friend."

"Which shelter are you staying at?"

"The one near the highway. It's a shelter for battered women."

Rose Brooks Frankie thought to herself. The shelter was in her sector when she was on patrol. Being one of the few female officers that worked nights, Frankie provided an escort to the facility many times.

"Okay. You said you were taken to Big Bruce's house. Do you know his address?"

Heather shook her head.

"Do you think you'd be able to show us where it happened?"

Heather thought for a moment before saying, "Maybe, but nothing really happened there. Well, except Tubby making me give him head. But that's it."

Frankie nodded, satisfied there were no identified crime scenes to process that night.

"One more question. Did you give the officers the license plate number for your car?"

Heather nodded.

"Okay, good. Can you come to my office tomorrow afternoon so we can get a full statement about what happened?"

"I don't know how I'll get there. I mean, they still have my car."

Frankie wanted to slap herself on the forehead at her faux pas. Instead, she said, "I can come to the shelter, and we can do it there."

"They don't let people just come to the shelter. They said we can't have visitors there and I can't give you the address."

"It's okay, I know how to get there. I can get your statement there if they have a quiet room. When we finish, we can drive around and find Big Bruce's house. Would that be okay?"

"What time would you be coming? I have classes I *have* to go to in the morning, so I might not be there. Then I have to meet with my case-worker to talk about getting a job. I have a lot of things going on right now. I don't know if I have time for all that."

"It would be after I start my shift. I could be to the shelter about 3:30."

Nodding her head, Heather said, "Okay. I should be done by then. I will tell them you are coming."

Frankie gave Heather her business card and then asked, "Can I take a couple of photographs of your injuries for my case file?"

"Yeah, I guess so."

Grabbing the camera from her bag, Frankie took several photographs of Heather and her visible injuries. If, no - when - she caught the men that hurt Heather, the prosecutor would have photographs of the injuries at their fingertips.

While she was taking the photographs, Heather continued to talk. The details she shared were in no particular order. Frankie was relieved she was recording it so she could re-listen before writing her report. She was finishing up with the photographs when she noticed something on Heather's forearm.

"Heather, can you hold your hands out like this?" Frankie asked, demonstrating what she wanted Heather to do by holding her hands straight out in front of her, showing the tops of her forearms and top of her hands.

Heather did as she was asked. Frankie captured a photograph.

"Can you flip them over now?" Frankie asked, demonstrating again what she wanted.

Heather complied, showing the thing that caught Frankie's eye. Frankie captured another photograph.

Heather asked, "How am I going to get home tonight? I don't think the bus is still running."

Frankie looked at the young girl and said, "The hospital will give you a cab voucher, but you have to go straight to the shelter. Okay?"

Heather nodded.

Frankie noticed Detective Steel did not give Heather his card or a number to call his office.

When they were in the hallway Steel looked at Frankie and said, "I won't be working this case. I'm leaving tonight to take care of my dad for the next few months. Give me your card, and I'll have the detective who gets assigned to this shit-show call you."

"I'm sorry to hear about your dad." Frankie handed him her business card, "I'm going to record her formal statement tomorrow. Have the case detective give me a call, and I'll burn off a copy for them. Or, if they get the case assigned tomorrow, they are welcome to join me."

"I'll pass the word."

Somehow Frankie doubted Steel would do any such thing.

CHAPTER
EIGHT

FRANKIE SAT in the police car, contemplating her next move with Derek. She thought he had been sincere when he said he ended things with Jessica, but if he had ended it with *her*, then who was the woman she saw in his car?

Frankie pulled out of the parking garage and started the drive back to police headquarters. "Maybe I'll know what to do when I get there," she said aloud.

The route was short and took her past the county courthouse. Frankie slowed down as she drove by the parking lot, seeing only one car left behind. A candy apple red Ford Mustang with vanity plates that read "Moonpie." Wherever Derek was, Jessica Moon was with him.

Frankie parked the police car and slowly walked to her old, red Jeep Wrangler. As if on cue, her phone jingled with an incoming text message.

"Are You still working?"

Frankie smiled despite herself. How did he always know? Instead of texting, she hit "send" on her phone. Her call was answered on the first ring.

"Why are you still up?"

Jim Craven was an FBI agent Frankie and Mia met while working on a rape case involving an organized crime syndicate. Jim and Frankie became friends during the investigation and since its resolution their friendship had grown.

"I got a late call to the hospital for a new case. More to the point, what are *you* still doing up?"

"After we left you and Mia, Fitz and I got called in on a wire. We are finally calling it. Do you want to grab a beer?"

Frankie hesitated and then said, "Yeah, I do. Kelly's in Westport?"

"I think that might be the only place still open. See you in 10?"

"Sounds good."

Frankie climbed into her Jeep. She navigated the empty streets with the skill of someone who had spent the better part of a decade working them. Frankie tried to clear her mind with loud music, pulling into the parking lot across from Kelly's Pub just as Jim was getting out of his SUV.

Jim spotted Frankie slipping out of the Jeep and called out. The faintest hint of his southern accent came through with the sound of her name.

"What's the good word?" Frankie asked as the pair walked to the bar for a beer.

"Usual?" Jim asked, looking down on Frankie's petite frame.

"Yep. I'll grab us a table."

To the bartender, Jim said, "Two Bud Light bottles."

Dropping the frosty bottle in front of Frankie, Jim asked, "What kind of case did you catch? I'm surprised Mia isn't with you."

"Cross-jurisdictional kidnap and rape. We got the call at the end of the shift and since I'm on call, I told her to go on home. We didn't have a scene, so it wasn't a big deal. I'm meeting the victim tomorrow to get a formal statement, then we'll try to track down the scenes after. I was going to call you. Guess what she had on her forearm?"

"A rose tattoo?"

Frankie nodded as she took a long drink of her beer.

"Do you think it's related to the other cases or just a coincidence?" asked Jim.

"Possibly, but I'm not a huge believer in coincidences. Did you and Fitz get any more information on the dead girls from the hotel?"

Taking a swig of his beer, Jim shook his head. "We were hoping to get something off the wire, but it came up cold tonight. Did Tessa give you anything?"

"Not really. She knew the girls, but when we brought up the tattoo, she said she didn't want to talk anymore. It was bizarre. She knows something but is either too scared to talk or too angry at me."

"If she wouldn't talk to you, you can be damn sure she won't talk to me. I think she might be the only female who's immune to my southern charm." Jim drew out the words southern and charm, letting his North Carolina drawl come out.

Frankie laughed and said, "You might be right about that."

"I almost didn't message you. I figured you'd be at the counselor's house since the kids are with Sophie."

Frankie began peeling at the label on the cold, wet bottle. With the label off the beer, she drained the bottle then returned it to the sticky high-top table.

"Not tonight."

Jim opened his mouth to say something, but sensing Frankie didn't want to talk about it, he shut it and fidgeted with his own bottle. After a moment, he asked, "Want another?"

"I'll get this round," Frankie said as she slipped off the stool.

CHAPTER
NINE

FRANKIE AWOKE to her cell phone beeping with an incoming text message. Looking at the message, she yelled at the screen, "Screw you!"

Her golden retriever, Isabelle, looked up from where she was lying as if to ask, *"What's wrong?"*

Rubbing the top of Isabelle's head, Frankie said, "Sorry Izzie. I didn't mean to startle you." She looked at the clock beside the bed and asked, "Do you want to go for a run?"

Isabelle jumped off the bed and started prancing around the room. Frankie got dressed, laced up her sneakers, and grabbed the leash. With an earbud in one ear, blasting Daughtry and others like him, Frankie took off to run in her neighborhood. Her pace started slow, but eventually her steps fell in time to the beat of the music. Forty-five minutes later she was filling Isabelle's bowls and getting ready for work.

Frankie was about to step into the shower when her phone beeped with another incoming text message. Realizing she had never answered Derek, she picked the phone up to see what the latest message said. But the message wasn't from him. It was from Craven.

"Emergency trip back home. Will call or text when I can."

Frankie quickly messaged back, *"Are you okay? What happened?"*

"Granddad is in the hospital. Probably a stroke. I'm okay."

"Call if you need anything – travel safe."

"Thx."

While Frankie showered, she realized she forgot to ask Jim if he was flying or driving, although she suspected he was driving. Jim grew up in a small fishing village on the coast of North Carolina, and all his family still lived there. Frankie and her two children had vacationed there for years but did not ever recall seeing Jim even though Frankie later learned they had been frequent visitors of his mother's bookstore.

Thirty minutes later, Frankie was dressed and on her way into work. The day shift told her Heather had called the office three times. She wanted to know if they had found her car, if they had arrested the men that attacked her, and if Frankie was ever coming into work.

Frankie sighed. She had specifically told Heather she would not be at work until 3pm. This girl was going to be a handful. Frankie hoped she would have a few minutes to get settled before Heather called again. She also hoped Mia would be willing to go with her to the shelter.

CHAPTER
TEN

FRANKIE THANKED the social worker that led her and Mia to a private room at the domestic violence shelter. No one from the Wyandotte County Sheriff's Department had called or emailed Frankie about the case. Frankie made a note to try to call and find out who the case had been assigned to so they could collaborate on the investigation.

Heather was sitting at a small table, fidgeting with the cross on her necklace. Shortly after they were seated, Alex, the victim advocate who had been at the hospital, was escorted into the room. Once she was seated, and pleasantries were exchanged, Frankie pulled out a digital recorder and laid it on the table.

Hitting record on the device, Frankie said, "Heather, can you tell us, *in detail*, what happened to you?"

Heather moved around in her chair, looked from Frankie to Mia, then back to Frankie before asking, "What did the kit show?"

Frankie sighed. It was a common question. Television made it look like evidence could be processed and results obtained in minutes. The reality was the lab didn't even have the kit and may not for a few more days. And once they had the kit, it could be months before they had the results of the analysis.

Frankie patiently said, "It will be a while before we have anything back from the lab. To be honest, it may be several months."

"What? Why?" Heather asked, exasperated.

"The lab has a lot of evidence to process. Yours will be a priority, but it will still take a while. It will help if you tell us exactly what happened. Then we can tell the lab exactly what to look for."

A slightly mollified Heather said, "Okay. I just moved here a few weeks ago, and they put me in a room with this girl named Audrey. I thought we were friends, but after what happened, I'm not sure."

"Is Audrey still staying here?"

"Yeah, but she's gone right now. Her baby had a doctor's appointment or something."

"Okay. Go on."

"Audrey said she wanted to go to a party, but she doesn't have a car. Her boyfriend, Tubby's car isn't running so she asked me if I'd take her to pick him up at his place and then I could go to the party too. Audrey told me they'd give me money for gas, but they never did."

"Where was the baby?"

"I think her mom took him, but I don't know for sure. We left here at 6 o'clock. It was early but we wanted to grab some food. She said her boyfriend would pay for it.

"After we picked him up and got food, we went to a house party over in Kansas. I told Audrey I really wanted to hook up with a guy. She must have told her boyfriend because he gave me the phone number for this guy Corey. We started talking on the phone and he said he'd like to meet up. Corey wanted me to pick him up at his house, but I told him I didn't have enough gas. He said he'd give me gas money if I promised to drive him back home later that night.

"I didn't want to go by myself, so Audrey and her boyfriend rode with me to pick up Corey. This other guy William decided he wanted to ride along too. We went back to Missouri to pick him up and then drove back to the party. I asked him about gas money, but he said he'd put gas in my car when I took him back home.

"When we got back to the house, Corey and I decided to stay in the car. We talked for a while then started making out. I was cool with it at first. We started to have sex and everything was okay until he got weird. He wanted to do some stuff I didn't want to do, so I told him to stop."

Heather's voice caught, "But he wouldn't stop and did what he wanted anyway."

"Do you know what Tubby's real name is?" Frankie asked.

"No. Everyone just called him Tubby which was a stupid nickname. He wasn't fat or anything."

"What happened next?"

"Corey got out, and I locked the doors and started my car. He got mad and started yelling at me, saying I better not leave. When I put the car in drive, he started hitting the car and making threats. I left and went to a friend's house. Dude really scared me.

"While I was at my friend's house, Corey started texting and calling me. He was threatening me and saying he was going to kill me. Tubby and Audrey started texting me too. They kept asking me to come back to the party and pick them up. They said they didn't have any way to get home. I wouldn't answer Corey, but yesterday morning Audrey called me. She said she needed me to pick her up. Her baby was sick and she needed to take him to the doctor. I told her I wasn't coming back because Corey scared me, and I didn't want to see him again. I believed him when he told me he'd kill me.

"Audrey called back a couple of times, and the last time she was crying. I asked if the guys were there, and she told me they had all left. She said she was there by herself. Audrey acted like she was really upset. She told me her baby was really sick and she needed to get him to the doctor. I ended up giving in and went back to the apartment.

"When I got there, I stayed in the car and called Audrey. She didn't answer her phone and I thought maybe she couldn't hear it, so I went up to the apartment door. I knocked on the door, but Audrey didn't answer. Corey answered the door and before I could say or do anything, he hit me. Like, in the face. With his fist. He hit me like I was a dude. I got really dizzy and fell. When I tried to stand up, he hit me again. Corey grabbed me by the hair and drug me into a room and threw me onto the bed. I could hear Tubby and Audrey talking to someone in the living room, but I don't know for sure who it was. Then I heard them leave. Corey raped me again and said if I was lucky, he wouldn't kill me.

"When he was finished, he left me lying there on the bed. I was crying and my whole body hurt. I was so scared. William came into the room next. I think he might have been who Audrey was talking to earlier, but I'm not sure. He tried to be nice, but I was still freaked out. He told me if I gave him head, he'd keep Corey from killing me."

The cadence in her voice was flat, but tears streamed down Heather's rosy cheeks as she shared the details of her assault. She laid her arms on the table and began clenching and twisting her hands. Frankie caught a glimpse of the tattoo and jotted a note onto her notepad, reminding her to ask about it.

"I did what William wanted me to do and when he was finished, Corey came back in and told William we were leaving. Corey held me by the hair and made me walk out to the car. Audrey and Tubby had come back to the apartment by then.

"When we got to the car Corey opened the trunk and told me to get in. I told him no. I wasn't going to get in there, but then he got this look…his eyes…they were cold and mean. He shoved me into the trunk. I kicked and did everything I could to keep him from getting me inside, but he was stronger than me. He punched me again. Hard. Then he grabbed the tape and taped my hands and feet. He pushed me down in the trunk and closed the lid."

CHAPTER
ELEVEN

FRANKIE WATCHED Heather shift and pull at her clothing as she calmly talked about her attack. Frankie nodded in acknowledgment as Heather described being in the trunk of her car and then Corey's threats to murder her and dump her body into the Missouri river.

Mia was taking notes, and when Heather stopped to take a drink of water, she pushed the notepad towards Frankie. Nodding, she asked, "Do you think you could show us where he stopped and threatened you?"

"Maybe. I'm not really familiar with the city, but I might be able to show you. I don't think it was very far from Big Bruce's house."

"Did you have a cell phone?"

"Yeah. They took it from me when they shoved me into the trunk and never gave it back."

Frankie felt a small smile lift the corners of her mouth. Finally, a break. Not only could they find the locations where they took Heather, but if the phone was still on, they might be able to find the suspects.

"Heather, can you excuse us for a second? I need to make a phone call to a friend who might be able to help us get your car back."

"Really? Like, seriously? Can I use the restroom while you make your call?"

Frankie nodded.

"Shit."

"What's up?" Mia asked.

"Craven's on his way to North Carolina." Frankie grabbed her phone and found Fitz in her contacts and pressed the call button. "But maybe Fitz will help."

Her call was answered on the first ring, "Hey Frankie, what's up?"

"Hey Fitz, do you think you could use some of your fancy equipment and try to find a phone?"

"Hmm. Maybe. Who does the phone belong to?"

"One of my victims. The suspects have her phone and her car. We were hoping to go up on it and find them."

"Do you know if the phone is still on?"

"No. I'll see if she can do a pre-text with them. Maybe they'll answer, and we can figure out where they are."

"Give me about ten minutes, then text me her phone number. I'll see what I can do."

"Thanks Fitz."

Frankie and Mia returned to the interview room just as Heather and Alex were taking their seats.

"Heather, I need to see if you'd be willing to try something that might help us find your phone."

"Okay. Yeah, whatever you need."

"I'd like you to try and call them."

"What? Call them? Like, actually talk to them. I don't know if I can do it. Corey scares me. What if he finds out where I am? He can hurt me. He knows people. He said he'd have me killed."

"We can spoof our number and record the conversation. We will be here the entire time. He won't be able to find you from this phone call. We might get lucky and get some admissions out of one of them. We also might be able to triangulate their location. The phone might not even be on, but it's the one play we have right now."

Heather hesitated before saying, "Okay. I'll do it."

Frankie grabbed the equipment and sent Fitz the information he needed. While waiting to hear back from Fitz, she explained the process to Heather.

"The earpiece is going to plug into this digital recorder. You will put the earpiece in your ear and hold the phone to that same ear. I'll hit record as soon as you push call."

"Won't the phone show up as a police department number?"

"No. We have the phone set to display a random number. It will dial this phone back if he doesn't answer but tries to call. If he tries to call back after I turn the phone off, it will come up as a disconnected phone."

"What do I say to him?"

"Ask if he still has your car. Ask why he had to rape you if all he wanted was your car. Ask why he had to duct tape your hands and feet then shove you in the trunk. Ask anything that will get him to admit to his wrongdoing."

"Okay."

Before Heather could ask any more questions, Frankie received a text message from Fitz saying they were ready.

"Are you ready Heather?"

Heather took a deep breath, exhaled, and then said, "Yes."

CHAPTER
TWELVE

HEATHER ENTERED her number into the phone and waited. She stared at the face of the phone for a moment before she hit "send." One ring was followed by a second, then a third. She was about to disconnect the call when a female voice said, "Hello?"

Surprised to hear a woman's voice answering her phone, Heather wasn't sure what to say.

Frankie mouthed, "Say something."

Heather said, "Hello? Who is this?"

"You called me. Who are *you*?"

"Is Corey there?"

"Who is Corey?"

"The dude that took my phone. The phone you have."

"Look, bitch, I don't know no Corey. My dude gave me this phone this morning."

Heather started to say something in response and realized the woman had hung up.

Frankie turned off the recorder and called Fitz.

"Were you able to get a location?"

"Barely. Looks like the address is 6923 Wabash. When are you and Mia going to roll out? Want some help?"

"Give us an hour to wrap things up. I'd like to drive her to the area to see if she can identify the house she was taken to. Can I call you when we are ready to go over there? We're already in the area."

"I'll start heading towards Metro Patrol. Meet me there when you are done."

Frankie affirmed then disconnected the call. She looked at her notepad, turned to Heather and asked, "Can I see your wrist?"

Mia and Alex both looked at Frankie with question in their eyes. Heather stretched out her arms and laid her palms on the tabletop.

"Would you turn them over, please?"

Heather flipped her arms over, palms facing upward. Mia nodded in understanding.

"Heather, when did you get that tattoo?"

Rubbing the rose on her wrist, Heather said, "It's been a while. Like a year or two."

"What made you get this particular tattoo?"

Heather looked down at her clenched hands. Pursing her lips, she said, "I don't want to talk about it."

Frankie thought better than to push the issue. She'd come back to it later. After she'd done some research on Heather. Instead, she asked, "Are you ready to drive around and try to identify Big Bruce's house?"

Heather nodded.

Mia said, "I'll go make space for you guys and bring the car to the door."

"Thanks, Mia."

Frankie waited in the lobby with Alex while Heather went to her room to retrieve her purse.

"What's up with the tattoo?" Alex asked.

"We have three dead women with the same tattoo and at least two others from cases I've worked. She probably worked with the women at the Shady Lady. If so, she may be able to help us – or she may be in danger. I'll press it after I've done a little more research."

"Damn, poor kid can't catch a break. Do you think you'll be able to find these guys?"

"I don't know, but we are sure going to try. It'll be extremely helpful if she can identify the house. Maybe Big Bruce will be a good guy and turn over the creeps that did this to her."

Alex started to say something then stopped when Heather walked into the lobby.

"I'm ready."

Frankie held the door for both women. At the car she said, "Heather, why don't you sit upfront. Alex and I will sit in the back."

"Okay."

Once they were all in the car, she said, "We are going to drive to the area where your phone is. If you recognize any houses or if you recognize where they stopped and threatened to kill you, I want you to point it out. If you see any of the men involved, I want you to point them out but do not get out of the car or do anything that will draw attention to us."

Heather nodded in understanding.

Mia drove out of the shelter gate and headed towards Wabash. The drive was brief with the only sounds in the car coming from the police radio. Mia turned off Gregory Boulevard onto Wabash and drove north. The car had barely made it through the intersection of 70th Street when Heather leaned forward in the seat and yelled, "Slow down! That's it! That's Big Bruce's house!"

Frankie noted Heather was pointing to 6923 Wabash.

CHAPTER
THIRTEEN

MIA DROVE the car past the house without stopping.

"Wait! Why aren't you stopping? My phone is in there. Go back!"

Frankie acknowledged Heather's frustration and explained, "We cannot stop with you and Alex in the car. We will take you back to the shelter, and then Mia and I will come back and try to get your phone."

"But what if she leaves? What if she takes my phone? What if Corey and Tubby are inside?"

"Then we'll find her and your phone. If they are there, we will arrest Corey and Tubby." Frankie paused for a moment and then added, "And Heather?"

"What?"

"You *cannot* come back here, and you *cannot* call her or Corey or Tubby. Do you understand?"

With a huff, Heather said, "Yes."

Mia turned the car towards the direction of the shelter. Operating on a hunch, she didn't immediately turn onto the main road. Frankie started to say something but stopped when she saw Mia give her a look in the rearview mirror. Frankie nodded, soon recognizing where they were going.

Silence fell over the car as it began to slow. Heather scooted forward in her seat and began moving her head from side to side, scanning the area. Where the streets had once been lined with houses, there were now trees. They drove down a hill and to their right was a plot of dirt with old, run-down mobile homes with no skirting to hide the axles. The homes did not look inhabitable, but cars parked on the dirt indicated people were living there. Dogs were chained to trees outside, and trash blew across the grassless yards. Frankie recognized the area officers in the district called "Little Arkansas."

Mia was preparing to turn and leave the area when Heather asked, "Can you go back? Past those trailers."

Mia nodded and slowly drove past the make-shift trailer park.

"Can we stop here for a minute?" Heather asked.

Mia slowed the car when they got to the wooded area, eventually bringing the car to a stop. Heather removed her seatbelt and opened the car door. Frankie jumped out of the back of the car with Mia and Alex close behind. They trailed Heather as she wandered up one side of the road and back down the other. She stopped and scanned the area, looking into the woods on both sides of the road then returned to the back of the police car. Heather closed her eyes and listened to the banging of the chain against a metal pool.

"I think this is one of the places where he stopped the car. He parked on this side of the road." She pointed towards the police car, "Not far from where your car is but facing the other way."

"How certain are you that this is where they stopped?" Frankie asked.

"Positive. I remember hearing a chain hitting a piece of metal when we drove away. When we drove by the trailers just now, I heard the same noise and I saw a big dog chained to a metal pole. That was the chain I heard. It was only a few seconds after he pulled away when I heard that sound."

Frankie shook her head in amazement. Mia's hunch and the sound of a chain got them another location. She hoped cellphone tower records would further corroborate Heather's statement.

The four women got back into the car and drove back to the shelter and when they pulled up to the front door, Heather asked, "Are you going to bring me my phone?"

"We will try Heather. I know it's not easy, but please be patient," Frankie paused then said, "And trust us. What kind of phone is it?"

"It's a silver iPhone. It has a pink case with Hello Kitty on it."

"Are there any other marks on it? Or anything that would identify it as yours if they took the case off?"

Heather did not immediately answer. Finally, she said, "There's a photograph of me on it. It's from this one night when my ex-boyfriend beat me up. He took a photo of me lying on the bed. I was naked and covered in blood. He said it was so I would remember what he did to me. As if…"

"I'm sorry he did that, Heather. We'll try to get your phone back for you."

Heather nodded and walked inside the shelter.

Outside Alex asked, "What's next?"

"We'll go do a knock and talk at that house. If we get lucky, we will identify Big Bruce and the rest of the clowns."

"What about her phone?"

"We'll recover it and then call the prosecutor. It will be up to them if we can release it after we process it."

CHAPTER
FOURTEEN

"HEY MAC! Are you and Payne working tonight?"

"We are," Mac responded.

Frankie was relieved her former patrol partner was working. "Mia, Fitz, and I want to go do a knock and talk. Can you join us?"

"Heck yeah. Where do you want to meet?" Mac asked.

"Put yourselves out at Metro Patrol. We'll meet you there."

Fifteen minutes later, Frankie and Mia were standing in the parking lot of the patrol station making small talk with Fitz.

"Jim's grandfather is in the hospital. Possible stroke," Frankie said.

"Man, that sucks. I hope he is okay," Fitz said. "Jim's super close with his granddad. He lived next door when Jim was growing up. Have you heard from him since he left?"

"No. He said he'd let me know when he gets back."

Mia started to say something but was interrupted by Mac's booming voice, "Frank-ee!"

Mac reached out to shake Frankie's hand then pulled her into a hug. They embraced with the comfort of siblings and the affection of people who had been to hell and back together. For the next five minutes, the group exchanged pleasantries about their families. After the niceties were complete, Frankie began to brief everyone on the case.

"Last night, I was called to County on a rape/kidnap that started in

Kansas and ended here. The offenders stole the victim's car and her cellphone. Earlier today we attempted a pre-text phone call and a woman answered. She said 'her dude' gave the phone to her. Fitz triangulated the phone to 6923 Wabash. When we drove by the house, the victim identified it as the house where she was taken. An oral assault occurred inside the house. The victim said Big Bruce lived at the address and took her back to the shelter because his lady friend was coming by and there would be 'trouble' if the victim was there. By all counts, it sounds like he helped the victim and did not assault her. I ran the address on the computer, and it comes back to a man by the name of Bruce Dolphus. We assume the woman who answered the phone is the lady friend he told the victim about. We don't have a warrant, so let's try a soft approach and hope he's there and cooperates."

"Did the victim mention any dogs or weapons?" Payne asked.

"No to both. She said he made her food and eventually dropped her at a bus stop by Rose Brooks. He didn't have the victim's cellphone when he dropped her off and since the woman who answered the phone was at his house, we can assume he has had contact with the men that kidnapped her."

While they were briefing, Frankie, Mia, and Fitz pulled on their bulletproof vests. The word "police" was imprinted on the front and back of the vest in all capital, reflective letters.

The drive to Big Bruce's house was less than five minutes from Metro Patrol Station. They parked in front of the house next to Bruce's and began a tactical approach, moving towards the front door through the yard at an angle. Mia and Payne walked to the rear of the house with Fitz while Frankie and Mac went to the front door.

Once everyone was in place, Frankie knocked on the front door. Before anyone could answer the sound of gunshots filled the air. Frankie and Mac carefully scanned the area while seeking cover behind a giant oak tree in the front yard.

"The shots are close. Where do you think they're coming from?" Frankie asked. Keying up the portable radio on her belt, she said, "*1061 to dispatch. Hold the air. Shots fired in the area of 69th and Wabash. 1064, 242, and 1712 are out with me.*"

"*Holding the air.*"

Mia keyed up the radio, "*1064 to 1061. The shots are coming from Olive. We're starting...*"

The sound of more gunshots erupted before Frankie could respond. Frankie and Mac began running towards the sound.

"*1061 to 1064. We're...*"

Mia reached the back of the house facing Olive, one block west of where they started. The sound of shots echoed and were followed with a guttural scream and tires squealing. Mia and Payne rounded the corner of the house as an older model Chevy Capris turned towards the highway. Mia caught a partial plate.

"*1064 to dispatch. Older model Chevy Capris, dark in color, partial Missouri license Frank Frank 3, headed north on Olive from 6916 Olive. Occupied one time. Looks like he's armed with a semi-automatic rifle.*"

The dispatcher sounded on the radio, "*246.*"

"*64th and Prospect,*" answered the officers holding radio number 246.

"*Respond to the area. 1845 hours.*"

"*242. We're a couple of doors from that residence. We will be approaching on foot. 1061, 1064, and 1712 are with us. Continue holding the air.*"

Together they began to move with a determined, yet steady, gait. Suddenly a man could be seen standing on the porch of the house in question. Mac started shouting commands, "Show me your hands!"

THE MAN STAYED CROUCHED DOWN with his hands hidden.

"Show me your fucking hands!" Mac and Frankie shouted in unison.

The man looked up with a vacant stare but still didn't move. The sounds of sirens from the approaching ambulance filled the air.

"Let me see your hands!" The officers shouted, their fingers on the trigger ready to fire if needed.

Shaking his head as if hearing the group for the first time, he said, "I...I...I can't. I have to apply pressure. My brother. He's been shot."

Frankie exchanged a knowing look with Mac. She kept her weapon ready, but started to walk towards the porch, ready to adjust her position if the man pulled a weapon. Stepping onto the first step, Frankie could see a young man lying on the floor of the porch, his brother hunched over his body. The man had applied a belt to the man's uninjured leg. A chrome-colored weapon lay on the floor an arm's length from the man's reach.

Frankie lowered her weapon, nodded to the group to come forward, and then asked, "Where was your brother hit? Is anyone else here?"

"In the leg," the man pointed to the leg without the belt. "My niece and my sister are inside."

Frankie said, "You might try putting the belt just above the wound on the leg that was hit if you want to stop the bleeding. Mia, you and Fitz come with me to clear the house."

They pushed the front door open, and before the trio could make entry a child ran and grabbed Frankie around the waist. The child clung to Frankie with a death grip as tears streamed down her toffee-colored cheeks. Frankie moved aside to let Fitz and Mia finish clearing the house before they called for the ambulance to come in.

Frankie holstered her weapon and kept hold of the little girl. She scanned the room. Across from where they stood sat a leather chair with a blanket and baby doll on the cushion. Just above where Frankie assumed the child had been sitting was a bullet hole. Frankie squeezed the child a little tighter, softly reassuring her she was safe.

CHAPTER
SIXTEEN

"246 COPY A CAR CHECK. Gregory and 71 Highway. Black Chevy Capris Missouri License Frank Frank 3 4 Nora 7. Occupied one time. Continue to hold the air."

"246. Gregory and 71."

"240's out with them," Sergeant Seever added.

The officers gave the man slumped over the steering wheel orders, but he didn't move. They approached the car slowly, carefully ensuring no one else was inside. As Sergeant Seever approached the driver's side door, he continued to shout orders. Seeing the limp body against the steering wheel, he holstered his weapon and grabbed a pair of latex gloves from his back pocket. With gloved hands, he reached in and felt for the man's pulse. Feeling a slight heartbeat, he ordered, "Grab some crime scene tape."

Keying up the radio he said, *"240. We have a party down. He's breathing, but barely. Start us an ambulance and at least two cars for traffic. Get crime scene en route as well. You can clear the air for us."*

The dispatcher went to the business of ordering an ambulance and getting additional cars to the scene for traffic.

"240 to 1061 on private."

"Go ahead, Sarge."

"I think we have your shooter. He wrecked out at Gregory and 71 Hwy. Looks like your guy got off at least three rounds."

"Copy that. We'll let the Assault Squad know when they get here."

Mia yelled to Frankie, "The house is clear, but we have an injured female in the kitchen."

Frankie keyed up her portable radio, *"1061 clear the air. Send paramedics in and start us a second ambulance."*

"The air is clear, and a second ambulance is en route at 2014 hours."

Frankie loosened the little girl's grip from her waist, knelt, and asked, "What's your name, sweetie?"

Wide, golden eyes bore into Frankie's.

"It's okay, we're here to help you."

Frankie's question was met with furrowed brows and tear-filled eyes, "Where's my mommy?"

"The ambulance is going to come and help her. Can you tell me your name?"

"London. What's your name?"

"Frankie."

"That's a boy's name."

Frankie stifled a laugh and said, "It's short for Francesca."

"Ches-ka?" she asked with a puzzled look. "Frankie is a lot easier."

"I agree. How old are you?"

"I just had my birthday. I'm four," London said, holding up her right hand with four fingers raised. "Where's my daddy?"

"He's outside. The ambulance is going to help him too. Can you tell me what happened?"

"Daddy was on his phone. He was yelling and I didn't like it. Mommy told him to stop 'cause he was scaring me, but he didn't listen; he just kept yelling. Uncle Dom come over and they was being real loud. He told daddy, 'let 'em come over. I'll have something waiting for him when he gets here.' Mommy told me to go to my bedroom while she and daddy went out to the porch with Uncle Dom. Frankie, I didn't do what my momma said 'because they was still fighting and I was scared. I climbed into my daddy's chair and turned the TV up real loud so I wouldn't have to hear them yelling."

Frankie never let her gaze falter as she listened to London describe what happened.

"I heard my mommy scream and then there were lots of loud pops. Like firecrackers. She ran inside and told me to get down. I slid down in daddy's chair, but I was too scared to run. I heard more loud pops and then my mommy fell. She was hurt and kept screaming at me to go to my room. I think she went to the kitchen, but I was afraid to follow her. I heard a whistle over my head after the last pop, and then you came."

Frankie looked over the child's head at the hole in the chair, knowing what made the whistling sound, but grateful London didn't.

"I'm sorry you had to go through that London."

Before Frankie could say anything more, the paramedics pushed the door open.

"She's back here," Mia said.

Frankie waited until the paramedics examined London and the ambulance had taken her parents away before she asked, "Where's your jacket?"

"On the hook by the door."

"Let's put it on so we can go for a ride, okay?"

"Where are we going?"

"How about we go to the hospital with your mommy and daddy?"

"Can Teddy and Uncle Dom come too?"

"Teddy can come, but Uncle Dom might have to talk to some other detectives, okay?"

"Okay."

London stood on the stool next to her coat hook. Frankie watched as the tiny girl stood on her tiptoes and pulled the jacket from the hook. She took great pains in buttoning each button of the purple garment. When she was finished, she said, "I'm ready to go now."

Noticing a backpack on the hook where her coat had hung, Frankie asked, "Do you go to school?"

"Yes. I go to Miss Ebony's class."

"Cool. Let's put some things in your bag for while you are at the hospital."

Frankie helped London get a coloring book, crayons, and her teddy bear and put them inside her backpack.

"Miss Ebony won't like me putting this stuff in my pack back. It's s'posed to only be for my papers from my school."

Frankie smiled at the way London transposed the words back and pack. Her son Tyler used to do the same thing.

"I think it'll be okay this one time."

"She says we can't bring stuff from home to school 'cause it makes kids fight."

Frankie pulled a business card from her badge holder, wrote a note on the back, and handed it to London. "If Miss Ebony says anything tomorrow you can give her this card, okay? It's a special, one-time-only, take stuff from home in my school bag, kind of card."

London's eyes lit up, "Really?"

"Yep. If you show her this card, she'll say it's okay this one time. Okay?"

London nodded vigorously.

CHAPTER
SEVENTEEN

LONDON'S GRANDMOTHER arrived at the house just as Frankie was preparing to take her to the hospital. Once the grandmother and child were gone, Frankie let out a deep sigh.

Mia turned to her partner and asked, "Do you want to hear the rest of the story?"

Frankie laid her head against the outside wall of the house and asked, "Do I want to know what this was about? Did you see the bullet hole in the seat by where London was sitting?"

"Yeah, and yes you do. Apparently, London's dad and this other dude got into it on the phone. Based on the kitchen, I'm going to say it was over drugs. Crack and maybe some weed. Anyway, the fight escalated, and the guy said he was going to come over and light the place up. London's dad Jerome, and his brother Dominick, told him to bring it, they would be outside waiting. Sure enough, the guy comes over and Jerome was true to his word. He was waiting on the porch with Dominick with a handgun and a SKS. Dude gets out of the car and starts waving his gun around. They exchanged a few rounds and the guy got into his car and left. Jerome and Dom both said they didn't know if they hit the guy. They were both repeating it was self-defense. Dom said as soon as he realized his brother, he tossed the SKS to the side of the house."

Frankie shook her head and said, "Can you believe that dumbass with the tourniquet? I don't know what he thought he was doing putting the belt on the wrong leg."

At that both women started to laugh.

Frankie looked at her watch then at Mia, "Want to try to go to the house on Wabash again? Mac and Payne are going to be out here all night, but I bet we can get Fitz to go with us."

Mia looked at her watch. 8:40 PM. "Sure, we can try it."

Frankie waved Fitzmeyer over and he agreed to go with the two detectives. The trio walked back through the houses, following the path they had taken earlier. The street was quiet compared to the scene they left, with only the occasional bark of a dog or sound of a car nearby.

Frankie stood adjacent to the front door, took a deep breath, and then knocked. A few moments passed before she heard a throaty, "What? Who is it?"

"Kansas City Missouri Police Department."

"Just a minute." The sound of boots hitting the floor echoed from behind the closed door. The door was opened slightly, chain still clasped.

Frankie held up her badge and asked, "Are you Big Bruce?"

"Why do you want to know?"

"Sir, we have reason to believe you may have some information on a case we are working. Can you open the door, please?"

The door slammed in Frankie's face. She raised her hand to knock again but stopped mid-air when she heard the chain being undone.

"Come inside. I don't want no one seeing me talk to you."

CHAPTER
EIGHTEEN

FRANKIE WALKED through the front door, scanning the room for people and weapons as they entered.

"You can have a seat at the table," Bruce said.

"Thank you."

Fitz asked, "Is there anyone else here with you?"

"No. It's just me. My girl's at the store."

"Mind if Detective Boden and I look? We're just looking for people. Nothing else," Fitz said.

Bruce shrugged his shoulders and said, "Go ahead. You ain't going to find nothing."

After collecting Bruce's demographic data, Frankie grabbed the piece of paper she had forgotten was inside her pocket.

"Do you recognize this girl?

Bruce looked at the photo carefully. Under his breath he said, "That didn't take long."

Frankie's expression didn't falter as she waited for him to explain.

"Yeah. I recognize her. Is she okay?"

"How do you know her?"

Bruce stood up and started to pace. Frankie sat patiently and waited. After a few moments he returned to his seat and flopped down loudly.

"A couple days ago, I got a call from one of my son's associates. He said he was coming by and needed to leave something at my house while he took care of some business. I told him no because I was getting ready to go to work, but about ten minutes went by and there was a knock at my back door. I looked out my kitchen window and see Corey standing there. I opened the door and asked him what the hell he wanted. I didn't have time for him or his nonsense. He told me he needed to stash that girl in the picture down in my basement while he used her car. I looked out at the car but only saw William and one other boy with him. I told him to quit playing and went to get my lunch from the refrigerator. Next thing I know he and that other boy are lifting that girl out of the trunk and bringing her in through the back door."

"How exactly were they bringing her in?"

"They were carrying her. Cory had a hold of her at her shoulders and the other boy had her feet."

"Did you notice anything about the girl?"

"She looked scared. She had duct tape on her hands and legs. Another strip was across her mouth."

"What happened next?"

"I asked what in the hell they were doing, that's what happened next. They told me the same thing again, and I told them to put her in the living room."

"Did they do what you told them to do?"

Big Bruce nodded. "Those boys know I don't play. After they put her down, Corey came back into the kitchen with William. Corey was spouting off about how that girl had disrespected him. He was going to leave her here while he went and took care of some business. He handed me a cellphone and said he was going to call it when he was on his way back to get her. He said not to worry about her seeing our faces because she wasn't going to be able to do anything about it when he finished with her."

"What do you think Corey meant by that?"

"What do *you* think he meant, detective? From what I hear, Corey isn't someone you want to mess with, and he was pretty pissed off when they got here. But let's be clear, I didn't see him do anything to that girl."

"Do you know where the third guy was?"

"I think he was in the living room with the girl. Keeping an eye on her, I guess."

"About how long were they alone?"

Bruce shrugged his shoulders and said, "I don't know. Five minutes? Ten?"

"What happened next?"

"The boys left. I called off work because I wasn't about to leave her or them boys in my house by themselves. When they were gone, I went in to check on her."

When it was clear Bruce wasn't going to say anything additional, Frankie asked, "What did you see when you went in to check on the girl?"

"She was on the couch. Her arms and legs were still taped up, but the tape was off her mouth. I asked her if she was hungry and made her some food. I also cut the tape on her legs and hands so she could move around a little bit."

Fitz asked, "Why didn't you call the police?"

Bruce looked over at Fitz who had been quiet until that moment and said, "I didn't want to get in the middle of their beef. I figured they was together and had gotten into it over something stupid. I figured with some time, he'd cool off and bring her car back."

Frankie resisted the urge to call the man a dumbass. To herself, she thought, *"Apparently, it's okay to duct tape someone and put them in the trunk of a car if you are having a lover's spat."*

"After a while, it didn't seem like they were going to come back, and my lady friend was coming by. I wasn't about listening to her bitch at me for having a girl in my house, so I took her where she wanted to go."

"How did you end up with her cellphone?" Frankie asked.

"I told you, Corey gave me the phone and said he was going to call it." Bruce said.

"Did you see the boys come back?"

"Yeah, they finally came back to the house a few hours after I dropped that girl off at the bus stop."

Frankie waited to see if Bruce would elaborate. When he didn't, she asked, "What happened next?"

"Corey started running his mouth, so I told him to leave. I told you he had plans for that girl, and he was pissed that I quashed them."

"Did he tell you exactly what his plans were?"

Bruce paused before answering, but then said, "All he said was if they ever found her body, it would be in pieces down the river."

"How did your lady friend end up with her phone?"

Bruce chuckled. "She saw it lying on the kitchen counter and thought I bought it for her. It made her happy, so I didn't say nothing."

"Do you know any of the boys' names? Or how we can reach them?"

Bruce hesitated, "They are my son's associates, not mine. I know William because him and Little Bruce played basketball together. I've only seen Corey a time or two. The other boy – I ain't never seen him before."

"Can you call Little Bruce and see if he has William's number?"

"He's locked up, so I can't call him."

"Is he in the county or state," Fitz asked.

"County. They got him on a bullshit dope charge."

"They are always bullshit," Frankie thought. To Bruce she said, "What about William's last name?"

"I'm not sure if he has his momma's name or his daddy's. I only know his momma."

Frankie was getting tired of playing games with Bruce but patiently, she asked, "What's his momma's name?"

"Miss Laronda. Cole, I think."

Frankie handed Bruce her business card, "Give me a call if you think of anything else."

Bruce nodded. He was about to escort them to the door when his lady friend walked in with a bag of groceries.

"Who the hell are you?" she demanded.

"I'm Detective Thomas, and these are my colleagues Detectives Boden and Fitzmeyer," Frankie said. "We understand Bruce gave you a new phone yesterday."

"What about it," was her gruff reply.

"We think it may belong to a young woman named Heather. Can I please see the one Bruce gave you?"

The woman shot Bruce a look filled with anger, then retrieved the phone from her bag. It was a silver iPhone with a pink Hello Kitty case.

CHAPTER
NINETEEN

FRANKIE LEANED her head against the headrest, "What a night."

"No kidding," Mia said.

"I just want to go home and give my kids a hug. That little girl could have died tonight. I wonder if her parents realize just how close that bullet came to their daughter?"

"I doubt it. I don't think we were dealing with the brightest bulbs in the box. I mean, Frankie the dumbass uncle didn't even realize the tourniquet was on the wrong leg."

With that both women broke into a sleep-deprived, stress-relieving laughter. The pair laughed so hard they fought to catch their breath as tears filled their eyes. Laughter was the release they both needed to cope with a scene that could have ended so differently. Amid their laughter Frankie's phone rang.

"You've got to be kidding me," Frankie said. "Sex Crimes, Thomas."

"Hey Frankie, it's Fitz."

"Don't tell me you scared up another scene."

Laughing, Fitz said, "No. I was driving home, and it dawned on me that we never talked about the tattoo."

Frankie put her cell on speakerphone.

"Heather's tattoo matched the tattoo on the other women. When I asked her about it, she clammed up, so I thought I'd do some research before I bring it up again. I don't think the guys that kidnapped and raped her are connected to the homicide cases, but I'd bet money she is connected to the women. The tattoo and its location are too unique. At the very least, I bet she can help us figure out who else is involved."

"Let me know what you find out. Do you want to try to talk to Tessa again?"

Frankie looked at Mia and chuckled.

"She shut Mia and me down pretty quick the other day but I'm willing to try again. Maybe tomorrow?"

Mia nodded.

"Fitz, we'll try again tomorrow."

After Frankie and Mia said their good-byes in the parking lot, Frankie sat in her Jeep and stared at her cell phone. She pulled up Derek's contact and was about to hit the send button but stopped herself. She wouldn't, no, she couldn't, call him. Frankie put the Jeep in first and headed towards home.

The ten-minute drive went by quickly. Frankie pulled into her dark driveway and shut off the engine. She leaned her head against the headrest for a moment before grabbing her bag and jumping out. Frankie cursed herself for not leaving the outside light on.

"Hey Frankie."

Frankie almost jumped out of her skin at the voice echoing from the shadows of her front step. Her hand instinctively went to her holster. She had been jumpy since her neighbor Bruce was shot in front of her house while preventing her daughter from being kidnapped.

"Dammit Derek, you scared the hell out of me! What are you doing here?"

"I needed to see you."

"What if my kids would have been here?"

"It's Sophie's night to have them." Derek smiled slightly, "You see I do listen when you

talk. You wouldn't answer my calls..."

Frankie started to speak, then stopped.

"What's going on, Frankie? I thought we were in a good place, then you started giving me the cold shoulder."

"Where were you last night, Derek?"

CHAPTER
TWENTY

DEREK'S JAW STIFFENED.

"Home. Why?"

"I was driving by the courthouse early yesterday evening and I saw you leaving with a woman who looked a lot like Jessica Moon. Then when I drove back by after a late call, I saw Jessica's car was still in the parking lot. You told me you were going to stop seeing her."

Derek shifted his weight from one foot to the other, "I have."

Frankie looked past Derek to the street.

Derek reached out and touched her on the arm and felt her body stiffen.

"I did end things with her just like I told you I would, but yesterday was a bad day. Your buddy Fitzmeyer came to my office with an FBI Agent. Jim something."

"Craven," interrupted Frankie.

"Yeah. We were discussing a homicide case they are working."

"Three dead people in a trunk."

"Yes. How did you know that?"

"Mia and I found two dead girls in a hotel. We think it's connected to that case as well as to another rape case we are working."

"Yeah, well apparently the dead woman in the trunk had reported a rape that Jessica was assigned to review. She had not done anything with it and seeing the victim dead hit her pretty hard. She was shaken by the photos and was beating herself up, wondering if she could have done something to prevent the girl's murder."

"You mean, like her job?" Frankie interrupted.

Derek ignored Frankie's outburst and said, "I gave her a drink from the bottle I keep in my desk. One drink turned into several. I didn't want her to get behind the wheel of her car, so I drove her home. I made sure she was safe inside and then went to my house. If you would have returned at least one of my calls or text messages, I could have told you that."

Frankie thought about what Derek said. She wanted to believe him. He leaned forward and reached his hands out to her as he cocked his head to the side.

"Come here."

Frankie reluctantly extended her hands and let Derek take them into his. He bent forward and gently kissed each hand.

"I need you to believe me."

Frankie leaned in and let her forehead rest against his.

"I know. I want to."

Frankie pulled away from Derek's grasp and put her keys into the door. She looked over her shoulder and asked, "Want to come inside?"

Derek answered with a gentle kiss on her lips.

Frankie felt her defenses crumble as the electricity coursed through her veins, igniting the desire within. She pushed the door open and let her bag fall to the floor. Frankie dropped her keys on the side table, took Derek's hand, and led him to her bedroom.

With only the light from the streetlamps illuminating the room, Frankie ran her hands up Derek's t-shirt, feeling the strength in his chest, as his manhood pressed against her body.

Their clothes fell and crumpled on the floor by the bed. Derek explored Frankie's body with the deftness of someone who knew it well. She let the doubts leave her mind as she let her hands and mouth explore his fit body.

Satisfied, they lay spent in one another's arms. Derek traced a pattern on Frankie's back as she lay with her head on his chest. His fingers gradually stopped moving just as Frankie fell into a dreamless sleep.

CHAPTER
TWENTY-ONE

THE 1050 SQUAD was packing up to go home when Frankie walked into the office.

"Anything brewing today?"

"Nope. It's been…" began Sergeant Kramer.

"Don't say it!"

Frankie laughed with Kramer then went about getting things ready for the night. Fitzmeyer had texted her before work to say he would meet her at the county jail at 4:00 PM. It would only take ten minutes to walk to the jail but might take a little longer to get access to Tessa.

"Hey Frankie, you got in early," Mia said.

Frankie looked up, shocked to see thirty minutes had passed.

"I wanted to make sure we got approval to talk to Tessa before we walked down there."

"Any luck?"

"Tessa's attorney wants to speak with us before we talk to her client. She wants to make sure we aren't trying to implicate her in anything else."

"Did you print the photographs of all the women with the tattoo?"

"Not yet. Do you mind?"

"Sure."

Frankie and Mia set about their tasks in relative silence. Another half-hour passed when the phone rang.

"Sex Crimes, Detective Thomas."

"Got any sex?"

"Hey Killer," Frankie laughed at the news reporter, with the odd nickname, who called multiple times a day, "We don't have anything for you tonight."

"You think you'll have anything for me later?"

"I hope not."

"Okay, I'll check back in before you head home."

Frankie hung up the phone just to have her direct line ring. "Sex Crimes, Thomas."

"Detective Thomas. Kristine Sallow. I am the attorney representing Tessa Kemp."

"Hello. Thank you for getting back to me. Is Tessa willing to meet with us?"

"With a few conditions, yes."

"Okay. What are her conditions?"

"She wants complete immunity."

"To the charges she has pending against her?"

"That would be nice, but no. She hopes her cooperation will provide leniency in that case, but that's not what she is talking about. She has information that may implicate her in other illegal activities and wants assurances she will not face additional charges from the information she provides."

Frankie was silent. She wasn't sure she could get Tessa leniency in the case pending, but she could almost guarantee no additional charges if she had information that would help solve three murders.

"Let me call the prosecutor handling the cases and I'll call you back."

"Who's handling the homicides, Detective Thomas?"

"Derek Kensington."

"If I had known it was Derek, I would have called him directly," Kristine said.

Frankie couldn't help herself, "Why's that?"

"Derek and I go way back."

Frankie said, "I'll call you back in a few minutes."

Mia asked, "What are her conditions?"

Frankie answered Mia while dialing Derek's number.

"Prosecutor's office, Derek Kensington."

"Hey Derek."

"Hey babe, to what do I owe this pleasure?"

"Remember the cases with the rose tattoo?"

"Yeah."

Frankie gave Derek the breakdown of the phone call.

"Can you give her anything?"

Derek paused before saying, "What is she offering up?"

"I'm not sure yet. Possibly something on at least one of the homicides you have. Her attorney wasn't very specific beyond saying she may have been involved in some illegal activities."

"Who's her attorney?"

"Kristine Sallow."

"Really? She's good. I haven't talked to her in a few years, but if she says Tessa has something good, she probably does. Tell her as long as she cooperates, I'll give her what she wants. I can't help her on the pending case, though."

"Good. I'll let you know what, if anything, we get."

CHAPTER
TWENTY-TWO

FRANKIE AND MIA made small talk while they walked the two blocks to the county jail. They signed in, locked up their weapons, and were escorted to a private room within the locked-down facility.

After a few moments, they were met by Tessa and her attorney.

"You must be Detective Thomas," Kristine said.

"I am. This is Detective Boden. You mentioned Tessa may have some information for us. We are very interested in hearing what she has to say. I intend to record our conversation if that's okay."

Kristine and Tessa both nodded their consent to be recorded.

Frankie hit record on her digital media recorder and identified the case number and people in the room.

"Tessa, I have a couple of photographs with me. Can you tell me the names of the women in the photographs?"

Frankie laid two photographs in front of Tessa. Each had a number written on the bottom.

"That one is Nicki. This one is Andi."

"Tessa would you mind stating, for the recording, which number is on the bottom of the photograph?"

"Nicki has a number one. Andi has a number two."

"What's Nicki's full name, and how old is she?"

"Nicole Andrews," Tessa looked at her attorney.

"It's okay, you can answer."

"Nicki is 16."

Frankie and Mia didn't blink.

"What is Andi's full name, and how old is she?"

"Andrea Tucker. She is 22, I think."

"Can you please provide us any information you may have about these two women?"

Tessa pressed her lips together, looked around the room, and let her gaze stop on the window in the door. Mia started to speak, but before she could say anything, Tessa said, "Nicki was so sweet. We all knew she didn't fit in. We kept waiting for her to go back home so when she disappeared… I'm sure no one really thought anything of it.

"Andi, well, she was something else. She took Nicki under her wing and looked after her. Nicki reminded Andi of her little sister, so she kept an eye out and made sure no one took advantage of her. I'd heard Andi let Nicki move in with her, but I lost touch with the girls when…" Tessa's voice trailed off.

Frankie waited to see if Tessa was going to say anything before asking, "Was Nicki from Kansas City?"

Tessa touched the photo of the sixteen-year-old girl, lightly tracing the girl's heart-shaped face.

"No. She was from a small town in Iowa."

"How did she get to Kansas City?"

Again, Tessa looked at her attorney for guidance.

"This is where Tessa needs assurances that she won't get in any trouble for what she is about to tell you."

"As I mentioned before, Mr. Kensington cannot do anything about the charges Tessa is currently facing, but he's willing to give consideration to additional charges based on any information she has that can help solve these murders."

"Go ahead, Tessa," Kristine said.

Tessa took a deep breath then said, "I drove her here."

CHAPTER
TWENTY-THREE

FRANKIE DISGUISED A LOOK OF SURPRISE.

"You know that I used to dance at the Shady Lady. I did a few private parties, but that's not everything. I also organized private parties and secured the entertainment based on the clients' demands. Our clients had a variety of tastes, but most liked the talent to be young. Do you know who owns the Shady Lady detective?"

Frankie nodded. It was common knowledge the club was owned by the Marzullo crime family.

"Then you should know what I was up against. If you worked there, and fit a certain need, you didn't just leave. The owners like to keep certain women beholden to them. For some of the girls, it's drugs and for others...."

"Money?" Frankie interrupted.

"Yeah. I'd worked there for a while when the Boss made me a deal. I had gotten a little old for the clients' taste, but I still needed the money. He said he'd put me to work at the dealership if I'd help him recruit new, younger talent. I found Andi working as a cocktail waitress in a little bar north of the river. She was pretty, confident, and had an attitude. I knew she'd be good and wouldn't take a lot of shit.

"Nicki was a recruit. Andi, Kat, and I went on a road trip to look for some girls that would be open to relocation. We found Nicki in Iowa."

"How exactly did you identify the girls you wanted to target?" Mia asked.

"I know it sounds trite, but we'd mainly go to malls. We'd set up a table as a talent agency searching for models and dancers. Which was sort of true. We were in Iowa, and this girl with a baby face and freckles came up to our table. I knew immediately Nicki would be in high demand. She was pure apple pie and girl next door. She didn't have any adults with her and seemed, well, lost. We worked our magic and she left with us the next day. I never asked, but I kind of assumed she ran away. All she had was a backpack when she got to the hotel, and we never saw any adults. We weren't exactly checking ID's or getting waivers signed, you know?

"We introduced her to the work as easily as we could. Nicki stayed with me for a few weeks in a loft we kept downtown. I was able to get a photographer to do a photoshoot like we told her we would and…"

"Was Alexandre Kristof the photographer?" Mia interrupted.

"Yea. He helped us out whenever we had a young girl we were breaking in. Nicki thought we were going to help her get auditions with dance troupes, so we mocked up a couple of dance auditions and gave her some drugs, telling her they would help her loosen up and enhance her performance. Eventually, we eased her into dancing and then other… activities with Alexandre. When she seemed more comfortable, we had her do a few private parties. She did a good job and after a few weeks, I moved her into an apartment with a few of the other girls. Eventually, she stopped asking about modeling and dance gigs. She seemed to get along with everyone okay, but you could tell she didn't belong there."

"To clarify, by 'activities' with Alexandre do you mean sex?"

Tessa nodded.

"How did she end up living with Andi?" Frankie asked.

"I'm not real sure. I know they did a few parties together and I think Andi was worried because Nicki was so young and convinced her to move in with her."

"Tessa, do you know how they ended up in that hotel? And when?"

Kristine nodded at Tessa.

"A few months ago, Andi called me and said she thought she was being followed by a guy in a white truck. She sounded strung out, and I had a few problems of my own," Tessa shot Frankie and Mia a dirty look, "I blew her off. A few days later she called me again. Andi said she and Nicki were on their way to do a private party at one of those big old houses off Gladstone. While we were talking, I heard Nicki say something about a white truck being behind them. Last thing I heard was Andi scream and the phone went dead. At the time I thought she might be drunk or high, but now I think maybe she was just scared."

"What happened next?"

"I don't know. I never heard from her again."

"Did you call the police?" asked Mia.

"And tell them what? That I was talking to a friend who sounded strung out, was driving somewhere in Kansas City, screamed, and then her phone went dead? Somehow, I doubt they would have done anything." Tessa locked eyes with Frankie and added, "Plus, I wasn't exactly a huge fan of the police at that point."

Frankie didn't waiver, "Do you know the address of the party they were going to?"

"I think it was at Johnny DiCapoli's house, but I'm not sure. If it was at DiCapoli's, it was off the books. I didn't book it, and the Boss would never have sent them there."

"Why is that?" Frankie asked.

"Johnny worked for the Finnegan family."

"What would happen if Andi got caught working at a party for the Finnegan family?"

"If the Boss found out, she'd be dead."

TWENTY-FOUR

FRANKIE LET the information sit for a moment before asking, "Why would Andi take a job working for DiCapoli if he worked for the Finnegan family? I assume she knew the dangers of working for the competition."

Tessa stared at the blank wall behind Frankie.

After a moment, she said, "Andi liked Johnny. I think they had been seeing each other, but she never admitted as much. The last time we hung out, Andi told me she was seeing a guy from Northeast, and he had offered her a way out from under the Shady Lady. Andi wanted to take his offer, but she didn't want to leave Nicki behind. I think the party was going to be a way to make introductions so she could take Nicki with her."

"Do you have any idea what Johnny's plan was?"

"No. He has a few front businesses so maybe he was going to put her up in one of them. Or maybe he was going to move her into his house. Andi and I were friends, but not that close. She didn't completely trust that I wouldn't tell the Boss what she was up to, so she didn't tell me everything."

Frankie thought to herself, *Smart girl.* Out loud, she said, "You mentioned Nicki said something about a white truck. Do you know if the Boss or any of his crew drove a white truck?"

"No. They mostly drive high-end luxury cars."

"Did any of Andi's exes drive a white truck?"

"Not that I'm aware of."

"Did any of her exes have a history of stalking her?

Tessa shook her head.

"What about clients?" Mia asked.

Tessa shook her head, "I don't think so. Working off the books was discouraged. The Boss did not exactly forbid it, but if he caught you... well, there would be consequences."

"What kind of consequences?" Frankie asked.

"Some of our clients have, shall we say non-traditional sexual appetites. When someone gets caught working off the books, they will spend time on that list. It is self-correcting."

Frankie looked through her notes and then said, "Earlier you mentioned you all did private parties. I need to ask, did the private parties always include sex? And did any of these parties ever happen at hotels?"

Once again Tessa looked at Kristine, who nodded at her to answer.

"Some of the clients wanted sex, but that was extra. I think Andi had a few regulars, but I don't know about Nicki. Most of the private parties were at houses." Tessa's eyes bore into Frankie's, "If I booked any of the girls at a hotel, it was at the casino, not some cheap-ass dive, pay-by-the-hour dump. When I was handling things, I made sure my girls were all well-taken care of Detective Thomas."

"Who's taking care of the girls now that you are locked up?"

"When I got busy at the dealership, Kat took over. When she disappeared, I heard Andi was handling things. Now, I don't have a clue."

"What's the deal with the rose tattoo?"

Tessa began rubbing the tattoo on her wrist. A small smile began to form on her lips. After a few moments of silence, she said, "I guess you could say it was a badge of honor. You had to earn the rose."

"What do you mean?" Frankie asked.

"See this?" Tessa pointed at the thorny stem of the tattoo. "The Boss makes all the girls get this tattoo when they start working for him. It's his way of letting you, and everyone else, know you belong to him. You get the rosebud when you start doing private parties. It's a symbol of moving up in rank, so to speak."

For the first time, Frankie noticed the rosebud on Tessa's wrist had a delicate symbol the others did not have.

"What's the significance of the symbol on yours?" Frankie asked.

Tessa smirked and said, "Trust. I am one of the few the Boss trusts."

Frankie noticed Tessa used present, not past, tense. It sounded to Frankie like the Boss still trusted Tessa which meant she was probably only getting part of the story.

"Is there anything else you think might help us find who murdered your friends?"

Tessa gave the question some thought before shaking her head.

As they were preparing to leave, Mia asked, "Do you know a girl named Heather?"

"Name doesn't ring a bell."

With that, Frankie and Mia left the interview room.

Walking back to police headquarters, Mia said, "I wonder why the Boss didn't do anything to Tessa for working with the Finnegan family?"

Frankie, lost in her own thoughts, said, "Huh? Wait, what?"

"Her partner in the rape conspiracy was Geoffrey Finnegan. Why would it be okay for her to work with them, but not Andi?"

"There's definitely something she's not telling us."

"Something tells me there is a lot she's not telling us Frankie."

TWENTY-FIVE

"WHAT THE HELL did you do, Big Bruce?" Corey's face was contorted in anger.

"Watch your tone with me, boy. The cops came to *my* house. I didn't tell them anything they didn't already know."

"You shouldn't have taken her anywhere. I told you we was coming back. Now I got to find that bitch. She needs to be dealt with."

"Just what exactly are you planning to do to her?"

"You don't need to worry about what *I'm* going to do to *her*. You should be worried about what *I'm* going to do to *you*."

"Don't you threaten me, boy." Big Bruce stood, puffed his chest out and let his dark eyes bore through Corey.

Corey immediately changed his tone. Bruce was an imposing man with a reputation.

"Did the cops give that phone back to her?"

"I don't know. Probably. They took it from me."

Corey took out his phone and called Heather's number. The phone was answered on the second ring.

"Hello?"

"You still want your car back, bitch?"

"Who is this?"

"Answer my fucking question. Do you still want your car back?"

"Ye..es."

"Meet me at 55th Street and Prospect at the Church's Chicken at 7 and I'll let you have your car back."

"How am I supposed to get there?"

"That's not my fucking problem. Meet me tonight. If you don't show up, the car will be gone for good."

Heather exhaled when she heard the phone disconnect. She stared at the bare walls in her room and wondered what to do next. She wanted… no needed…her car back. It didn't really belong to her, and if she didn't get it back, she would be in trouble. Her grandmother…with thoughts of what would happen if her grandmother found out about the car, she pressed the numbers on her phone.

"Sex Crimes, Detective Thomas."

"I need your help."

"Okay," Frankie said then asked, "Who is this?"

"Heather. Corey wants to meet me at some chicken place to give me my car back. Will you take me to get it back?"

Frankie sat up in her seat and firmly said, "Heather, do not go and meet him."

"…but…I need my car," Heather interrupted.

"It's a set up. Did he give you the address for the meet?"

"It's by Prospect. Some chicken place. I think he said it was at 55th Street."

Recognizing the location Frankie said, "Good."

"Will you go with me to get my car?"

Frankie was relieved Heather could not see her eyes rolling. She took a deep breath and firmly said, "No, Heather. I mean, yes. We are going to get your car but no you cannot go. Do you understand he is not planning to give you the car? It's a trick to get you there. My guess is he wants to snatch you again. Or worse. We will set up surveillance and as soon as we see your car, we will stop him. What time does he want to meet?"

"7."

"Okay. I need you to stay at the shelter. I'm serious, Heather, this could be bad if you try to meet him on your own. Do you understand?"

"Yes, but…"

Frankie's voice raised, "No 'buts' Heather. You have to stay at the shelter."

Heather responded with a sullen, "Okay."

Frankie told Heather she would call her when it was over, and she could get her car. Once the call was disconnected, Mac.

"Hey Mac, are you and Payne working tonight?"

"Yeah, what's up?"

Frankie explained the situation and asked if they'd be willing to be the takedown crew while she and Mia did surveillance. Silently she hoped all three men would be in the car, but something told her that was wishful thinking.

Mia was listening and began gathering her vest and supply bag. When Frankie hung up the phone, she said, "Want some help?"

"I was about to ask you if you wanted to go get these guys."

"Heck yeah. What's the plan?"

"We are going to meet Mac and Payne at the car wash at 59th and Prospect in about thirty

minutes to watch for the car. If we see it, they will initiate a felony car stop. We will hang back until everyone is in custody. Of course, if the shit hits the fan…."

"We move in."

"Yep," Frankie replied as she gathered her keys and vest. "As satisfying as it would be to put handcuffs on these guys, I want to keep a little distance. It'll benefit us in the interview if we don't have to go hands-on."

"Agreed," Mia said.

CHAPTER
TWENTY-SIX

MIA AND FRANKIE slowly drove the streets around Prospect. There were many ways Corey could approach, and they wanted to get him before he got to the busy restaurant. At the last minute, she had called Fitz to join them. He was sitting in a parking lot across the street from the Church's Chicken in an unmarked, undercover car.

"What are the chances Corey will be the one driving," Mia wondered aloud.

"Slim to none. If I was a betting woman, I'd say he'll have one of the other guys driving. Probably William. Or he could send a cutout."

"You really think he plans to kill her?"

Frankie thought for a moment before responding, "Yeah. She can identify him and, my guess is, he's been to prison and doesn't want to go back."

"Check that car out," Mia said.

As soon as she said the words, a car matching the description of Heather's car drove past. Frankie waited, then pulled in behind the car. Checking the license plate number, she confirmed it *was* Heather's car then turned onto a side street.

"I'm surprised they didn't switch the tags out," Frankie said.

Mia picked up the radio mic and said, "1064 to 242 on private."

"Go ahead for 242."

"The target vehicle is heading north on Wabash. Looks to be occupied one time. He's going to turn east on 59th and should be coming right at you."

"Copy that. We'll initiate the car check as soon as he's on Prospect."

"We'll circle around and come in behind you."

"242 copy a car check. 59th and Prospect. Northbound. Silver Ford Taurus. Missouri license Adam Adam 3 7 George 1. Occupied one time. Hold the air."

"Holding the air for 242. 59 and Prospect."

Frankie and Mia pulled in behind Mac just as he began ordering the driver out of the car at gunpoint. Payne stood on the passenger side, gun drawn, carefully scanning the vehicle for other occupants or threats.

"Using your right hand, open the door from the outside. Step out of the vehicle facing away from my voice. Put your hands above your head."

The driver complied with the initial instructions. Frankie and Mia exited their vehicle but remained in the doorframe for cover, their hands on their holster just in case they needed to act.

"Step backward towards the sound of my voice."

Once the driver was a safe distance from the car, Mac ordered him to stop.

"Keep your hands above your head and get on your knees. Now, lay face down and put your hands straight out. Keep your hands where I can see them."

Fitz circled around behind Frankie and joined them at their car. Traffic on Prospect slowed down and passersby watched curiously at the scene playing out before them.

Once the driver complied with his instructions, Mac and Payne quickly moved towards him. Frankie, Mia, and Fitz moved forward to the patrol car and continued to scan the area for threats.

Mac put his knee onto the driver's shoulder while he put handcuffs on his wrists. Once he was secured, Mac began searching the driver, rolling him on his sides to check the front of his waistband for a weapon.

"242. You can clear the air. One in custody. Start us a wagon."

"219, I'm almost 10-23."

"Copy 242. The air is cleared. 219 I have you out with 242 at 1853 hours."

Frankie and Mia approached the car Payne was about to search.

"Hey, hold off on that for a minute. I think I'm going to have the Crime Scene Unit process it. The victim said she was held in the trunk for several hours. There's bound to be all kinds of evidence in this car."

"Do you want to have them come here or take it to the garage?"

Scanning the area, Frankie said, "Let's tow it. Then I can bring the victim to pick it up when we are done."

"242. Start a tow to this location."

"Copy 242. Tow en route."

Frankie glanced at the vehicle, then turned to Mac. "Did he have an ID?"

"Yep. William Kennedy. I was just about to run a check on him."

Frankie took the ID and said, "I'll do it. Go ahead and load him up. Tell the wagon driver I'll bring the May-I up when I get back to Headquarters."

Frankie slid into the driver's seat of Mac's patrol car. She entered William's information into the computer and within a few minutes she had a complete criminal history on William R. Kennedy.

"What's he got," Mia asked.

"Couple traffic violations and one pop for possession. Doesn't look like he has any violent criminal history. At least not as an adult. He only has one address listed. My guess is it's his momma's house. I'll have the Perpetrator Information Center pull his associates when we get back. Maybe we can get Tubby and Corey's information that way."

TWENTY-SEVEN

"WE CAN MEET you at the lot if you are ready to process the car now," Sierra said.

Frankie smiled to herself. Sierra Planck had been a crime scene technician as long as Frankie had been with the department. They had worked many scenes together over the years. She was smart, funny, and very easy to get along with.

"That sounds good. See you in twenty." Frankie turned to Mia, "Looks like we can process the car before we talk to William. I'll have somebody on 4 take the May-I up for us."

Frankie called Mac to tell him they would not be meeting him at Police Headquarters. The Investigative Arrest form, otherwise known as a May-I, would be waiting for them in the Domestic Violence Unit on the 4th Floor. All felony arrests required a completed May-I before the jail would let the officer book in the arrest.

Sierra arrived just as Frankie and Mia entered the gates of the tow lot. The wind had picked up, making them glad they had a garage bay out of the elements to process the car. Sierra jumped out of the van with a camera around her neck and a notepad in her hand.

"What do we have, ladies?"

Frankie explained the case facts to Sierra along with the evidence they hoped to find in the car. Once she had all the notes she needed for her report, Sierra began taking photographs. Mia started a photo log and Frankie began taking notes on the car.

After taking photographs of the exterior, they all donned gloves so they could look inside the car. Frankie started on the driver's side, looking underneath the seat first, then in the gap between the seats and emergency brake.

"What do you know?"

"What did you find?" Sierra and Mia asked in unison.

"Sierra, would you take a photograph of this for me?" Looking at Mia, she said, "He had a handgun next to his seat."

"What do you want to bet he wasn't planning to give her the car back?" Mia asked.

While Sierra photographed and recovered the gun, Frankie moved to the passenger side. A McDonald's bag was sitting on the seat with a couple of French fries lying next to it. Almost as an afterthought, she opened the bag.

"Yeah, I'd say that's a pretty good bet," Frankie said. "Sierra, when you are finished there, please photograph this."

Mia peeked in and said, "Are you freaking serious? When did you start getting a roll of duct tape with your combo meal at McDonald's?"

Frankie started laughing at the ridiculousness of the situation.

"I guess instead of a toy, you get a roll of duct tape. I hear it can fix anything."

Laughing with Frankie, Mia said, "Yeah, too bad it can't fix stupid."

Sierra joined in the laughter while she worked.

After they finished with the front of the car, Sierra prepared to open the trunk so she could capture photographs of the contents.

Frankie said, "Damn, I hope there's not a body in there."

Sierra paused and then asked, "Do you think that's a possibility?"

"Heck, anything is possible with this crew," Mia said.

Frankie hit the trunk button, and they all held their breath as it popped open. The laughter of relief as they realized there was nothing but a bunch of clothes inside subsided as the odor of stale urine hit their noses.

"Damn!" Mia exclaimed. "You didn't mention this."

"She didn't tell me she urinated in the trunk, but it doesn't surprise me. She was in there for a long time and was terrified. It would be embarrassing to admit, too. I'll ask her when I call just to make sure it wasn't one of the men trying to punish and humiliate her more."

"Can you imagine being stuck inside this trunk?" Sierra asked as she looked through the clothing. "With all these clothes? Especially if she urinated. She's lucky she didn't suffocate."

Sierra grabbed paper sacks from the van and began the methodical process of inventorying the contents of the trunk. Frankie and Mia took note of the remnants of duct tape among all the pieces of clothing.

"I hope they used their teeth to tear the tape," Frankie said.

"Do you need these clothes recovered as evidence or just the tape?" Sierra asked.

Frankie looked to Mia, "What do you think? I'm leaning towards photographing and releasing the clothes."

"We should confirm the item she said he tried to put over her head, but otherwise, I'm not sure what we can get from it. Especially if she is the one that urinated. She was wearing the clothing she was raped in when she went to the hospital, so we already have those. I don't see signs of anything else and she didn't say anything about them doing anything to her in the trunk."

"Agreed." Frankie looked to Sierra, "Why don't we inventory the clothes and put them in our car. I'll photograph everything at the unit. If we decide to recover anything, we'll do it there. Chain of custody should be good since we are all here."

"Sounds good, let's finish the inside of the car."

Sierra began examining the car for trace hairs and fibers, specifically on the driver's side of the car. The men could claim they had been in Heather's car with her consent, but she had been driving when she picked them up. Unless they admitted to driving her car, it would be hard to explain anything they found on the driver's side. Sierra collected hinge lifts of the seats and floorboard, documenting the location of each lift carefully.

"Did you see this, Frankie?" Mia asked.

"What?"

Mia was in the back, looking underneath the front seats.

"Sierra did you already capture photographs under the seats?"

"I did. What did you find?"

Mia removed an EBT card from the floorboard and held it up for Frankie and Sierra to see. "Looks like it belongs to Laronda Cole. Didn't Bruce say one of the boys' mommas was named Laronda?"

"Yeah, I think it was William's," Frankie said.

"Do you want me to dust the car for prints?" Sierra asked.

"Yes. They can argue anything we find, but the prints will help iden-tify their specific locations in the car."

Once she had finished processing for fingerprints, Sierra began collecting swabs of areas the men may have touched for possible touch DNA. Heather did not mention anyone wearing gloves, so the chance of finding DNA was pretty good.

With the last swab collected, Frankie looked at her watch, "Dang ladies, we have been at this for over 2 hours. I don't know about you, Mia but I think I'm ready to go talk to this guy. He's got some explaining to do."

TWENTY-EIGHT

FRANKIE CHECKED her phone when she got back to the car, hoping it wasn't too late to tell her kids good night. 9pm. Tyler's bedtime was 8:30, but if she hurried, he might still be awake.

"Hey Keith, is Ty still awake?"

"Of course, he is. He said he wasn't going to sleep until you called. Hold on a minute."

Frankie stared out the window into the darkness as she waited. It never got easier not being there to tuck her kids into bed at night. Her shift rotated every twenty-eight days, making a routine very challenging. She was lucky her neighbor and best friend Keith was willing and able to help. When he wasn't available, her parents and sister pitched in. She couldn't do her job without their help and support.

"Hey mom! Catch any bad guys today?"

"As a matter of fact, we did. I'm heading to HQ now to talk to him. How was your day at school?"

"It was okay."

"What was your favorite part of the day?"

"Recess. Tommy and I played a new game." Tyler regaled Frankie with the rules of the game he and his friend invented. She smiled at his never-ending imagination.

When he had finished, Frankie said, "Sounds like a fun game, Ty but you need to get some sleep now."

"I know. Will you come and tuck me in when you get home?"

"You know it. I love you, buddy."

"I love you too, mom. And good job today."

"Thanks, Ty. Is Dani awake?"

"Yeah, here she is."

Frankie could hear Tyler telling his sister she was on the phone. Softly she said, "Night buddy."

"Hey mom."

"Hi Angel-girl, how was your day?" Frankie often called her teenage daughter the nickname she had given her as an infant.

"It was okay. School is so boring. Are you going to be home soon?"

"You'll be asleep when I get home. Mia and I are getting ready to do an interview."

"Okay. Are you taking us to school tomorrow?"

"That's the plan. Do you have any homework?"

"I'm doing it now."

"Okay. I love you, Dani."

"Love you too, mom. See you in the morning." Dani disconnected the phone before handing it back to Keith.

Frankie sent a quick text, *"Doing an interview. May be late."*

"Okay. Bruce is working. Going to sleep on the sofa."

Keith was such a good sport when Frankie had to work late. He rarely, if ever, complained. Keith's partner, Bruce, spent almost as much time with the kids as Keith. Frankie felt very fortunate to have them nearby and willing to help.

Frankie said, "You ready to get a confession from this guy?"

Laughing, Mia answered, "Hell yeah."

"If you'll take my bag and start the recording, I'll go grab him from the jail."

"Sounds good, Frankie."

CHAPTER
TWENTY-NINE

"WHO ARE YOU HERE FOR FRANKIE?" asked Claire, one of the detention facility officers assigned to the jail.

"William Kennedy. Mac brought him in a few hours ago."

"Yeah, he's been asking when a detective was going to come to talk to him. The May-I said he's being held for kidnapping?"

"Yep. He and two other men stuffed a woman in the trunk of her car and drove her from an apartment in Wyandotte County to a house here. I'm hoping he'll give up his buddies. The vic said this guy was pretty decent, but the other two were not. We may be looking at adding conspiracy to his charges once they are identified."

"I hope he gives you what you need."

Before Frankie could respond, the man she watched get taken into custody on Prospect was standing before her.

"Mr. Kennedy?"

He grunted a response.

"I'm Detective Thomas. My partner, Detective Boden and I would like to speak to you for a few moments if that's okay."

Looking down on her slight frame he grunted another response.

Frankie guided William onto the elevator.

"What's this about, man?" William grunted.

"I'll explain everything when we get into the interview room."

The ride to the fourth-floor interview room was brief. Mia was waiting with a bottle of water and notepad in hand.

"Please have a seat in that chair," Frankie said, pointing at the chair farthest from the door and most visible by the camera.

Reluctantly William sat in the chair with a thud.

Frankie spent the next half hour asking William questions unrelated to his arrest. Frankie and Mia worked to build rapport with William so he would relax and let his guard down.

"What's your mother's name?" Frankie asked.

"Laronda Cole."

Frankie and Mia shared a knowing look and continued to ask general demographic questions. When William began joking with them, Frankie knew it was time to switch to business. She pulled a photograph of Heather from the file folder.

"Do you recognize the woman in this photograph?"

William did not immediately answer. He picked up the photograph and stared at it, paying close attention to the purple bruises lining Heather's eyes. Frankie opened her mouth to ask him again but stopped when William dropped the photograph face down onto the table.

"Yeah, I recognize her."

Handing him an ink pen Frankie said, "Can you please sign the photograph? It's just to acknowledge that you recognize her."

William scribbled his signature on the front of the photograph then returned it face down.

"Where do you recognize her from?"

Once again, William hesitated, seemingly giving careful thought to his response.

"She was at a party I went to the other night."

"Do you know her name?" Mia asked.

"I didn't concern myself with that white girl's name," William answered.

"Where was the party?" Frankie asked.

"Over in Kansas. At my friend's apartment."

"Do you know the address?" Frankie asked.

"Naw. I just know it's off Parallel."

"What is the name of the complex?"

"I don't know. That was my first time being there."

"What's your friend's name?"

"Regina."

Frankie waited to see if he would volunteer a last name. When it became clear he wasn't going to give her one she asked, "Last name?"

William shrugged his shoulders.

Frankie continued asking questions about the apartment and Regina, hoping to get something usable from him. Satisfied she had gotten all she could, Frankie switched her line of questioning.

CHAPTER
THIRTY

"TELL me about the night you met the girl from the photo."

"What about it?" William asked.

"Was she there when you got there? Did you talk to her at the party? Anything you remember."

William leaned on the table and looked from Frankie to Mia then back to Frankie. Resigning himself he sat back, crossed his arms and said, "I didn't do anything to that girl."

Frankie waited. She wanted to ask what he didn't do but knew if she sat quietly, he would want to fill the silence.

"They got there after me. That girl carried Tubby and his girlfriend over in her car. She told Audrey she wanted to hook up with a guy, so we called this dude from the neighborhood. They talked on the phone, and she said she'd go get him and bring him back to the party. It was still early, so we all climbed in her car and rode over there."

"What was the dude's name?"

"Corey."

"What's his last name?"

"Simpson."

Frankie glanced over to see Mia writing the name on her notepad.

"What happened next?"

"We got Corey and brought him back to the apartment. We hung out for a while, then they went to her car. I don't know what happened between them two, but he came back, and she left. I figured she got what she wanted and decided to leave. It kind of made us angry though because she was supposed to bring us back to the city the next day. That was our agreement."

Knowing the answer, Frankie asked, "Did she come back?"

"Eventually. Corey was mad as hell. He really needed to get back the next day. He had some stuff to do and when she bailed like that, it put him in a bad spot."

"Why did she come back?"

William chuckled softly and a smirk lifted the corner of his mouth.

"Man, Corey was blowing up her phone. Bitch said she wasn't coming back, but he kept calling. About midnight she stopped answering the phone. Corey started yelling at Audrey and anyone else who would listen. Finally, Audrey started calling her. That girl didn't answer at first, but I guess she got sick of the phone ringing. About the time the sun came up she answered. They conversated for a minute and the girl came back and picked us up."

Frankie noticed William did not say why Corey needed to get back to the city.

"What did Audrey say to her to make her come back?"

"I don't know precisely what she said, but Audrey put on the waterworks."

"Did Heather know Corey was still there?"

"Who?"

"The girl from the photograph."

"Oh, I think Audrey may have told her that Corey, Tubby and me were gone and that her kid needed to go to the doctor."

"What happened when the girl got back to the apartment?"

William's account of what happened was like what Heather had told her, albeit downplayed.

"That girl came back, and when she came to the door, Corey hit her in the face and knocked her off her feet. Her car keys flew out of her hands. Tubby grabbed them off the floor and he and Audrey took her car to pick something up for Corey. Dude grabbed that girl by the arm and pulled her to a back room.

"Did you hear anything from the back room?"

William didn't immediately answer. He began fidgeting in his seat, obviously uncomfortable with what he was about to say.

"She might have yelled a few times."

"Why was she yelling?"

"I wasn't in that room. I don't know what happened behind closed doors."

"Why do you think she was yelling? What did it sound like was happening?" Frankie struggled to keep the annoyance out of her voice.

William looked towards the floor and said, "It sounded like he might have been hitting her."

Frankie waited before asking, "Do you think she wanted to be in that room with him? Or wanted to have sex with him?"

William didn't hesitate with his reply, "No. She definitely didn't want to be in that room."

Mia asked, "Why didn't you do something about it?"

"I wasn't getting in the middle of their business."

"What happened next?" Frankie asked.

"Corey came out, and a little while later, Tubby came back with the car."

"Did you go into the room where the girl was?"

William began picking at something on his pants that only he could see.

"What did she tell you?"

"Heather said you came into the room. She said you were pretty nice to her," Frankie intentionally downplayed William's participation to see if he would tell them more.

"Yeah, I went in there."

"What happened when you got in the room?"

"That girl was all over me, grabbing my junk and shit. I finally told her she could suck it if it would help her calm down."

Frankie and Mia gave each other a sideways glance.

"And did *that* help her *calm down*?" Mia asked without trying to hide the sarcasm in her voice.

William did not flinch when he answered, "Seemed to."

"What happened next?" Frankie asked.

William squirmed in his seat, "I got up and left the room."

"What did she do?"

"Sat there, I guess. Corey went in to get her and we all left."

Frankie noticed he glossed over putting Heather into the trunk of the car. She decided to let it go and see what he said next.

"Where did you all go?"

"They dropped me off at my girl's house in the city. I don't know what they did after that. I assumed they took the girl home. I wasn't with them, so I don't know what they did."

Frankie knew William was minimizing his involvement in the kidnapping but wanted to lock him into his statement before calling him on it.

"Where was everyone sitting in the car?" Frankie asked.

William tapped his foot under the table, "What do you mean?"

"Who was driving?"

"Audrey."

Frankie took a deep breath. They were going to have to work to get the answers they needed from this guy.

"Where did Corey sit?"

"He was in the passenger seat. Tubby and I sat in the back."

"Where was the girl?"

"She was chillin' in the trunk," William said.

"What do you mean she was chillin' in the trunk?" Frankie asked.

"That's where she was," William answered.

"How'd she get *into* the trunk?" Frankie asked.

William grunted.

"Can you repeat that?"

William mumbled a little louder, "They put her inside."

Frankie concealed the smile threatening to appear.

"Who put her inside?"

"Tubby and Corey."

"How did they put her inside," Frankie asked.

"They picked her up and put her inside," William said.

Frankie asked, "What did you and Audrey do?"

"We got into the car."

Mia asked, "How do you get in contact with Corey?"

"He always calls me. I don't really have a number for him."

Seeing an opening, Frankie said, "Then you won't mind if we have a look at your phone?"

William looked from Frankie to Mia before saying, "Why do you want my phone?"

"We need to reach Corey, and you might be able to help us with that."

"I don't know, man. There's private stuff in there. My girl…"

Mia interjected, "If you give us Corey's number, we may not need to look at your phone."

Mia knew they would most likely seize his phone anyway, but it was worth a shot.

William hesitated before he said, "Let me think about it."

"What's Tubby's name?"

"I ain't knowin' him like that. I just know he's a skinny dude that goes by Tubby."

"Why were you driving the girl's car today?" Frankie asked.

"Man, dude told me the girl was going to pick it up. It wasn't no big thing."

"HOW DID YOU GET THE CAR?" Frankie asked.

William started to say something, then stopped. He rubbed his hands roughly against his pants, took a deep breath, and then said, "Corey brought it to me. He told me he'd hook me up with some cash if I delivered the car to the girl."

"How were you supposed to get home after she took the car?"

"I was either going to walk or see if that girl would take me home."

"Where did you take Corey after he brought you the car?"

"I just dropped him on the block."

Frankie was about to ask what block, but before she could say anything, William spoke again.

"68th."

"What exactly did Corey want you to do?"

"Man, I told you. Give the car to that girl."

Frankie asked, "William, do you own a gun?"

"Naw. Man, I don't mess around with stuff like that. Shit'll get you killed."

"Can you explain why a gun was found in the car you were driving. Next to the driver's seat."

William hesitated before saying, "It probably belonged to that girl. She's not right in the head."

"Is there any reason we would find your fingerprints or DNA on the gun, the magazine, or the bullets?"

"Well, um, maybe. If it was by the driver's seat, I might have brushed against it."

Mia made a note to have the gun fumed for prints. They would check the ammunition and magazine too.

"Did you go to McDonald's today?"

The pupils of William's eyes expanded, making his eyes appear black.

"Naw, man, I haven't been to McDonald's in a while."

"Whose trash was that in the passenger seat of the car?"

"Must have been that girl's. Or maybe Corey's."

"Is there any reason we would find your fingerprints or DNA on the roll of duct tape found in the McDonald's bag?"

William pursed his lips and began to rap the tips of his fingers on the table. The speed and intensity of his bouncing knee increased, causing his knee to hit the underside of the table.

"William…"

"I think I should talk to a lawyer."

Mia checked the time on her watch, notating it for the report. Frankie pushed her chair back and stood as William looked on.

"That's it?" William asked.

"William, we will present all the facts we have gathered to the prosecutor in the morning. We can hold you up to 24 hours, but they will most likely decide about charging you by 5pm. Ready to go upstairs?"

William didn't rise from the chair. He rubbed the top of his head and then leaned back in his chair as though he wanted to continue talking.

"William, you understand when you asked for a lawyer that meant we cannot continue asking you questions."

"Man, it's not that simple."

Frankie returned to her chair thankful the interview was being video recorded.

"Actually, it is. You said you wanted to talk to an attorney. Are you saying you want to continue talking to us without a lawyer present?"

William mumbled, almost imperceptibly, "I'm not going down for this by myself."

The sun hadn't yet dawned when Frankie and Mia walked out of police headquarters. They had secured William's confession, finished up their reports, and left the case file with a note for their sister squad to give to the prosecutor.

"What a day," Mia said.

"No kidding. I wonder if Heather has any idea how much danger she's in?"

"I doubt it. I don't think she realizes just how bad those dudes are. You think William would have gone through with it?"

Frankie gave the question a little thought before answering, "I think William would have taken her to Corey or Tubby and made one of them pull the trigger. I don't think William could have done it alone."

"Agreed. I think he's just a pawn. See you tomorrow, Frankie."

Frankie nodded and climbed into her Jeep and drove home.

CHAPTER
THIRTY-TWO

FRANKIE AWOKE a couple of hours later to the familiar sounds of morning in her household. Dani and Tyler were arguing, and the dog was chasing the cat. She smiled despite her exhaustion. Frankie climbed out of bed, put on her workout clothes, and went into the kitchen to make Dani and Ty's lunches.

"Why can't I buy lunch like the rest of my friends," Dani whined.

"Because you said you wanted to take your lunch this week, and I bought the stuff for you to do it. Don't forget you and Ty are going to Grandma's tonight. Your dad will pick you up there."

"I'm going to Grandma's tonight?" Tyler asked excitedly. "Can Izzie come?"

"You'll have to ask Grandma, but I'm sure that'll be fine. I'll pack your bags and leave them on your beds. She will pick you up here, so ride the bus like you always do. Grandma's going to take you to school Monday morning, and I'll pick you up after, okay?"

"You have a day off on Monday?"

"Yep."

"Hooray! Can we go to the park?"

"If it's not too cold, bud. Now get your backpack before you guys are late."

After dropping the kids at their respective schools, Frankie went about her morning routine. In between dishes and laundry, she fielded calls from the prosecutor's office regarding William and talked to Fitz about what they had learned from Tessa. Her head was spinning trying to keep the cases straight.

Frankie walked into the squad room an hour before her shift started. Her sister squad was finishing up at a crime scene, so she had the space to herself. Frankie used the quiet to organize her thoughts and write her reports.

As Frankie typed the images flashed through her mind. Two women dead; their bodies hidden in the bedframe, under the mattresses in a hotel room. Both women had a rose tattoo on their wrist; the same tattoo Heather had on hers. Frankie knew there was a connection between the women, but Heather's kidnapping didn't appear to be related.

The ringing phone pierced the silence in the room.

"Sex Crimes, Detective Thomas."

"Detective Thomas, it's Jessica Moon from the prosecutor's office."

Frankie cringed. Jessica and Derek had a brief affair after they were both shot by an angry gang member. Jessica knew about Frankie and, out of jealousy, tried to tank some of her cases. Even though Derek ended the affair, and Jessica had been more professional since he called her out on the casework, Frankie wasn't sure she could trust her.

Frankie asked, "How can I help you?"

"Are you the case detective on William Kennedy?"

"Yes." Frankie's jaw clenched. "I thought Pierce was reviewing that case."

"He got called away on a family matter and asked that I review it for him. I am going to release Mr. Kennedy until we get lab results back from the car. I'd also like to see what the men he implicated say in this case before making any charging decisions."

"You do realize once they figure out he flipped on them, he's as good as dead."

"Detective Thomas, contrary to what you may think, I am not an idiot. I think you are being just a bit dramatic. Release him."

Frankie started to say something, but instead put the phone on the cradle and stared. They had a confession from Kennedy, and Moon wanted to let him go.

"Any word from the prosecutor?" Mia asked as she entered the room.

Through clenched teeth Frankie said, "Moon did the case review, so what do you think she decided to do?"

"Well, he did confess to kidnapping the girl and transporting her across state lines in the trunk of her own car. But let me guess, she wants us to release him?"

Frankie nodded.

She and Mia discussed the situation with Sergeant Baker, who directed them not to release Kennedy until he spoke with the prosecutor.

A half-hour passed before Baker exited his office and told Frankie to call the jail and have Kennedy released.

"For the record, I agree with you that she is making a stupid judgment call," Baker said. "But we cannot hold him without the warrant, and I can't get her supervisor on the phone. You'd think they'd charge him with the gun, but she argued until the lab results are back, she can't be sure it's not the victim's gun. She is hell-bent on letting him go."

"Well, if something happens to the guy, she can't say she wasn't warned," Frankie said as she dialed the jail and gave orders to release Kennedy.

CHAPTER
THIRTY-THREE

THE PHONE BEGAN to ring just as Frankie, Mia, and Sergeant Baker walked into the office after a quick pizza.

"Sex Crimes, Detective Boden."

Frankie held her breath, silently praying they did not have a new crime scene.

"Sure, here she is," Mia put her hand over the mouthpiece of the phone and said, "Frankie, this is a detective from Wyandotte County. He says he wants to talk to you about the Whitaker case."

"Okay, send him over." Frankie introduced herself to the detective and after about five minutes, said, "Okay, see you tomorrow."

"Are you going there or is he coming here?" Mia asked.

"He's coming here. I'll make copies of everything we've done. Hopefully, this guy will be more eager than the original detective that responded."

"What was his name?" Mia laughed. "Not that I really know anyone over there,"

"O'Brien. Kelly O'Brien."

CHAPTER
THIRTY-FOUR

DEREK AWOKE IN A COLD SWEAT. It wasn't the first time this had happened. Over the years, since the helicopter crash that killed his best friend, he had nightmares. They had subsided for a while but then he got shot and technically had died. Since then, the nightmares had come back with a vengeance. As a prosecutor who dealt mostly with homicides, he seemed to always be surrounded by death and after all these years, it was finally starting to take its toll.

As if on cue, his phone vibrated with an incoming text.

Hey babe. You still awake?

I just woke up. You coming by?

Finishing up now. See you in 20.

Derek was relieved Frankie had texted. He needed to see her tonight. She could help exorcise the demons that were haunting his dreams. Derek got out of bed and padded into the kitchen with Bear, his Labrador Retriever, following close behind. He picked up the bottle of Johnny Walker Black from the counter and poured two fingers into a glass. He finished it in one gulp then poured another. Lately, it was the only thing besides Frankie that helped him get back to sleep. After he unlocked the back door and turned on the porch light, he went into the living room and stoked the fire that had faded into embers.

Derek stared as the flames began to rekindle, thinking about the dream that had awakened him. The blades of the helicopter whirred loudly in his ears. The crackle of the growing fire reminded him of the flames that engulfed the machine, but tonight, instead of watching the helo crash, he felt the piercing of the bullet into his own flesh and saw Jessica lying dead at his feet. The tattoo of a rose caught his eye. Derek's experiences were beginning to meld together. His mind was no longer treating them as separate events. It was as if he was being shot when the helo crashed, and Jessica was dead at his feet with a rose tattoo. He was beginning to think he might be losing his mind. Sensing his unease, Bear laid his head on Derek's knee. Without thinking, Derek began stroking the dog's fur. With each stroke, he felt the stress begin to leave his body.

Derek's heart rate had returned to normal when he heard Frankie's Jeep ramble up the driveway. A few moments later, she was opening the back door.

"Hey there. I was surprised you were still up!" Frankie said with a smile.

"I had just woken up a couple minutes before you texted."

Something about the look on Derek's face caused the smile to fall from Frankie's. She knew he had struggled with nightmares in the past but thought they had subsided.

Sitting on his lap she asked, "Nightmare?"

Derek wrapped an arm around her waist and ran his hands through her short, dark hair. His ebony eyes looked deeply into her blue ones. Without answering the question, he pulled her in and kissed her fully on the mouth. Frankie's arms circled his neck, and her fingers grazed the back of his head.

As the flames licked the wood in the fireplace, Derek ran his fingers down the side of Frankie's neck and whispered, "Let's go to bed."

Frankie nodded and led Derek to the bed they had shared on so many nights. When they were both satisfied, they lay spent in one another's arms.

Letting her fingers trace the arm he had thrown across her body. Frankie asked, "Do you want to talk about it?"

Derek sighed and said, "No. I think I can sleep now."

With those words he pulled her body closer and nuzzled her, resting his chin on her head. As they lay there, as close as two people could be, Frankie sensed Derek was a million miles away.

THIRTY-FIVE

FRANKIE WOKE before Derek and quietly slipped out from under his arm. She grabbed his t-shirt and went to the kitchen to start a pot of coffee for him and make a diet Coke for herself.

As the smell of coffee filled the kitchen, she scrounged around looking for something to cook for breakfast before going for a run. After turning on the radio, she pulled out some eggs and a slab of bacon. The sounds of Daughtry provided the perfect background to the sound of sizzling bacon and percolating coffee.

Derek came into the kitchen, wrapped his arms around her waist, and kissed the top of her head just as Frankie was plating the bacon.

"Mornin' sunshine! I was going to bring you breakfast in bed."

"How about we skip breakfast and just go back to bed?"

Frankie smiled and laid the back of her head against Derek's chest. "We need to eat a good breakfast so we can go for a run. We can take Bear with us on the Trail of Heroes."

Frankie enjoyed running the trail near the regional police academy. Normally they took both of their dogs, but this weekend her golden retriever Isabelle was with Tyler.

"Do we have to? I think we can get a good cardio workout in right here," Derek raised his eyebrows flirtatiously.

Frankie smiled and said, "Yes, I'm sure. Let's eat and get out there."

Reluctantly Derek took the plate and coffee and went to the table. Frankie grabbed her diet Coke and joined him.

"Tell me about your latest case," Derek said.

Frankie sighed, "This one is a doozy. Three unidentified suspects. Well, technically, we only have one that is unknown now. At least two different jurisdictions."

"What is the other jurisdiction?"

Frankie spent the next half hour telling Derek all she knew about the case. He listened intently, occasionally interrupting to ask questions. It was common for them to discuss their cases. They looked at things through different lenses; therefore, were able to give each other ideas they may not have considered on their own.

"You ready to go for a run?" Frankie asked.

"Honestly, I'd rather take you back to bed, but you seem to have your mind made up."

"You will thank me later."

Twenty minutes later, they were at the Trail of Heroes with the sun was climbing into a deep blue sky. They started off with a slow jog, gradually increasing their pace to a level that made it difficult to talk.

When they were about 400 yards from the trail's end, Frankie asked, "Race? Winner gets to shower first?"

Derek smiled and said, "Go," and took off.

Frankie broke into a sprint, barely finishing after Derek. "I guess you get the shower first!"

Derek grabbed her around the waist, pulled her body close to his, and said, "Maybe you can join me."

THIRTY-SIX

"HEY SARGE, ANYTHING GOING ON?"

"Nope. You ready for the phones?" asked Sergeant Kramer, supervisor for her sister squad.

"Yep. Have a good night."

"You too, Frankie."

Just as she parked the car, her phone began to ring, "Sex Crimes, Thomas."

"Detective Thomas, this is Officer Davis out of Metro. I've got something I need to run past you."

Frankie grabbed her notepad and pen from her bag and said, "Go ahead."

"We are out at the station with a woman who says she found a video recorder hidden in the bedroom at her boyfriend's house. She found a couple tapes and said there is some disturbing shit on them. She has had consensual sex with him, but never consented to being videotaped. First, is this even a crime? And if it is, is this something Sex Crimes handles?"

"It *is* a crime, and *it is* something our unit will handle. I'll need you to take an Invasion of Privacy report. Did she happen to say what was on the videos that was so disturbing?"

"Just that the women in the videos did not appear to know they were being videotaped and at least one did not appear to be conscious."

"Is she still there with you?"

"Yes."

"Good. I just got to the unit. Let me run upstairs and talk to my partner. I am meeting with a detective from Wyandotte County and a witness coming in about ten minutes. Can you ask the victim if she'd be willing to come to headquarters in about an hour? If not, Detective Boden and I'll drive down to Metro after O'Brien leaves."

Frankie waited while Officer Davis talked to the woman.

"She said she'll drive downtown."

"Great. Tell her to park in the PD parking lot across from the Federal Building. Let her know she won't get towed since it's the weekend. She can come in through the basement. I'll let the guard down there know she's coming and to let her in. What's her name?"

"Keeley LaCorte. She'll be down in about an hour."

"Okay. Does she have the videotapes?"

"No, she said she was afraid to take them."

"Okay. Give me a call when you get a case report number."

"Will do."

Mia was parking her car when Frankie jumped out of the Jeep. The pair walked in together, stopping at the guard desk to tell them they had a Wyandotte County detective, a witness, and a victim coming in.

"What do you think the deal is with this one Frankie?"

"Honestly, I have no idea. Davis didn't refer to the suspect as a 'former' boyfriend, so I don't get the idea they are estranged."

"Should be an easy case. Get her statement. Find the cameras. Arrest him. Easy peasy," Mia said.

"Let's hope so."

CHAPTER
THIRTY-SEVEN

FRANKIE SMILED at Detective Kelly O'Brien as they walked towards the elevator.

"I'm sorry we have to take the jail elevator, but they close the others down over the weekend."

"It's not a problem, Detective Thomas."

"Call me Frankie, please."

O'Brien stood no more than a head taller than Frankie. His eyes were coal-black, his skin the color of dark chocolate, and his smile infectious. During the ride to the 4th Floor, Frankie learned that he had just made detective and had only handled one other rape case.

"Do you think this girl will talk to me?" O'Brien asked.

"I think so. Especially if you let Alex be there with her, but why don't you listen to the statement Mia and I got before you decide if you need to bring her in."

"That would probably work."

Frankie escorted O'Brien into the squad room and introduced him to Mia.

"Audrey's waiting in the interview room," Mia said.

Frankie looked to O'Brien and asked, "Want to sit in?"

"How about I watch from here and let you two talk to her?"

Frankie nodded and followed Mia into the interview room. They spent about fifteen minutes gathering demographic data before pulling out Heather's photograph from the file folder.

"Do you know this girl?"

Audrey nodded.

"Can you please sign your name on the photograph and tell us how you know her."

As she signed her name, Audrey said, "Heather is my roommate at the women's shelter."

Frankie noticed Audrey did not use past tense and wondered if they were still roommates. She asked, "How long have you known her?"

"A few weeks. She got there a few days after me. I don't have a car, but she's been helping me see my son and get to my appointments."

"Sounds like she's been a good friend," Mia said.

Audrey didn't say anything.

"Tell us about the party in Kansas," Frankie said.

THIRTY-EIGHT

AUDREY SAT QUIETLY and stared at her hands. After a few moments passed, she said, "A few days ago, my boyfriend told me there was going to be this house party over in Kansas. His car is broken down, so I asked Heather if she'd take me to pick him up. He said he'd take us to McDonald's and put gas in her car if she'd do it. Heather was excited. She tried on different shirts and fixed her hair up. She talked non-stop while she was doing it too. I swear that girl never shuts her damn mouth.

"We finally got in the car and started towards my man's apartment. While we was driving, Heather told me she hoped there'd be a cute guy there. She said she wanted to feel a man tonight and hoped there'd be somebody up for that."

"What's your man's name and where is his apartment?"

"Tubby. He lives off 87th Street."

"What's his given name?" Frankie asked. Noticing the question in Audrey's eyes, she clarified, "What did his momma name him?"

"Lamont. I don't know his last name."

"What happened after you picked up Lamont?"

"We went to McDonald's then to the party. Heather was disappointed that everyone there seemed to be with someone, so Tubby told her his boy Corey might be willing to come over and keep her company. She talked to dude on the phone and then we all got in her car to go pick him up.

"They seemed to hit it off okay, and when we got back to the apartment, they stayed in her car. I don't know what happened in the car but after about thirty minutes, he came inside the apartment alone. He was mad as hell too. He said the bitch had left us there when she said she'd take us home the next day. That kind of freaked me out too.

"I had a visit scheduled with my son and she was supposed to take me, so I called her a few times, and when she finally answered, she said she wasn't going to come back. Corey kept calling her too, but she wouldn't answer him either."

"What finally made her come back?" Frankie asked.

"About 8:00 AM, I called her and begged her to come back. I was crying and told her I was going to miss my visit with my son. She knows how important those visits are to me. Heather asked if the guys were still there, and I lied to her. I told her they had left so she would come back."

"What happened when she came back?"

Audrey shared a similar story to what Heather and William had provided. Audrey and Tubby had left to pick up a package for Corey, and when they got back, they all left in Heather's car. She described the drive back to Missouri, glossing over the fact that Heather was in the trunk during the drive.

"They let me out on 77th Street, and I walked to the shelter. I don't know what they did after that. A few hours later, Heather came back to the shelter and asked the night staff to take her to the hospital."

"What was in the package you picked up for Corey?" Mia asked.

Audrey glared at Mia, "I didn't ask. I figured it was probably best if I didn't know."

"Why didn't you stop them from putting Heather in the trunk of her car?"

Audrey squirmed in her chair and, at first, did not act like she was going to answer the question. Just as Frankie prepared to ask the question again, Audrey looked up with tear-filled eyes and said, "Because I didn't want to end up in the trunk with her."

THIRTY-NINE

AUDREY EXPLAINED to Frankie and Mia that she was at the shelter because of an incident between her and Tubby. Tubby was her baby's father, but he had accused her of stepping out on him and the baby belonging to someone else. During a fit of rage, he had hit her while she was holding the baby. She fell and she and the baby ended up with a few bumps and bruises. The neighbors called the police and as a result, their baby went into foster care. Audrey had gone to the shelter because the Department of Family Services told her she had to get away from Tubby or she wouldn't be able to get her son back.

"But you are still seeing him?" Frankie asked.

"We're trying to work things out. He said he's sorry, and it was just momentary lapse. He says he'll never hurt me again but that day…I couldn't risk it. Corey is a bad dude and after seeing the way he was with Heather I know he would have thrown me in the trunk too."

"Can you help us get in touch with Tubby?"

Audrey gave it some thought before saying, "I can give you his number, but that's it. He told me he was moving. His momma told him she was tired of his stuff and kicked him out. He pretty much stays wherever a friend will let him crash."

"Is there anything else you think is important for us to know?"

"Will they know I talked to you?"

Frankie saw the fear in Audrey's eyes. She considered her answer carefully, "We won't tell them, but if this goes to court, it will likely come out."

Audrey nodded then got up to leave the room. Mia escorted her to the elevator and out of the building while Frankie returned to the squad room to talk to O'Brien.

"You guys going to charge her with conspiracy?" O'Brien asked.

"I don't know. I am trying not to judge her, but damn, with friends like her who needs enemies?"

O'Brien nodded.

"Do you want us to call you when we get the other two in custody? We can interrogate them together, or I can burn you copies of the video," Frankie said.

"Please give me a call. If I'm not out on anything else, I'd like to come and at least observe. Have any of the lab results come in yet?"

"No. We put a rush on them, but it will still probably take a few days."

"Okay. Is there anything I can do to help?"

Frankie thought for a moment before saying, "She mentioned an apartment off Parallel. Any ideas on where she might be talking about?"

"There are only a couple of complexes over there. I can run by and see if they can pull surveillance footage. Maybe we'll get lucky. Also, I can take Heather driving around and see if she will identify anything," O'Brien said.

"For what it's worth, I think it will help keep her focused and on point if you have Alex with you," Frankie described what happened when they took her driving around. "Make sure you give her specific instructions about staying in the car. She's a bit of a handful. Well-meaning, but a handful nonetheless."

"Sounds good. Did you all want to go with me when we do it?"

"It depends on when you go, I suppose. I would appreciate any information you can share, though."

"Will do. Thank you for making copies for me, but I really should go and let you get back to work."

"I'll walk you out," Frankie said.

Frankie walked O'Brien to the door of the garage.

The guard at the door said, "I was just about to call and tell you a visitor was here to see you, Frankie."

CHAPTER
FORTY

FRANKIE ESCORTED Keeley to the waiting room and said, "Can you wait here for just a moment?"

"Sure," Keeley answered.

Frankie closed the door to the squad room, walked to her desk, and took a long drink of water. She reached her hands over her head and stretched, then bent in half, exhaling with force. She was returning to a standing position when Mia walked into the room.

"Hey, did you know there is someone in the lobby?"

"Yeah, that's the woman Metro called about. I just need to stretch a bit before I went back to the interview room," Frankie explained.

"Want some help?" Mia asked.

Frankie nodded.

Mia grabbed her notepad and a couple bottles of water. When Frankie opened the door into the waiting room, she found Keeley pacing between the interview room door and the wall with her hands clasped in front of her.

Frankie opened the door into the interview room and gestured to a chair across the table. Once Keeley was seated, Frankie gathered her demographic information. When she got to the space for place of employment, she was surprised to hear Keeley was a schoolteacher.

"What grade do you teach?"

"Kindergarten."

Thinking she looked familiar, Frankie asked, "What school?"

"Crestview."

Frankie disguised her surprise. That was where her kids attended.

Frankie said, "Keeley, why don't you explain to Detective Boden and I what brought you

here today."

Keeley's hands were folded and resting on the table. Her eyes filled with tears, but none fell. She unclasped her hands and began rubbing her arms before responding.

"I think my boyfriend has been videotaping us having sex, but that's not why I'm here. I mean, it's weird, but it's the videotapes I found that made me file a report. I think he's been videotaping more than just us."

"What's his name?"

"Alexandre. Alexandre Kristof."

Frankie looked at Mia. They knew the name. Kristof owned a marketing firm and was associated with executives from Stevenson Automotive. Frankie and Mia had investigated a rape case connected to a sexual harassment lawsuit involving Stevenson Automotive who had deep connections to organized crimes. During that investigation, one of their witnesses told Craven about an experience she had at a party at Kristof's house. After hearing the details, the three of them speculated the woman had been drugged and raped. She didn't identify it that way, so no investigation had been opened. After talking to Tessa earlier that week, Frankie and Mia were beginning to think Kristof may also be involved in trafficking women and possibly a series of murders. So much for an easy case.

Keeley caught the look and asked, "Do you know him?"

"We met him during an investigation we were conducting last year."

"Really? He never mentioned it." Keeley took a drink of her water and said, "But I guess that shouldn't surprise me. Anyway, Alexandre left to go into the office this morning but told me I could hang out at his house if I wanted to. I was going to meet a friend for lunch in Brookside, so I decided I'd relax there instead of going all the way back to my house before meeting her. He had just left when I decided to turn on the television. I was expecting to see a cable channel but instead it was me on the screen. At first, I thought I was just seeing things. As dumb as it sounds, I started to move around on the bed. For a full minute I watched myself on the television doing the same movements.

"I grabbed a t-shirt to cover up then tried to figure out where the camera was. I looked all around his TV and finally found it hidden inside a wooden statue of a woman. I couldn't believe it. I never gave him my permission to videotape us having sex. I was pissed, but instead of calling him I decided to see if I could find the tape and just get rid of it. I found a couple of tapes lying by the TV, so I grabbed the first one and put it inside the VCR."

"He has a VCR?" Mia asked.

"Yeah. I thought it was weird too, but figured he just liked watching all the old videotapes he had. Turns out it wasn't *Top Gun* he was using it for. I put the first tape in the VCR and this time it wasn't me on the video. I'm not positive, but I think it was a girl he used to date named Melissa. I wasn't mad at the fact that he had a video recording of her, it was the content of the video that freaked me out."

CHAPTER
FORTY-ONE

FRANKIE WAITED while Keeley took another drink of her water.

"The girl looked like she was unconscious. She was just lying there naked with her eyes closed. I could see there was someone in the shadows, but I couldn't see his face. Then Alexandre started doing stuff to her. Every now and then I would hear a grunt and see a flash like someone was taking photographs."

"What kind of stuff was he doing?"

"He was putting stuff inside her vagina. He pinched her breasts and bit and twisted her nipples."

"Did she ever wake up, open her eyes, or respond in the video?" Frankie asked.

"I don't know. She seemed out of it, and after a few minutes, I shut it off. I grabbed another tape, and it contained a different woman. She wasn't unconscious but she was *really* out of it. She looked more than drunk, if that makes sense. I think she may have been drugged. There was a close-up shot of her eyes and they were… vacant. I know that may not make sense, but I'm not sure what other word to use. It was like the lights were on, but nobody was home. The third video contained two women."

"Were the videos all done in his bedroom?"

Keeley shook her head and said, "No, two of them looked like his living room. The third looked like it was in his hot tub. I swear I had no idea he had video cameras in his house. I feel sick."

"Did it look like the women were aware they were being videotaped? Other than the one who you think was unconscious?"

"No, I don't think so. If they knew, they were a lot less self-conscious than I would have been."

"Was there penetration in the second and third videos?"

"In the second, he was using stuff on her. It looked like she was trying to push his hands away, but it didn't matter; he didn't stop. In the third video, he was directing the girls to do stuff to each other. I didn't get the impression they were girlfriends either. It's hard to explain. You'd have to see it to understand. It looked like they were high or really drunk and completely unaware."

Frankie began asking pointed questions about the layout of the house, weapons, animals, and the neighborhood. She was thinking they were going to have to get a search warrant, but she wanted to talk to the prosecutor first.

"MIA, who's the on-call SVU prosecutor this weekend?" Frankie asked.

"Looks like it's your favorite prosecutor, Jessica Moon."

"I think it might be better if you give her a call."

Jessica answered the phone on the first ring.

"Hey Jessica, it's Detective Boden, KCPD Sex Crimes Unit. I have a case to run past you for a possible search warrant."

Mia crossed her eyes and stuck her tongue out sideways. Frankie stifled a laugh.

Mia explained the circumstances of the case and what they thought they could gain from a search warrant. When she was finished, Jessica asked a few clarifying questions before asking how long they needed to draft the warrant. She agreed to meet them at police headquarters.

Frankie's next call was to her supervisor, Sergeant Myles Baker. "Hey Sarge, sorry to bother you on a Saturday, but it looks like we're going to be serving a search warrant in Brookside tonight."

Frankie provided Baker with all the details and then waited. He was a man of few words who gave careful consideration before making any big decisions.

After a few moments, Baker said, "Let's call the on-call Tactical Response Team. This guy has a history with us and based on the people he hangs out with I don't trust him."

"Agreed. Are you coming in?" Frankie could hear him rustling things on his end of the phone.

"Yeah. It'll be an hour or so."

"Sounds good. You'll be here about the same time the prosecutor gets here."

Mia had already started drafting the search warrant by the time Frankie disconnected the phone. Frankie called the on-call Tactical Response Team and gave their sergeant, Tony Carmody a quick synopsis of what they were looking at.

"Let's plan to meet at Metro Patrol in two hours to do a drive-by. That should give us plenty of time to get the judge's signature and get there."

Sergeant Carmody said, "Sounds good. Call my cell if there are any changes."

"Will do." Frankie disconnected the phone and turned to Mia, "What do you need me to do?"

"Read over this and tell me what I'm forgetting."

They were making copies of the warrant when Sergeant Baker escorted Jessica into the squad room.

"Good timing, we just finished."

Frankie was steeling herself for any pushback Jessica might give on the content of the warrant, but after reviewing the documents, she asked for a pen and signed off.

"Need anything else," Jessica asked.

"Do you happen to know which Judge is on call?"

Jessica looked in her day planner and said, "Looks like Judge Maron is on call this weekend."

"Thank you, that's great. She lives in Brookside. That will make our lives a bit easier."

"Please give me a call and let me know what you find at the house."

"Will do. Thanks again."

Frankie and Mia grabbed their vests and started putting their duty bags together while Baker escorted Moon from the building.

FORTY-THREE

AN HOUR LATER FRANKIE, Mia, and Baker were in the briefing room at Metro Patrol Division Station listening as Sergeant Carmody updated his team on the necessary plans in the event there was a medical emergency. Sergeant Carmody and Frankie had already conducted a drive-by of the address to ensure the description on the warrant matched the house they were going to hit. The last thing any of them wanted was to make entry into the wrong house. Especially in Brookside. A fair number of attorneys and judges lived in that neighborhood, and they were certain to get sued and publicly vilified if they breached the wrong door.

"They're all yours, Frankie."

Frankie briefed the team on the case facts and the safety concerns based on Kristof's associates.

"The victim has never known him to have any weapons, but his associates do. We also know the house is wired to record. I am not 100% certain where all the cameras are, but we should assume he has them outside as well as inside so he may see you coming and may be recording."

"Alright men load up. You guys follow us," Carmody waived to the detectives. Carmody looked directly at Frankie and said, "*No one* goes inside until we are certain it's clear. Copy?"

"Copy Sarge."

The drive to Kristof's house took less than ten minutes. He lived in a large three-story 1920's neo-classical style home. As they approached, Frankie noticed not only was the front porch light illuminated, but the party lights on the back patio were illuminated as well. It was almost as though he were waiting to host a party.

Frankie and Mia watched as Team 2 announced themselves at the front door. They were preparing to ram the door when it opened slightly. Alexandre Kristof stood just inside the doorway in a pair of blue jeans and white t-shirt.

"What the he…" Kristof began to ask.

"Show me your hands," shouted Carmody.

Kristof immediately raised his hands with a look of terror on his face.

"He looks like he's going to piss his pants," Mia said.

Team 2 searched the house for any other people, and when they were finished, they called the detectives inside. Frankie noticed the look of recognition when she approached Kristof.

"You've got to be kidding me," Kristof said, revealing a slight accent.

"I guess you remember me, Mr. Kristof. Has Sergeant Carmody advised you of the reason for the warrant?"

"No. Is this related to those damn bitches at Stevenson? Because I have nothing to do with all that."

"Actually, Mr. Kristof, this is all about you."

"Regarding?"

"We will get into the details downtown but as you will see by this warrant," Frankie held up a copy of the search warrant for Kristof to see, "a judge has granted us authority to search your property for evidence."

"Are you being serious right now?"

"Yes, we are serious." Looking towards Carmody, Frankie asked, "Do you have a wagon coming?"

"Yep, one's on the way."

"Thanks. Mr. Kristof, you will get a ride downtown courtesy of KCPD. Once we have concluded with the execution of the search warrant Detective Boden and I will come talk to you."

Sergeant Carmody guided Frankie, Mia, and Baker on a walking tour of the house.

"We didn't see any cameras or monitors. Are you sure she was videotaped?"

"Yeah. She said one of the cameras is in his bedroom inside the statue of a woman. Maybe he has the others cleverly hidden as well."

When they reached the basement, Frankie noticed a wall of painted beadboard. A padlock attached two panels.

"What's this?" Frankie asked.

Carmody gave Frankie a quizzical look.

"I can't believe no one noticed this. Why the hell is there a lock on the wall?"

Frankie looked closer and noticed it was a false door. Drawing her weapon, she stood back as Carmody broke the lock. Both aimed their guns at the opening the door created.

"What the…"

FORTY-FOUR

THE DOOR OPENED into a small cellar. The floors were bare, and the block walls were lined with two rows of wooden shelves. The first row of shelves contained numerous video cassette recorders and the second contained a monitor attached to each VCR. Most of the wires fed from the ceiling, but two wires appeared to lead outside to the backyard.

"I can't believe my team missed this," Carmody said.

"It would be easy to miss," reassured Baker. "The door was built to blend in with the walls."

"I'm going to go call the Crime Scene Unit," Mia said.

Frankie started sketching the basement, making a note of the placement of all the electronic equipment. She scanned the walls carefully making sure there were no more hidden doorways.

When she was finished, she started back up the stairs in time to hear Mia finishing her call with the Crime Scene Unit.

"They aren't coming out. There was a double homicide *and* an officer-involved shooting. Rhino had to call in another team to cover the scene with the officer involved. I've got our camera, and our cars are stocked. Hopefully, this will be an easy scene."

Frankie nodded and started sketching the main floor, taking note of the antique furnishings and the expert photography adorning the walls.

It appeared as if Kristof had traveled extensively and knew his way around a camera.

"This guy's photographs belong in a gallery," Frankie said.

"I agree," Mia replied. "I'm going to start photographing the scene. Can everyone get outside please?"

Frankie thanked Team 2 and watched Baker escort them outside. Frankie followed Mia, creating a log of the photographs she was taking. Baker waited with Team 2 until Mia called him back inside.

Mia photographed the first floor before stepping into the backyard.

"Dayum," Frankie said.

"Looks like he was gearing up for one hell of a party," Mia said.

A cooler full of ice and bottled beer sat next to the tiki-style bar on the patio. Twinkle lights were strung over the bar, by the pool, and over the pergola covering the hot tub. A rock fountain poured water into a softly lit pool. A sandpit with a volleyball net flanked the pool deck. A covered stage stood at the edge of the court, seemingly waiting for a band to walk on and perform.

"The only thing missing are the people," Frankie said.

"No kidding. It's like he was planning to have a party tonight. I guess we foiled his plans."

Frankie started looking at the fencing surrounding the pool, shining her flashlight across metal rods. About midway between the fence, near the gate, the light reflected at a different angle. A small camera, almost imperceptible, was located on one of the iron posts. Baker looked around the post and located a cable in the seams of the concrete. He followed the cable to a basement window.

Frankie followed the same process on the pergola over the hot tub. The camera was hidden almost directly above the hot tub. The cable led to the same basement window.

"Looks like we found the two outside. Based on the monitors, there should be at least three, possibly four inside. We can speculate the one in the master bedroom may be recording there. Based on what Keeley described, there should be one in the living room. I'm not sure where the others will be."

The trio located the camera in the living room easily and moved the search to the second floor. The second camera was easy to find in the bedroom since Keeley had told them where to look. With it identified, they started methodically searching the rest of the house.

Kristof's home office was located on the third floor of the house. Frankie scanned the space carefully. Something about the space made a chill run down her spine.

Kristof's home office was not in keeping with the rest of his house. There were file folders stacked around the room and miscellaneous papers scattered across his large library-style desk. Two wingback chairs flanked the desk, and a large, plush rug covered the floor.

After Mia photographed the space, Frankie began scanning the documents and files scattered about the desk. As she navigated herself around the desk, she bumped into the mouse pad, causing the two monitors atop the desk to wake up.

"What in the....?" Mia and Frankie said in unison.

CHAPTER
FORTY-FIVE

"SARGE, you need to come and see this," Frankie shouted.

Frankie wanted to look away but found her gaze transfixed on the monitor. It appeared to be a live feed coming from a little girl's bedroom. The child did not look like she was any older than nine, but the angle of the camera and position of her body made it difficult to be certain. She was wearing pajamas and appeared to be sleeping in a twin-size bed. A nightlight illuminated a dollhouse flanking the bed.

Sergeant Baker walked in and, upon seeing the video feed, repeated what Frankie and Mia had said.

"Does the search warrant cover the computer?"

"Yeah. We didn't know if he had videos linked to his computer, so we threw it on there. I'm going to see if we can get Brad out here. We need to figure out where this feed is coming from and do a scan to see if there is any child pornography on this computer. If there is, we may need to get a piggy-back warrant."

Mia and Baker watched the little girl sleep while Frankie talked to the cyber unit and made a follow-up call to Jessica for the piggy-back warrant. It didn't look like she was being held against her will or was in distress, but it didn't make the video any less creepy.

"Jessica is on board with us writing another warrant if needed. Brad will be here in thirty minutes. Did we figure out where the other camera is? Or where this little girl is?" Frankie asked. "Is she in this house? I don't remember Keeley or anyone else mentioning children."

"I think the other camera is in one of the extra rooms, but I haven't found it yet. He doesn't have any kids, so it's not a nanny cam," Mia said.

Just as Frankie was preparing to go back to the second floor to look for the camera, Baker called out, "Come back up here, you are going to want to see this."

Frankie and Mia joined Baker behind the desk and watched as a man entered the room. They each held their breath to see what he was going to do. Frankie observed the man sit on the edge of the bed and watch the little girl. He reached down and gently touched her face, then brushed her hair to the side. Frankie and Mia held their breath when he touched the blanket resting on her shoulders, exhaling only when he stood up. Frankie stared intently at his face, certain she had seen the man before, but unsure where.

"Mia, does this guy look familiar to you?"

"I was just thinking the same thing, but I can't figure out where I know him from."

The man walked closer to the camera, giving them a better shot of his face. Frankie grabbed her cell phone and snapped a photo.

"Maybe we can try to run him through facial recognition. Dammit, he looks familiar."

They continued to watch the man until he finally left the room.

"Thank God," mumbled Frankie to herself.

"Where you guys at," came a booming voice from below.

"3rd floor," Baker responded. "Come on up."

Brad Stephens, a detective from the Cyber Unit, took the stairs to the third floor two by two. He wore a KC Royals polo and a baseball cap with blue jeans. The only thing identifying him as a detective was the badge hanging from his neck, and the gun holstered on his belt.

"What kind of stuff did you all stir up tonight?" Brad asked.

Frankie explained what they had found and showed him the monitor.

"What's this?" Brad asked.

"We aren't sure. Is there any way you can identify the IP address or anything that will tell us where this child is?"

"Give me a few minutes, and I'll see what I can find." Brad grabbed his equipment and got to work.

CHAPTER
FORTY-SIX

"YOU MIGHT AS WELL START WORKING on your piggyback warrant," Brad announced. "I ran a scan on the computer and found at least two dozen images of child sexual abuse material. I suspect we will find more when we do a forensic exam of the hard drive. I also got you an IP address on that live feed. You may not need a warrant if you site exigent circumstances, but I think I'd get one just in case and add the exigent circumstances to the formal request."

"Thanks Brad. I'm going to run and get the warrants. Mia and Sergeant Baker will be here looking for that last camera. Are you going to hang around?"

"Yeah, I have one more preview scan I can run, and I want to make sure everything gets disconnected properly."

"There is a whole recording set up downstairs in the basement. Would you mind disconnecting all of it as well?" Frankie asked.

"You bet," Brad answered while simultaneously watching the computer scan.

Frankie drove to Metro Patrol Division and quickly typed up the second and third warrants. She decided she might as well get one for the IP address while she was working on them. If she got lucky, she might be able to get an address for that little girl by morning. She was back at the house in less than two hours.

"Anything new since I left?"

"We found the other camera," Mia said. "You won't believe where it was."

"Do tell."

"In the guest bathroom. From the angle of the camera, it appears he likes to watch people using the toilet."

"Gross."

"I know, right?" Mia said.

Based on the scope of the second warrant, the four detectives began searching the house for anything that could contain images of child sexual abuse material. At Brad's direction, they collected all the video-tapes, DVDs, compact discs, and USB drives along with the computer.

"It's not uncommon for guys collecting and manufacturing CSAM to tape over commercial VHS tapes. They will cover the security tab, fast forward a bit, and then record. It's a good way to hide the CSAM in plain sight."

Frankie started looking through the desk drawers, looking for any type of printed images. A stack of photographs filled an envelope in the top drawer. The first few photos looked like a birthday party. Frankie almost returned the envelope to the drawer, but something told her to continue looking. Midway through the stack, Frankie was glad she did. The first few photos were of pre-pubescent girls, wearing bikinis, and playing in his pool. The next few photos were, Frankie assumed, the same girls. However, in these photos, the angle of the camera focused on their buttocks. The last photos Frankie pulled from the envelope were of an adult woman. The photographs depicted the woman's body in varying sexual positions. In some, her body appeared to be covered in oil. In all of them, she appeared to be unconscious.

"Hey Mia, don't these photographs look like the video Keeley described?"

Mia looked at the photographs Frankie was holding before saying, "Yeah, they do. This guy is sick."

Frankie continued to go through the desk, finding varying images on photo paper and some on plain copy paper. She pulled out each file, wondering with each one what she would find. When the files began to look like financial records, she almost stopped searching. Frankie began to put the files away when something caught her eye.

"Mia!" Frankie yelled.

Mia ran upstairs from the second floor and breathlessly asked, "What? Did something happen to that girl?"

"What? No, she's still asleep. Check this out. Look at Kristof's credit card statement, then look at what's attached to it."

Mia scanned the documents carefully, then began to laugh. "We've got you, you stupid son of a bitch!"

FORTY-SEVEN

FRANKIE ESCORTED Alexandre Kristof to the interrogation room located on the fourth floor. It was after 3 AM, and she was completely sickened by what she had found at his house. Frankie dismissed the pleasantries she normally attempted with people she interviewed and moved directly to why they were there.

"Alexandre, we received a report you were videotaping people having sex at your house without their consent. As a result of the search warrant, we identified other misdeeds, but let's talk about the videotaping first. How many cameras do you have set up in your house?"

"How many did you find?"

"Don't be cute, Alexandre. It's late and I'm not in the mood. Give me the number."

Alexandre sat, silent.

"Let's talk about *these* photographs first." Frankie laid out the photographs of the naked woman, posed in varying positions. "Who is she?"

Alexandre continued to sit in silence.

"Is that really how you want to play it?" Frankie was tired and irritated but took a deep breath and tried to change her approach. "Look, Alexandre, in the morning, I'm going to tell the prosecutor everything we found. I would like to give them your side of the story too. I can't do that if you won't talk to me."

Alexandre seemed to give what Frankie said some thought. After a few moments, he said, "I have five cameras in my house, but I suspect you know that already. They are purely for security purposes. I entertain a considerable amount and own quite a few antiquities. I would be very unhappy if any were to come up missing. I also have a lovely outdoor space, one that some could construe as having a certain element of risk. As a result, I keep cameras outdoors as well."

Mia fought the urge to ask what his reason was for having one in the powder room aimed at the toilet. She would ask about it later.

"And who is this girl?" Frankie showed Alexandre a photograph of a naked young woman covered in baby oil, wearing only a yellow tie.

Frankie thought she saw a small smile begin to form on Alexandre's lips then quickly disappear.

"That is an old friend of mine. Actually, she is a former lover."

"What's her name?"

"Sonja Lincoln." The name seemed to roll off Alexandre's lips.

"How can we get in touch with her?"

"I'm afraid I don't know. We had a bit of a nasty breakup and sort of lost touch. I think she's somewhere in Kansas. Possibly one of the little college towns."

Well, that narrows it down, Frankie thought.

"Did Sonja know you were taking her photograph?"

Alexandre didn't immediately answer. Once again, he appeared to be weighing the risk of being honest.

"Of course, she did. She was posing in any of the photographs you may have found. What kind of pervert do you think I am?"

Frankie filtered the answer that popped into her mind. Instead, she decided it was time to ask him about the other photographs.

"Alexandre, you had beautiful, framed photographs in your home. It appears you have traveled a bit."

"I have been fortunate to have had the means to see the world."

"Who took the photographs lining your staircase?"

"Why, I did, of course."

CHAPTER
FORTY-EIGHT

FRANKIE PULLED out the photographs of the young girls in bathing suits and asked, "Who are these girls?"

"Those are my niece and her friends."

"Do you remember when these were taken?"

"I believe it was her 12th birthday," Alexandre stated. He hesitated then added, "She asked to use my pool for her party."

"Did you do the photography for the party?"

"Of course. I wanted to document the memorable experience for her so I created an album as part of her gift."

Frankie turned over the photographs that appeared to be of just the girls' buttocks.

"Did you include these in the album? Was this part of the 'memorable experience'?" Frankie asked.

"Of course not," Alexandre stated, seemingly horrified at the question."

"Why did you take them?"

"Detective, I believe you are fishing. Do all your photographs turn out perfectly? It's obvious I snapped the camera before I had it in focus."

To herself, Frankie thought, *"Not likely given the photographs on the walls of your home."* Instead, she laid down the other photographs of various young girls' behinds.

Alexandre sat quietly.

Not challenging his silence, Frankie laid a photograph of a naked, pre-pubescent girl in front of him and said, "We found this one in your desk. Did you take it as well?"

"Detective, I collect art, but to answer your question, no, I did not take that photograph. It is obvious you do not know much about the fine arts if you think this is in any way vulgar. It is purely a work of art."

Frankie fought the bile rising in her throat and the desire to physically harm him. Instead, she asked, "Alexandre, who is the little girl on your computer?"

"What are you talking about?"

"The live feed of the little girl and her bedroom. Who and where is she?"

"Oh, you must mean my niece. It's a nanny camera my sister wanted me to test for her."

"What is your sister's address?"

Alexandre hesitated before answering, "11760 North Corrington."

Sergeant Baker was watching the interview on the monitor. Frankie trusted he was calling dispatch to have a radio car complete a residence check.

"Have you ever visited any child pornography websites?" Frankie asked, already knowing the answer.

Alexandre physically recoiled at the question. Regaining his composure, he said, "Why would you ask such a thing. Of course, I haven't. As I said before, I'm not a pervert."

Frankie allowed silence to fill the room, hoping Alexandre would attempt to fill it. He didn't disappoint.

"Well, there may have been a time or two when I was doing a search on the internet that something came on the screen that I wasn't expecting. It's happened to everyone at one time or another. You click on a link in an e-mail or a pop-up advertisement and end up with something perverse on the screen. If you saw something like that on my computer, that's all it was."

"Just to confirm, you are saying you've never paid for access to a site that depicted children engaged in sexual acts?"

"Absolutely not," Alexandre emphatically stated.

Frankie pulled out a manila folder full of documents and asked, "Alexandre, what is your email address?"

"ARKristof@gmail.com."

Frankie opened the folder and pulled out a printout from an internet site. The printout identified a username, email, and subscription information.

"Alexandre, is this your email address?" Frankie asked, pointing to the email address listed on the printout, which matched the address he provided.

"Uh, um," Alexandre stuttered. "Yes."

"And are these the last four digits of your credit card number?"

"I'd have to have my wallet. I have a plethora of credit cards and do not have all the numbers memorized."

Frankie pulled another document from the folder. She laid it in front of Alexandre. The color drained from his face.

"We found this bank statement in your desk and the name on the statement is yours. The transaction number for a charge of 21.99 is the same as the transaction number on this printout," Frankie said, tapping the printout from the internet site.

Alexandre scanned the documents and then said, "I want to speak to my attorney before we go any further."

CHAPTER
FORTY-NINE

MIA RETURNED Alexandre to the jail while Frankie talked to Sergeant Baker.

"The address doesn't exist, Frankie. We'll have to wait for his internet provider to respond to our warrant."

Frankie was disappointed but not surprised and since Alexandre had asked to speak to an attorney, she couldn't confront him. Once Mia got back to the office, they returned to Alexandre's residence. With the help of Baker and Brad, they did one more scan of the house. Frankie couldn't get the images of the unconscious women out of her mind. Something in the photographs was nagging her, like there was something she was supposed to remember but couldn't.

Almost as an afterthought, Frankie opened the minifridge at the bar by the pool. She stood and stared at its contents. Three bottles of Blue Moon, two oranges, a chilled bottle of Chardonnay, a bottle of diet Coke and a bottle of Captain Morgan spiced rum. Frankie closed the refrigerator and stood staring at the pool.

Jerking the refrigerator back open, Frankie said, "Mia, come here."

"What'd you find?" Mia asked.

"Does anything seem off about the contents of this fridge?"

Mia stared for a moment before saying, "Why is it clear?"

"Exactly."

Baker and Brad joined the pair on the patio.

Baker said, "Want to invite us to the party?"

Frankie held up the bottle of Captain Morgan and showed it to Baker, "Anything seem unusual about this bottle?"

"I thought Captain Morgan was brown," Baker said.

"It is. So why is there a clear liquid in this bottle?" Frankie asked, a smile creeping up her face.

"You don't think?' Baker asked.

"We won't know until we send it to the lab, but my bet is GHB. It would explain the women in the photos and maybe even the behavior Keeley described observing on the videos."

"This was supposed to be a simple invasion of privacy case," Baker said. "I should have known with you two there would be nothing simple about it."

Frankie started laughing, nudging her shoulder against Baker's, "It's one of the reasons you love Mia and me so much. We keep things interesting."

Baker couldn't help but laugh. Frankie was right, there was rarely a boring shift when those two were working.

They finished their walk-thru of Kristof's house and headed back to headquarters. Frankie sat at her desk, staring at the computer monitor. The sun was beginning to rise and her energy was waning.

"Sarge, do you mind if we go catch a few z's before finishing up this file for the prosecutor? I'm falling asleep at my computer," Frankie said.

Mia rubbed her eyes and said, "I agree Sarge." Looking at her watch, she added, "It's almost 7. I can be back by noon. What do you say?"

Baker stood, stretched his back, and said, "Yeah. Let's take a break and come back at noon so we can get this son of a bitch charged."

CHAPTER
FIFTY

FRANKIE GOT HOME in time to talk to Tyler on the phone before he left for Sunday school. Ten minutes later, she was sound asleep with her cat curled up on the pillow next to her.

The sound of the alarm jolted Frankie from a sound sleep. Rolling over, she cursed at the phone as she silenced the alarm.

Frankie stretched and groaned, then got off the bed and went to the kitchen for a banana and a bottle of water before hitting the shower. Before she could start the water, her phone began to buzz.

"Thomas."

"Hey kid. Miss me much?"

Frankie smiled at the southern drawl on the other end of the line.

"Hey Jim, how's your grand-dad?"

"He's doing much better, thank you for asking. I'm actually on my way back to KC. What's going on with you? Any good cases cooking?"

Frankie entertained Jim with stories of the cases he had missed out on. When she got to the Captain Morgan bottle, Frankie stopped and waited for his response.

"Are you thinking what I'm thinking?" Craven asked.

"If you're thinking we need to go by the Brooksider and try to talk to your girlfriend Candi, then yes."

Frankie and Craven met Candi while they were working on a rape involving two women from Stevenson's Automotive. Candi was a receptionist who had taken a keen liking to Craven. He met her at the Brooksider to extract information on their case, and while they were there, Candi disclosed, what they believed to be a drug-facilitated rape at a 4th of July party at Alexandre Kristof's house. Craven wanted to go after him then, but Candi didn't identify herself as a victim so they could not pursue. This new evidence might be enough to compel Candi to make a report and ultimately hold Kristof accountable.

"When will you be back?"

"I'll be rolling in around 6. Do you want to try to catch up to her tonight?"

"Are you sure you'll feel up to it?"

Craven laughed, "Darlin', I'm always up for working with you."

Frankie smiled and disconnected the call. Forty-five minutes later, she was walking into police headquarters with Mia.

"Sarge called and said he wasn't going to come in unless we need him. By the way, Craven is on his way back and is going to meet us at the Brooksider around 7."

"You think Candi will talk to us?" Mia asked.

Frankie laughed and said, "Maybe not you and I, but I don't see her turning down a chance to talk to Craven."

CHAPTER
FIFTY-ONE

IT WAS BEGINNING to get dark when Mia whipped the unmarked police car into an empty parking space in the back lot at the Brooksider and waited. Craven told them he would be there by 7 PM so they could all make entry together.

"You think Kristof will make bail?" Mia asked.

"Maybe, but I hope not. I'm surprised she didn't ask for more than $50,000. He appears to have the means to easily afford 10% of that."

"True. She only charged him on one count of invasion of privacy since we don't have any other named victims…yet. I wonder what they will do with the CSAM?"

"Brad is working to secure federal charges, which will make it a bit harder for him to get out."

"How do you want to approach this interview with Candi?" Mia asked.

"Honestly, I hadn't thought that far ahead. I guess we will let Jim start up the conversation with her and then follow her lead. I have no idea how this girl is going to react – hell, she still may not want to make a report."

"I wonder if we should have brought someone from MOCSA with us?"

Frankie thought about what Mia said. It might have been a good idea to bring a victim advocate from the Metropolitan Organization to Counter Sexual Assault with them. Candi might be triggered by the realization of what happened to her.

"Good call. Let's introduce her to the idea that something is up and get her to come to HQ. We can have someone from MOCSA meet us there," Frankie said.

A black SUV pulled up next to their unmarked car and lowered its window.

"Hey there, pretty ladies. How are you doing tonight?"

Frankie smiled and noticed Jim's accent was a bit thicker than it had been before he left for North Carolina.

"You might want to save some of that charm for Candi," Mia said.

"There isn't anything to save Mee," Jim used Frankie's abbreviated name for Mia and flashed a smile. "It's all natural."

Mia couldn't help but laugh.

"Jim, did you call her, or are we just hoping she will be here?"

"I didn't call but I'm pretty sure she will be here. I got the impression this is a regular place for her. If not, we'll find her address and pay her a home visit. What kind of approach do you want me to take?"

Mia spoke up, "Low key. Let her know Kristof is in jail and see if she'd be willing to talk to us about the party on the 4th of July. We'd prefer not to talk about it in the bar. If possible, we'd like to get her down to HQ. We'll be at a table waiting for a nod from you."

"Sounds good."

The trio made their way to the front entrance in perfect cadence. Jim opened the door, allowing Mia and Frankie to enter first. All three scanned the room, thankful the crowd was a light one. Jim glanced at Frankie and nodded at the bar. Sitting with her back to them was the slender figure of the person they were looking for.

CHAPTER
FIFTY-TWO

FRANKIE AND MIA found a table close to the bar so they could hear what Candi told Craven. They watched as he walked up behind her and gently touched the middle of her back. A smile lifted the corners of Candi's mouth in recognition.

"How've you been, Candi?" Jim noticed a glint of water in her eyes.

"I'm doing better now," she said. "Want to join me?"

"I'd love to. What's new with you?"

"Oh, you know, same ole stuff. Work. School. Parties. More work."

"You still working at Stevenson's Automotive?"

"Ha, it's funny you should ask that. As of yesterday, I have two weeks left at Stevenson's. They notified me today that they are making some changes at the dealership, and my services will no longer be needed as a receptionist. And, since apparently, I don't have any other skills they can use, I will be left without a job."

"I'm sorry to hear that, Candi. Do you have any idea what you're going to do next?"

"Apply for other jobs, I guess. I tried to call Alexandre to see if he needed any help at his firm, but his phone went straight to voice mail."

"Do you really think you want to work for him?" Jim asked.

Candi appeared to give his question some thought before saying, "Not really, but if I don't, then I'll have to pick up some extra shifts at the

Shady Lady and maybe work a party or two. I'm already working there a couple of nights a week, but I'd rather not do any more if I can find something else."

Jim knew he had to pursue the issue of the party carefully in light of everything Candi had just told him. The sleeve of Candi's sweater receded as she reached for her drink, revealing the bud of a rose on the inside of her wrist.

"Candi, may I see your tattoo?"

With a wink, Candi replied, "Which one?"

Jim smiled, "Let's start with this one. He took her hand in his and gently pushed the sleeve of her sweater up to reveal the rose tattoo.

"Oh, this one." A cloud shadowed her face. "That one's nothing."

Jim's tone took a serious note, "Candi, would you be willing to come talk to me and some of my colleagues? It's really important."

"Tonight? I have to work in the morning. Can it wait?"

"No, it really can't. I think you may be able to help us with a couple of homicide investigations."

"I don't see how I can be of any help. I haven't had anything to do with any homicides."

"I know you haven't, but I think you may know who has. Will you come downtown tonight?"

"Can I drive my own car?"

"Of course. You aren't in any trouble I just don't want to talk about this stuff in here where people can overhear us."

Candi rubbed her covered forearm and bit her lower lip. She looked around the room, then back at Jim. Nodding at Frankie and Mia, she asked, "Are they going to want to talk to me too?"

"Yes."

"So, I guess this wasn't just a coincidence, huh?"

Jim could hear the disappointment in her voice.

"Not entirely, but the tattoo is not what we initially wanted to talk to you about."

"Would you care to enlighten me before we drive downtown?" Candi asked with a bit of irritation.

Jim took a deep breath then said, "Alexandre Kristof is why we initially wanted to speak to you."

CHAPTER
FIFTY-THREE

"THANK you for coming down here, Candi. Detective Boden and I appreciate you agreeing to speak with us. Special Agent Craven will be joining us in a minute, but we wanted to speak to you alone for a few minutes while he grabs his files on the homicides." Frankie looked over at Alex and said, "This is Alex. She is a victim advocate with the Metropolitan Organization to Counter Sexual Assault. We asked her to join us to serve as a potential support person for you. If, at any time, you would like to speak to her privately, or if you would like her to leave, just say the word."

During the drive to Police Headquarters, Candi had determined what she believed to be the reason for the interview with the Sex Crimes Unit, but she hadn't decided how much she wanted to tell them. Sitting in the interview room, she still was unsure, but she was grateful to have Alex there with her.

Frankie and Mia had spent their drive to headquarters discussing how much they would put on the table. They ultimately decided to tell Candi about the videos but, at least initially, to leave out the information on the possible drug found.

"Back when we were investigating the rape involving Stevenson's Automotive, you met with Special Agent Craven at the Brooksider.

During that meeting, you mentioned an incident that occurred at Alexandre Kristof's house. We recently received a report that he was videotaping people in his home without their consent. As a result, we obtained a search warrant and when we executed the warrant, we recovered hundreds of videos and a mound of physical evidence. We'll be going through the videos and photographs while we wait for the lab results on the physical evidence. We also wanted to talk to you about the incident from the 4th of July and see if it may be related."

Frankie paused to let the information sink in.

Candi's face was ashen. The silence in the room was palpable as the realization drifted over her face.

"There are videos?" she softly asked.

"Yes. We haven't had a chance to watch all of them yet, so I don't know if there are any with you in them. If we find any, I promise I'll let you know."

Candi nodded.

"Did you go to a lot of parties at Alexandre's?" Mia asked.

Candi looked up, snapping out of her thoughts, and said, "Yeah. He was always throwing great parties. And if he wasn't hosting the party, the after-party was at his house. It didn't matter what day or what time we went over there it was like he was always ready. The bar was always stocked and there was plenty of food in the house. I think he liked having people around. Especially women."

"What kind of alcohol did he usually keep in the bar?" Frankie asked.

"You name it and he had it. Wine, liquor, beer, mixers. Everything."

"Did people mix their own drinks?"

Candi seemed to give the question some thought before answering.

"I never really thought about it, but now that you ask, no. I mean, you could grab a beer on your own but he or one of his friends would pour the wine and mix any drinks that had liquor. He was always making a big deal about how he had a 'special recipe' no matter what the drink was."

"You said he or one of his friends poured the wine and mixed the drinks. Who was the friend or was there more than one?"

"Luka."

"Do you know Luka's last name or where he lives?"

"I don't know. I only met him a few times."

"Tell us about the 4th of July party."

Candi sighed.

"It was one of Alexandre's killer parties. He had pulled out all the stops. There was a live band playing, everyone was swimming and dancing, and of course, drinking. Even the general manager from Stevenson's Automotive, Anthony Maggio, showed up. I saw Anthony walk in but didn't really care. I was hanging out with one of the guys from the repair shop. I waved hello and went back to doing shots with Josh.

"Josh got hammered. I mean stupid hammered. Alexandre has a rule about not letting people drive home after drinking at his house, so when he saw how lit Josh was, he helped me take him to one of the guest rooms to sleep it off. When we laid him down Alexandre touched my ass and told me I could stay with Josh that night or if I wanted to, I could sleep with him. I just laughed it off and told him I'd be back down to the party after I used the bathroom.

"I was coming out of the bathroom and almost ran into Mr. Maggio in the hall. I told him, 'it's all yours' and gestured towards the bathroom. He reached over and grabbed my waist and asked, 'Really?' I pushed on his chest and told him I was referring to the bathroom, but he kept a hold of my waist and tried to kiss my neck. I had heard about his antics from the other girl and told him to knock it off. I was about to show him how serious I was and use the heel of my shoe to stomp on his foot when he let me go. I walked away and went back to the party. He waited upstairs for a couple of minutes and then came back to the pool.

"Almost everyone else had left the party and I was trying to decide if I wanted to go back upstairs with Josh or catch a cab home. I knew I couldn't drive but I wasn't sure I wanted to stay at Alexandre's. I'd never stayed there before and it kind of creeped me out. Mr. Maggio came up to me again and this time asked me if I liked my job and if I thought Josh liked his. I told him we both liked our jobs, why was he asking? He took his finger and traced it along my shoulder blade and told me I should think about how much we both like our jobs before I start running my mouth off about the 'misunderstanding' in the hallway. I told him there was no misunderstanding and I had no intention of saying anything as long as he left me alone. He smiled at me, offered me a glass of wine, and asked, 'truce?'

"Just as I accepted the glass of wine, Alexandre asked Anthony and me if we wanted to join him and his girlfriend in the hot tub. That's really the last thing I remember about that night. When I woke up the next morning, I was in bed with Josh. Naked and sore." Tears were trickling down Candi's cheeks as she said the word naked. "I didn't think I drank that much, but I guess that wine really pushed me over the edge."

"What happened when you woke up?"

Candi brushed the tears from her cheeks and gave a half-hearted laugh, "What do you mean? I got dressed and went downstairs. Alexandre cooked me a gourmet breakfast, gave me a tall glass of water, a shot of tequila, and a couple of aspirin. When Josh woke up, we both left. Josh and I talked later and both of us are pretty sure nothing happened between us. He was out of it and, well, I was too. I probably took my own clothes off when I got back to the bedroom. I mean, after all, I was drunk. I never did figure out why I was sore though."

"Do you remember anyone else being at the house when you got into the hot tub?"

Candi seemed to give the question some thought.

"Now that you mention it, I think Luka was there."

"What was Alexandre's girlfriend's name?" Frankie asked.

"Keeley."

"You mentioned you were sore. Tell me more about being sore."

Candi lowered her head and said, "My whole body but especially… down there." Candi pointed to her lap.

"Did it feel like someone had penetrated your vagina?"

Tears fell from Candi's eyes as she nodded.

"Did you consent to having sex with anyone that night?"

"No. I mean, I was drunk, but I don't think I did."

"Is there anything else you remember about that night?" Frankie asked.

"No," Candi paused. "I remember the wine tasted different and when I asked Alexandre about it, he said it was a new blend he was trying. I don't know a lot about wine, so I didn't question it."

"How did you feel when you woke up? Besides sore."

Laughing, Candi said, "Like shit. My head was pounding, and I felt pretty nauseous. I've been hungover plenty of times, but this was different. It took me a couple of days to shake it."

Frankie was preparing to end the interview when Mia asked, "Can I speak to you in the hall?"

"LET'S show her the guy from the computer. He looks familiar to us. Maybe she can tell us why."

"Good call," Frankie said.

"Do you want to talk to her about the tattoo, or shall I?" Craven asked.

"You can join us. We probably should show her the photos of the girls too," Frankie answered.

"I think all of us in the room would be a bit overwhelming, so I'll watch from here and start working on the report," Mia said. "Why don't you guys go talk to her."

Frankie grabbed the photographs, and she and Craven returned to the interview room.

"Hi Jim," Candi looked up and smiled sweetly.

"Hey there. Do you feel like you can answer a few more questions for us?"

"Whatever you need," Candi said as she winked at Jim.

"Candi, do you know this guy?" Frankie showed Candi the photograph of the man with the little girl.

"That's Luka."

"Is Luka related to Alexandre?"

"Not that I know of. I don't think they are family, but Alexandre mentioned they grew up together, but I'm not sure where."

"Great. Do you know how to get in touch with Luka or where he lives?"

"No, I've only seen him at Alexandre's house."

"Thank you. I have a couple of other photographs to show you." Frankie flipped over the photograph of Katarina Schlovik and asked, "Do you know her?"

Candi touched the face of the woman in the photograph, "Yeah, that's Kat."

Frankie flipped over the photograph of Andrea Tucker and Nicole Andrews.

"Do you know these women?"

Candi gasped and put her hand over her mouth. Frankie heard a groan escape through Candi's fingers.

"What happened to them?" Candi cried. She touched each woman's face, letting her hand rest on the image of Nicole.

Jim laid his hand across Candi's and said, "They were murdered. Were they friends of yours?"

Candi cried openly and nodded. "Andi and I used to live together. She was a hard ass, but if she liked you, she'd do anything in the world for you. And she liked me. Nicki hadn't been here very long. I only saw her a time or two. Actually, the first time I met her was at the 4th of July party at Alexandre's. She and Andi weren't there very long though. I think they had booked a private party that night."

"Did Andi ever tell you she thought she was being followed?" Frankie asked.

"No, but we haven't really talked much the last couple of months."

"Do you know anyone who drives a white truck?" Frankie asked.

Candi looked at her with a questioning look, "Not that I can think of."

Frankie showed her a photograph of Heather, "Do you know this girl?"

"What the hell happened to her?"

"You didn't answer my question," Frankie said gently. "Do you know her?"

"I thought she was…yeah, I know her. Heather used to dance with us. She disappeared about a month ago. Honestly, I thought she was dead." Candi's face had grown ashen.

"Why did you think she was dead?" Frankie asked.

"She dated this guy that worked as a bouncer at the club. Bobby something or other. He was a total prick. She used to show up at the club sore and with bruises all over her body. He was careful not to touch her face, though. All the other bruises could be explained away, but bruises on her face would keep her from dancing. Midori is particular about that. Anyway, about a month or so ago, she stopped dancing, and Bobby was gone."

"Did you ask anyone about either of them?" Frankie asked.

Candi shook her head.

"Candi, where did you get your tattoo?" Craven asked.

Candi traced the rose stem on her wrist, "All the girls get a rose stem tattoo when they go to work for Midori at the club." Candi cocked her head to the side and smirked, "You have to earn the bud, though."

"How do you do that?" Craven asked.

"After hours, of course," Candi said with a laugh.

Candi told Frankie and Craven the same story Tessa had told. When she finished, they thanked her for talking to them and told her they would be in touch.

CHAPTER
FIFTY-FIVE

"FRANKIE, we have an address on that IP," Mia said excitedly.

"Is it the sister's address like he said?" Frankie asked.

"Not even close. In fact, it's Kristof's office building. Sarge is on his way in, and I've already started the search warrant."

"I'll bet money the girl isn't his niece either," Frankie said sardonically.

"I'll get Fitz and go sit up on it, see if we can see anyone coming or going from the building. Do you know if there are any apartments or anything in that building?" Craven asked as he typed a text message to Fitzmeyer.

Mia stopped typing and turned to Frankie, "I looked it up on google maps, and it looks like a warehouse converted into an office building and loft space. Didn't Tessa mention an apartment they used for the girls they recruited?"

Frankie nodded, "I wonder if Candi knows where it is?"

Craven called Candi and quickly confirmed the apartment was in an old warehouse that had been converted. She didn't remember the exact address but said it was in the west bottoms.

"I'll be in touch once I get out there. I'll video chat with you to help with the description for the warrant."

"Thanks, Jim. That will save us some time," Frankie said.

Mia worked on the warrant while Frankie called the on-call prosecutor who said she'd drive to police headquarters to sign the warrant.

"Do you think it's weird Moon doesn't want us to come to her?" Frankie asked.

"Maybe she's a slob, or maybe she just wasn't home," Mia answered. "Or maybe she doesn't want you to know where she lives because she's scared of you."

Frankie laughed out loud, "As if. I have no interest in jeopardizing my career over her."

Frankie looked at her watch, 9:30PM. It was going to be another late night by the time they got a judge's signature and served the warrant. She had planned to go to Derek's after work but looked like those plans were about to change.

"Hey babe, it's going to be a late night. We are working on a warrant now."

"Okay. Come by anyway if you aren't too tired ;)"

"K"

"Be safe. D"

Frankie smiled at the exchange and then began an inventory of her duty bag. The last warrant left the contents bare, so she quickly replenished her supplies in case the Crime Scene Unit couldn't respond.

"You two are determined to keep me from having an entire night at home with my wife, aren't you?" Baker's voice broke the silence. Jessica Moon followed him into the office.

"Sorry, Sarge," Frankie and Mia said in unison.

"It's okay. She's used to it," Baker said. "Is there anyone out on the address?"

"Craven and Fitz are out there. I heard from them about ten minutes ago, and they said it was quiet with only one light on in the building," Frankie said.

Jessica reviewed the warrant, requesting one minor correction before signing the document.

"We are going to run and get the judge's signature, then meet you in the lot down the block from the building," Mia said.

"Sounds good. Is Judge Maron still the on-call judge?"

"Yeah. I emailed her the affidavit to save some time, so it should be quick."

FIFTY-SIX

FRANKIE MADE her way into the renovated warehouse with Mia close behind. The brick building loomed over the empty streets and neighboring parking lots. Frankie used the key she got from Kristof's property and unlocked the door to the dimly lit lobby.

"I wonder if they use the freight elevator?" Frankie asked, nodding at the gated elevator in front of her.

"Looks like the gate is unlocked." Pointing at the black sign next to it, Mia said, "ARK Marketing has offices on the first and second floors. Midori Enterprises has offices on the third floor. Check out the name on four."

Frankie read aloud, "L. Petrov. We know Midori has a place where he keeps his recruits. What do you want to bet L. Petrov is Luka?"

"What does the warrant cover? The entire building or just ARK Marketing?" Baker asked.

"None of the above. It actually covers the location of the IP address, which is registered to the fourth floor. We don't have probable cause to get into Midori Enterprises…yet. We can probably get a warrant for ARK Marketing but I'm not up to that tonight," answered Frankie. "Maybe the other squad can work on getting it tomorrow."

"Okay. Let's check out who, or what, is on the fourth floor. There's a good chance that the door opens directly into the loft, so be alert," Sergeant Baker said.

Baker scanned the group to make sure everyone had their vests on, then led the way into the freight elevator.

No one said a word as the elevator slowly made its way to the fourth floor. A collective exhale could be heard as the doors opened into another lobby-like space. Baker took the lead as Mia and Frankie stacked behind him. Craven and Fitzmeyer posted up on the opposite side of the door. Baker glanced at his watch, 11:57PM, just under the wire. He raised his hand to knock, then waited. He was preparing to knock harder and louder when they heard the clopping sound of shoes hitting the floor on the opposite side of the door.

A cough was followed by a thick accent asking, "Who zee hell is it?"

"Kansas City Missouri Police Department. Open the door," Baker asserted.

The sound of the chain dropping, and the deadbolt being disengaged echoed in the silence.

"What can I do for you?"

Baker put his foot inside the doorway and pushed the door open. "We have a warrant for this apartment. My detectives are going to search the space based on this," thrusting the warrant into the man's hand.

Frankie and Mia scanned the living room, seeing no threat they moved hastily towards the hall. Fitz and Craven followed close behind. The doors in the hallway were all closed. Before leaving the living room, Frankie called back, "Is there anyone else here?"

"No. I mean, yes. My niece is in the bedroom asleep."

"How old is your *niece*?" Frankie asked, disbelief obvious in her tone.

"Fifteen. No, I mean sixteen."

Frankie remembered the girl from the video feed. She did not look sixteen. She pushed open the first doorway, only to find a laundry room. Mia opened the second door to a desk with a computer and a chair. Craven opened the third door to a scream.

FIFTY-SEVEN

"IT'S OKAY. We're the police," Frankie said. "Do you know where you are?"

The young girl stared at the group of detectives with a puzzled expression. "Of course, I do. I'm in Kansas City. Why would you ask me that?"

Frankie nodded at Craven and Fitzmeyer, gesturing for them to leave the room. She noticed a chair at the end of the bed and asked, "Do you mind if I sit down?"

The little girl nodded. Her voice trembled as she asked, "What's going on? Why are you here? I don't understand."

Mia grabbed a stool and sat down. "What's your name?"

"Julia Christenson."

"Where are you from?" Mia asked.

Frankie grabbed her notepad to take notes.

"Alton, Illinois."

"How old are you?"

"10. Will you please tell me what is going on?"

Frankie marveled at how articulate this child was at the age of ten. It was almost as if she had been coached how to answer the questions.

Mia calmly explained, "My partner, Detective Thomas, and I are with the police department. We served a search warrant at a house yesterday and found a computer with a live feed into this room. We watched you sleeping on the camera. Did you know there was a camera in this room?"

The color drained from Julia's rose-colored cheeks.

"How did you get here, Julia?"

Julia pulled the covers tightly around her petite frame. Tears glistened in her emerald-colored eyes. With her head lowered, she began to mumble into the blanket.

Mia touched the girl's foot and softly said, "Can you please speak a little louder, it's hard to understand you through the blanket."

Julia looked up slightly and said, "They promised me I was going to be famous, so I came here with them."

"With who?"

"I can't remember her name, but it started with a T. The other girl's name was Andi. I told them I was 13."

"How long have you been here?" Mia asked.

"Since October. I left on Halloween."

"Do your parents know you are here?" Frankie asked.

Julia glared at Frankie and said, "My parents are dead. I'm sure as long as my foster family gets a check every month, they won't care that I'm gone."

"Julia are you the only girl that lives here with Luka" Mia asked.

Julia shook her head but did not volunteer any information.

"Who else lives here?" Mia asked.

"Heather was staying here, but I haven't seen her in a few weeks." Julia reached up to brush golden strands off her face, revealing a tattoo of a thorny rose stem.

Mia made eye contact with Frankie and nodded. Frankie felt her stomach roll as she asked, "Does anyone else stay here?"

"Just Emma. She should be asleep next door if you all didn't wake her up."

"I'll go check," said Frankie. "How old is Emma?"

"11 or 12. I can't remember. She hasn't been here very long."

Frankie fought the anger growing inside. Stepping out of the room, she leaned against the wall and took a deep breath. The children in this loft were similar in age to her own children and it broke her heart. When she looked up, Craven was staring down at her.

"THERE'S a little girl sleeping in the next room. We thought she might be less scared if she was woken up by Mia, or the girl with the boy's name." Craven winked at Frankie.

It was just the lightness Frankie needed. She said, "I'll be right back."

Frankie slowly pushed the bedroom door open. The room was laid out identically to Julia's. She turned on the lamp and said, "Emma?"

The girl groaned something unintelligible.

"Emma, wake up."

Frankie watched the tiny girl's eyes flutter, then open wide with a look of fear.

"It's okay, I'm the police. I'm not here to hurt you." Frankie pulled a chair next to the bed and sat down. "My name is Frankie. Do you know where you are, Emma?"

Emma rubbed the sleep from her hazel eyes and nodded.

"What's your last name, Emma?"

"Brandt. Why are you here?"

Frankie explained why they were at the loft, then asked, "Emma, where are your parents?"

Tears created a trail down Emma's freckled cheeks. She brushed them away and said, "My momma's in Heaven and my dad's in hell."

Frankie thought Emma's choice of words was interesting.

"How old are you, Emma?"

"I just turned 13."

"Where were you living before you got here?"

"With my mom's sister and her husband."

"How did you get here?"

Emma fidgeted in her bed. She grabbed a worn, brown teddy bear and clutched it close to her chest. After a few moments, she said, "I ran away." The tone of Emma's voice deepened when she added, "You can't make me go back there. I won't go."

"Why did you run away?" Frankie felt a tightness forming in her chest as she waited for the answer.

"I don't want to talk about it, but I won't go back. They are not good people."

"We'll see what we can do. How did you end up here? In this apartment?"

Emma hesitated before saying, "Heather and Andi found me at a rest stop on the highway. They said I could stay with them. They told me I was going to do some modeling or something."

"How long have you been here?"

"I'm not sure. A few weeks. Maybe longer…"

Frankie knew she needed more information but decided not to push the issue in the tiny bedroom.

"Why don't you get dressed and we'll go for a ride to my office?"

"Why? I haven't done anything wrong. Why can't I stay with Luka?"

"Because you are a minor, and he doesn't have custody of you. We have to sort some things out and it will be easier to do it downtown."

CHAPTER
FIFTY-NINE

FRANKIE RAN her hand through her hair as she stared out the window of her office, trying to process all she had learned. They had gotten statements from Julia and Emma who were in the waiting room watching television and eating potato chips from the vending machine. Mia was trying to get someone from social services on the phone.

"Dammit!" Mia shouted, drawing Frankie from her thoughts.

Turning around, Frankie asked, "What's wrong?"

"The on-call Division of Family Services worker is a freaking idiot, that's what's wrong."

"What did they do now?"

"It's not what they *are* doing, it's what they are *not* doing. They told me to take these girls down to JJC like they were…"

Frankie interrupted, "They told you to take these two victims of sex trafficking to the Juvenile Justice Center?"

"Yes, like a couple of criminals. I'm not going to do it. I'll stay here with them all night before I do that."

"Maybe we can get them into…" Frankie paused for a moment before saying, "Wait, I have an idea. Hold on."

Frankie started looking through her desk, frantically.

"What are you looking for, Frankie?"

"There's a place in Parkville that might be able to help them, but I can't find their number. You know the SAFE PLACE signs at Quick Trip and the fire stations?"

"Yeah."

"I used to volunteer for them. If a child goes where a SAFE PLACE sign is, the workers have a number to call. Volunteers transport the kids to the shelter in Parkville. I thought I had their number in my desk," Frankie said as she continued to rifle through business cards.

"Hey Dawn," Mia said to the dispatcher on the phone. "Yeah. Do you have a phone number for the SAFE PLACE in Parkville? Mm Hmm. Yeah. Okay. 9055. Okay. Thanks Dawn."

Frankie listened to the one-sided conversation, thinking how brilliant Mia was to call the dispatcher. Aloud she said, "You da' bomb girl!"

Mia smiled and shrugged her shoulders as she dialed the number to the shelter. Frankie listened to Mia describe the circumstances to the on call worker. Five minutes later, they were explaining to Julia and Emma that they had a safe place for them to stay until their families could be notified.

Julia began to cry.

Emma put her arms around Julia and tried to comfort her, looked at Frankie and Mia and said, "You can't make me go back to those people. I'll run away again."

Frankie sat in a chair next to Emma and said, "I need you to explain why you won't go home. You don't have to do it tonight, but you're going to have to tomorrow, or they will send you back to your aunt and uncle. They have legal custody of you."

Julia looked at Emma and said, "Em, you have to tell them. I'll even come with you if you want."

Emma grabbed a tissue from the side table and wiped her nose. Her eyes searched Frankie's then fell to her lap. Quietly she stated, "Can we talk in the morning? I'm really tired."

Frankie said, "Of course. I'll come and talk to you at the SAFE PLACE tomorrow after breakfast, okay?"

Emma nodded.

The drive to the shelter was silent. Frankie glanced in the rearview mirror and saw Julia and Emma huddled together with their eyes closed.

She wondered what traumas they had experienced that made them so… old. She wondered what nightmares haunted their sleep.

Softly Mia said, "Frankie, you remember we are off tomorrow, right?"

Frankie nodded, "Yeah. I'm going to go talk to her after my run and while the kids are at school. You don't have to come in. I'll call you after. I don't want to bring anyone else into this if I can help it."

Mia nodded.

CHAPTER
SIXTY

THE SCREECHING of the alarm roused Frankie from a restless sleep. She had been dreaming about finding a young girl being held captive only instead of Emma or Julia, the face was that of her daughter, Danielle. The image left her shaken.

Before she could get out of bed, Frankie's phone began to vibrate. A smile filled her face at the incoming text messages.

"Hey girl with a boy's name! Sorry I had to cut out on you. Did you get what you needed?"

"Mornin' Jim! Got what we needed on Kristof. Got time for a run?"

"Macken Park in 15?"

"See you there."

Frankie opened the second message.

"Hey babe. Missed you last night. Enjoy your day off. D"

"Was another late one. Will call you tonight."

Frankie let Isabelle into the backyard while she changed into her running clothes. Five minutes later, she was climbing into her Jeep with a bottle of water. The drive to Macken Park was brief, giving her time to stretch while she waited on Craven.

"Hey girl, don't you ever get tired?"

Frankie laughed. "I wouldn't know what it was like to not be tired. The bags under my eyes have bags."

Craven made an exaggerated effort to look for bags under Frankie's eyes. Seeing none, he said, "You look bright-eyed and bushy-tailed to me."

Frankie began to blush. Before he could say anything else, Frankie asked, "Ready?"

"Let's do it. Take it easy on me though. I didn't run at all while I was gone."

The pair started off slow, finding a steady rhythm before the first turn on the track. Craven talked about his trip to North Carolina, entertaining Frankie with stories about his grandfather and the coast. Frankie updated Craven on what the girls told her and her plans to talk to them after their run.

As they started the final mile-long lap, Craven asked, "When do you have your next VISION meeting?"

Frankie smiled at the mention of the mentoring club she had started while on patrol. Craven had recently gone with her to a meeting and talked to the kids about career goals.

"Thursday. Want to join us? We are going to talk about our next volunteer project."

"What's your project?"

"We actually have two scheduled this year. We always cook a few meals at the Ronald McDonald House, but this year I want to do something more. I have three ideas, and I'm going to let them vote for their favorite."

"Don't leave me hanging. What are your ideas?"

Frankie slowed to a walk, "Make blankets for the elderly. Gather toiletries and distribute them to individuals trapped in the sex trade. Collect socks and gloves for the homeless."

"Those are great ideas. Where would you get the stuff from?"

"I've been thinking about that. We could probably get toiletries from the hotels if we write something up and go around to the various high-end hotels in town. We might be able to get a small grant or collect donations to buy fleece to make blankets or to buy gloves and socks."

"Which one do you think they will choose?"

Frankie laughed, "I have absolutely no idea."

"Fair enough," Craven said. They had stopped at the gate by where their cars were parked, "What's the rest of your day look like?"

"I'm going to go talk to those girls from last night, then usual mom stuff. I told Ty I'd pick him up from school so, for a few minutes at least, I'll be getting updates on everything I missed over the weekend. You?"

"I think Fitz and I are going to see what kind of intel we can get on those homicides."

"Let me know if you find anything good!"

SIXTY-ONE

FRANKIE SENT Sergeant Baker a text to tell him she was going to meet with Emma at the shelter. Frankie had promised Tyler she would pick him up from school and that was a promise she did not intend to break. She figured she had three hours to conduct the interview and make it to the school on time.

Frankie patted Isabelle on the head and said, "I'll be back before you know it, Izzie."

Frankie checked her bag to ensure she had her digital recorder, notebook, and a pen. At the last minute she threw in some snacks for the girls. Confident she had everything she needed she signed in and was escorted to a small conference room.

Emma walked into the room wearing a pair of blue jeans and an over-sized hooded sweatshirt. Julia stood in the doorway with a questioning look in her eyes. Frankie normally did not want other people in the interview room other than a victim advocate, but something about the girls' bond made her ask, "Emma, do you want Julia to sit with you?"

Emma gave a barely perceptible nod.

"Julia, you can sit with Emma, but it's really important that only she answers the questions, okay?"

"Yes."

"Okay. Emma, you told me last night that you'll run away again if you have to go back and live with your aunt and uncle. Can you tell me more about that?"

Emma kept her head down and did not immediately answer. Frankie didn't push. She was comfortable in the silence but knew Emma would not be. After a few minutes, Emma raised her head.

"My mom died when I was in first grade." Emma looked at Julia and said, "I was with her did you know that?"

Julia shook her head.

"We were driving kind of fast, and the roads were wet. That's what my aunt told me. She says she doesn't know why we were even on the road, but I know." Emma took a drink of the Coke Frankie had brought her. As she sat the bottle on the table, she added, "Momma and me were running away from home. She was trying to protect me. From my dad."

The weight of the words felt heavy in the air as Frankie waited for Emma to continue. Julia reached over and held Emma's hand.

"Dad used to get mad at mom, and sometimes when they fought, he would hit her, but that night…that night was different. They were fighting and I got really scared. I wet my pants and started to cry. I don't usually wet my pants and I knew I was going to be in trouble. My dad turned around and…."

Frankie thought Emma was going to cry but instead, she fought for control. Emma began to take deep breaths and fought back the tears threatening to fall from her eyes.

"I don't really remember what happened. He grabbed me, and my mom kept screaming at him to stop. The next thing I remember is being in the car. Momma was crying and telling me how sorry she was. She said she wouldn't let him hurt me again. I heard her saying something about the hospital right before the car started spinning. When it stopped, my momma was no longer in the driver's seat. She was…she was…"

Emma's voice cracked, and she couldn't hold back the tears any longer. She apologized for the emotion as she swept the water from her face.

Frankie grabbed a tissue, handed it to Emma and said, "Take your time."

Clearing her voice, Emma said, "She was lying through the windshield. The tree had pushed the driver's side seat up against me in the passenger seat. An ambulance came and took me to the hospital but I'm not sure they took her. They told me when my dad came that my momma was dead, but I already knew it. The doctors all thought my bruises and the blood on my body were from the accident, so no one asked me about them. They sent me home with my dad not realizing he's the one that beat me. But…he's dead now too."

Frankie let the gravity of what Emma said sink in before asking, "What happened to him?"

Emma half-laughed, half-coughed.

"Well, he liked to use drugs."

When Emma did not expound any further, Frankie asked, "Did he overdose?"

"Right after he beat me for the last time."

SIXTY-TWO

EMMA TOOK a deep breath then released a sigh so heavy Frankie could almost feel it. Julia clenched Emma's hand tighter in support.

"The beatings only got worse after my mom died. He blamed me for her death, even though it was *his* fault. If he hadn't beat me in the first place...one night he was on a binge, yelling at me for something stupid and then said he was going to kill himself. He took a few pills and then drank some alcohol. He closed his eyes and I really thought he was dying so I called 9-1-1. By the time the ambulance got there, he was awake and mad that I had called. He didn't like outsiders at the house. When they left..." Emma's voice caught in her throat. More tears threatened to fall but she fought them back. "When they left, he beat me. Bad. He beat me so bad that I started throwing up. When he finally finished, he picked up his pipe and took another hit, all the while telling me how much he hated me and how much he wished I had died instead of my mom. I told him I was going into the bathroom to clean up but instead, I climbed out the window. I ran to my neighbor's house and asked them to call the police. The cops got there and took me back to my dad. I begged them not to take me back, but they said they had to. They told me they were going to talk to my dad and get his side of things. He didn't know I was gone and so when they started asking him questions, he got really worked up. He fell and white stuff started coming out of his mouth. The officer tried to help him, but he was dead by the time the ambulance got there."

Frankie sat in stunned silence. She couldn't believe what this girl had experienced in her young life; what she had to witness.

"Some social workers came to my house, and they took me to my aunt's. That's when the real nightmare began." Emma stopped. Frankie could tell she wasn't sure if she should continue. "Can I take a break? I need to use the bathroom."

"Of course. Take your time."

Julia waited until Emma left the room before she said, "Does she have to go back to her Aunt's house?"

"It depends on what she says, Julia. She cannot go back, neither of you can go back, with Luka. You are minors and what he is doing to you…"

"What he is doing is giving us a safe place to stay. A place where no one comes into our rooms at night and…"

The door opened, leaving Julia's words to hang in the air.

"Emma, do you feel like you can finish telling me about your Aunt and Uncle?"

Emma nodded and took a drink of her soda.

"It started the day I got sent home from school. I had to change schools after my dad, uh…anyway, I didn't fit in very well in the new school. Everyone there knew each other their whole lives, and I didn't exactly have nice clothes or anything, so the kids started teasing me. One day one of the kids started making fun of me and said my mom was lucky she didn't have to see what a loser I was. I got mad and punched her in the face and I got sent home. My uncle picked me up and when we got to the house, he made me stay in the living room with him. I figured he was going to beat me or ground me, but he didn't. He got ice for my hand and then sat next to me on the couch. He talked to me and told me how pretty I was. He said we should just keep this between us. I was suspended from school for a day, but he said he'd tell my aunt he was taking me to school and then just hang out with me. I thought he was cool and was going to take care of me. Be a dad, you know?"

Frankie thought she knew where the story was going. It was a story she had heard before way too many times.

"The next day my aunt left for work, and my uncle and I went out and got some breakfast. He talked to me and for the first time since my mom died it seemed like someone was interested in what I had to say about things. When we got back to the house, I laid down on the floor to watch TV with him. Jared, that's her husband, laid on the floor beside me and threw his arm across my back. At first, it was nice. No one had done that in a long time."

Frankie watched as Julia began to fidget in her chair, and Emma began to tap her fingers rhythmically on the table.

"Before I realized what was happening, he had me on my back and had put his hand down the front of my pants."

Emma described the sexual abuse that followed with a flat voice. She described the frequency of abuse and her fear of him trying to put "it" inside her.

"I ran away before that could happen."

CHAPTER
SIXTY-THREE

FRANKIE GOT to Tyler's school just before the bell rang to signal the end of the day. As she predicted, he immediately began describing all she had missed over the weekend. Frankie smiled when Tyler's non-stop chatter continued after they got home.

Interrupting his monologue, Frankie asked, "Are you hungry, Ty?"

"I'm starving. I didn't have any lunch money, so the lunch lady would only give me a peanut butter sandwich today."

Frankie was engulfed by a wave of guilt. The kids did not usually take their lunch when her mom dropped them off at school, and she was supposed to pay Tyler and Danielle's lunch accounts online but had forgotten. Frankie squeezed Tyler's shoulders and said, "I'm so sorry bud. I forgot to put money on your account."

"It's no big deal mom. I know you get busy."

Frankie smiled at the easy way her son always forgave and excused her errors, but it was important to her that he learn one had to own their mistakes. She said, "I appreciate that, but I still shouldn't have forgotten to put money on your account. What do you want for dinner? You get to pick tonight."

Danielle walked through the back door and asked, "What does he get to pick?"

"I get to pick dinner! How about Panda Express? Can we do that mom? Puhleeeease?" Tyler drew out the word, the sound just short of a whine.

"What do you think, Dani? Do you want Panda?"

Stomping down the hallway, Danielle answered, "Whatever."

"What's wrong with her?" Tyler asked.

"She's probably just tired, Ty. How about we have an apple while you do your homework, then we can go get dinner."

"Ok."

Frankie cut up an apple and placed it on the table while Tyler worked on his math. Once he was settled, she said, "I'm going to go check on Dani. I'll be right back, okay?"

"Mmhm."

Frankie knocked on her teenage daughter's door, "Dani?"

"What?"

Frankie opened the door, scanning the room. Posters of pop singers hung on the walls, and piles of clothes sat stacked on the end of her bed and atop her dresser. Dani lay across the comforter, headphones in her ears with a textbook open in front of her. Frankie sat on the edge of the bed.

"How was the weekend at your dad's?"

"Fine."

Frankie sighed at the one-word answer.

"What did you all do?"

"Not much. Watched TV and played games. I went to church with the girls yesterday. They want me to join the Bible quiz team, but I told them I didn't think I could."

The girls. Dani had stepsisters, which made it a slumber party every time she went to visit her dad. Frankie knew she couldn't compete with that, especially with her erratic work schedule.

"That sounds like fun Angel-girl. Where does the Bible Quiz team meet?"

"At their church down there."

"Well, that would be really hard for us to do. Maybe we can find a church that has a Bible Quiz team a little closer to us."

"Never mind, it wouldn't be the same without my *sisters*." Danielle turned back to the textbook lying in front of her.

Frankie felt the comment like a punch in her gut. She was glad Dani was close to her stepsisters, but it didn't take away the twinge of jealousy she felt or her fear of being replaced.

CHAPTER
SIXTY-FOUR

"THEN AUSTIN TOLD the teacher his dog ate his homework. She didn't believe him, but when he got his paper out of his backpack, you could see the slobber and teeth marks on the paper. The teacher gave him an extra day to turn in his assignment."

Tyler laughed at Dani's stories from middle school. In his eyes, she was grown up and worldly. Frankie laughed despite the questions going through her mind. How did the dog get the paper? And why was it still wet when Austin got it to school?

"What was the funniest thing that happened at your school today, Ty?"

"Brittany *kissed* me at recess."

The Diet Coke Frankie was drinking came out her nose as she choked in surprise.

"She did what?"

"Ugh," Tyler grunted. "She *kissed* me. It was so gross. We were playing tag, and when I caught her, she turned around and planted one on me."

"Did you kiss her back?" Dani asked.

Tyler's face turned a bright shade of pink. Tears of anger and embarrassment filled his eyes. Turning to look at his sister, he shouted, "NO!"

Dani laughed at the discomfort she had caused.

Softly Frankie asked, "What *did* you do, Ty? Did you say anything to her?"

"I wiped my face and then the bell rang so I went inside."

"If she tries to do it again, and you don't want her to, don't be afraid to tell her no. Make sure she understands you don't want her to kiss you. You can do it without being mean too."

"Okay, mom."

"Why don't you go take a shower while Dani and I clean up in here."

Tyler took his plate to the sink. He was barely out of earshot before Dani asked, "Why do I have to help you clean up, but Ty doesn't have to do anything around here?"

Frankie sighed. It was going to be one of those nights. Lately, it felt like she was always battling with Danielle about something.

"Tyler does do stuff around here, but tonight you and I are on kitchen duty. I thought it might be nice for us to spend some time together."

"Whatever. All he does is take the trash out and *occasionally* cleans out the litter box. Usually, you make me do it. I have to do everything while you baby him."

"Danielle, you know that is not true. He also unloads the dishwasher and feeds the cat. You have to remember he is seven years younger than you, so he isn't going to have as many responsibilities. He also isn't going to have as many privileges. You get to stay up later and watch movies he can't watch. You get to hang out with your friends at the park, but he always has to have an adult with him."

"Whatever," Dani said, throwing the dishtowel on the counter. "I'm going to go do my homework."

Frankie picked up the towel, slung it across the oven handle, and leaned against the counter. All she wanted was a few minutes with her daughter without an argument, but it had become impossible. Isabelle sat at Frankie's feet and looked up.

Frankie rubbed the dog's head and said, "I just can't win with that one."

ONCE DANIELLE and Tyler were in bed, Frankie poured a shot of rum into her diet Coke. She felt like the weight of the world was resting on her shoulders. Her day had been spent moving from one thing to another and there had been no time to process what she had been told by Emma. Child Protective Services had been called, and all Frankie could do was pray they wouldn't send the girls back to their families and that the foster family they were sent to wouldn't do more harm. The only positive was the social worker said she would try to keep them together if possible.

Frankie sank into her overstuffed chair and released a loud sigh. As if work wasn't enough, Danielle was pushing every button she had. Some of it was definitely her age, but Dani had gotten noticeably worse since the attempted kidnapping. She was perpetually angry, primarily at Frankie, and refused to talk to the therapist she had taken her to. Parenting was the one area in her life where Frankie felt like a complete failure.

The ding of her phone interrupted Frankie's thoughts. She wasn't on call and debated on looking at the message. Frankie took a sip of the smooth drink, and she picked up her phone.

"We have a hit on the duct tape. Give me a call. B."

Frankie recognized the number from Boyd Miller, a technician in the crime lab. Her call was answered on the first ring.

"Well, that didn't take long," laughed Boyd.

"Your text was a bit of a tease." Frankie chuckled then took another drink.

"I can't give you too much via text, or I may never hear your voice."

Frankie laughed and redirected the conversation back to business, "What did you find on the duct tape?"

"There was a mixture of DNA, but it may be a few more days before we get that back. The reason I texted was because we found a couple of fingerprints." Boyd said, following with a dramatic pause.

"And…" Frankie drew out the word in mock frustration.

"One of the prints belongs to Lamont Foster. The other was to Corey Simpson. I've already emailed you the report but figured you would want the news."

"You know me too well, Boyd. Thank you for texting me. I'll let you know if the victim identifies them. Please keep me posted on the DNA, okay?"

"Of course. Talk to you later."

Frankie sat in her chair, staring at her drink. She was resisting the urge to call the office and have Foster ran through NCIC. Before she could give in to her impulses, her phone began to ring.

"What are you wearing?" Derek's velvety baritone voice sent a quiver up Frankie's back.

"Nothin' but a smile. What are you doing?"

"Finally driving home from the office and thought I'd see what my girl was up to."

Frankie smiled. Derek always seemed to sense when she needed a call to distract her from the craziness in her life. The pair talked mindlessly for the time it took Derek to get to his house. Even though they had not discussed any of what had happened that day, Frankie felt a sense of ease when she hung up the phone.

THE NEXT FEW days were a blur. Frankie created photographic line-ups to show Heather, but new cases prevented Frankie from contacting her and she had been playing phone tag with Detective O'Brien. Frankie and Mia had been going non-stop since they returned from days off.

"Did I read the schedule correctly, are you taking Saturday *and* Sunday off?" Mia asked.

Mia knew her too well. Normally when they were on the night schedule, she worked weekends so she could be home with the kids a couple of nights during the school week.

"Yeah. We are going to the farm on Saturday. Dad and Jake are smoking a brisket."

"How's your dad doing?"

Frankie smiled at the question. Frankie's dad, Frank, suffered a heart attack and almost didn't survive. It was one of the scariest moments in Frankie's life. She could not, no did not want to, imagine a world her dad wasn't in.

"Dad's doing great. He went for a check-up recently and came back with a clean bill of health. He and Jody are back on the trail every day. He told me the other day they were going to start taking scuba diving lessons!"

"That's fantastic!"

"Yeah, I think this was a wake-up call for them. Dad said it's time to start doing all the things they've been putting off."

"Good for them. And Jake?"

"Ah, little brother Jake. I think he's actually going to settle down."

"What?" Mia did not try to hide the surprise in her voice. "With the girl he brought to the party. Ann, something?"

"Yep, Ann Marie. She is super sweet. Sophie and I approve." Frankie chuckled. "As if that matters."

Frankie and Mia spent the next few hours working on paperwork. The darkness had set in when Mia said, "I need a diet Dr. Pepper. Do you want to run to Quick Trip?"

Frankie looked at the clock and nodded.

Twenty minutes later, they were circling the block of one-way streets to find a parking spot in front of the sally port. As they drove past the courthouse, Frankie couldn't help but glance into the parking lot, noticing Derek's SUV in its regular parking spot. The only other cars in the parking lot were a red convertible with personalized tags and a dark blue RAV4.

CHAPTER
SIXTY-SEVEN

FRANKIE FOUGHT the urge to call Derek and see if he was with Jessica. She had jumped to conclusions before and been wrong, but the pain of his past indiscretions was still fresh. It was probably just a coincidence that they were both working late. She'd send him a text and see if he responded.

"Hey babe. How's your night going?"

Frankie laid her phone back on her desk, screen down. How long would it take Derek to answer? She tapped her pen on her desk as she stared at the computer screen, finding it difficult to concentrate on the report she was writing.

"You okay, Frankie?"

Mia's words jolted Frankie from her brooding.

"Huh? Oh, yeah. Just lost in thought."

Frankie's phone began to buzz, indicating an incoming message.

"Working late. Tying up some loose ends at the office. Are you working this weekend?"

Frankie read the message and thought to herself, *this might be a good way to ask Derek if he wants to go to the farm on Saturday. Or maybe help with the cookout on Sunday?*

"Took the weekend off. BBQ at the farm Saturday. Want to join us?"

Frankie watched the screen of her phone for what seemed like forever. Just when she began to believe she wasn't going to receive a response, the phone vibrated.

"I need to work. Sorry babe. Maybe another time."

"Want to come to the park on Sunday for a BBQ? I'm having the VISION kids come up to Macken."

"I'll be working. Have fun. XO D"

Frankie recognized the signature "conversation is over" text. She didn't understand. One minute, things were great and the next, he was putting a wall up between them. The ringing of the unit phone broke the silence.

"Sex Crimes, Detective Boden."

Frankie looked at the clock. Ten o'clock.

"Uh-huh. Okay. Mm hmmm. Okay. Put me down as notified. Boden. B-O-D-E-N."

"What do we have?"

"A weeny-wagger up north."

Frankie let out a sigh of relief.

"White male, average height. No other descriptors. It sounds like the cases Coleman is working."

"Did the victim in this case get anything additional the others did not provide?"

"A car with a partial plate."

"Good. More than Coleman has, I think," Frankie said as she took a drink from her diet Coke.

"That's good because I really doubt they'd let us do a penis line-up."

Frankie choked, trying to keep the soda from coming out of her mouth. She and Mia broke into a fit of laughter. It was the best way to end the night.

FRANKIE AWOKE TO A PERFECT SATURDAY. The sun was shining, and not a cloud was in the sky. It was a perfect day to go to the farm. She grabbed the kids and had them help her take the top off the Jeep. Danielle and Tyler giggled and had fun as they rendered the Jeep topless.

Thirty minutes and a stop at Quick Trip later, they were off to the farm. Frankie let her mind wander as the sun warmed her face and the sound of the kids singing along to the radio warmed her heart. This was not the first time she had asked Derek to meet her family or the first time he evaded her invitation. Frankie knew there was an unspoken meaning behind it, but she wasn't ready to face it. Earlier that day she had received a text from him saying he was sorry to miss the cookout. Frankie resisted the urge to say something smart back – in the end, it wouldn't do anything but put a wedge between them. Instead, she told him she would miss him and to not work too hard. In the back of her mind, she wondered if he was working or if he was playing. With Jessica Moon.

Tyler's voice interrupted Frankie's thoughts, "Hey mom, is Grandpa Frank going to be at Jake's?"

"Yep. Aunt Sophie, Jody, and Ann Marie's boys will all be there."

"Anyone my age?" Tyler asked.

"I think Ann Marie's boys are about your age."

"Yahoo!"

Frankie smiled and looked over at Dani, sitting in the passenger seat.

"Why can't I go to dad's house? The girls are there. It's not like anyone my age is going to be at Jake's. You could drop me off on your way."

Frankie forced herself to continue smiling as she said, "Because I took the weekend off for a *family* cook-out and you are part of *this* family too."

Dani put her earbuds back in her ears and mumbled, "Whatever."

Frankie worked to stay present while Tyler asked more questions about Ann Marie's boys.

"Bud, I don't know. I haven't met them. You'll have to ask them when you see them."

Frankie turned onto Moonglow Road, the gravel road that led to the family farm where her brother lived. At the top of the hill, she reflexively looked to the right and caught a glimpse of the old barn playhouse her dad and uncle renovated when she was a kid. It had been a staple of her childhood. As she began the descent down the hill, Frankie's breath caught at the beauty of the property that had been in her family longer than she had been alive. Water met the bottom of the bridge that crossed the creek bordering the edge of the property. The trees were dressed in their spring leaves and the pasture was a deep, lush green. The air was fresh and smelled of the season.

The old white farmhouse sat on a hill with a new barn to its left. A huge tree with roots older than the farmhouse sat in the front yard with a tire swing hanging from a branch. Frankie couldn't help but smile at the memories of swinging on that old tire for hours, only stopping when the fireflies came out, and her dad or grandfather called for her to come inside.

Frankie didn't even have the Jeep in first before Sophie was yelling, "Hurry up!"

"Hey sis! What's the rush? I thought dinner wasn't for a few hours."

Sophie was at Frankie's door, "It's not, but Jake said he had something he wanted to tell us before mom and dad got her. I have a feeling it's about Ann Marie. I bet she's knocked up!"

"Sophie!" Frankie glared at her little sister and nodded her head towards Tyler.

"What's knocked up mom?" Tyler asked.

"Never mind, Tyler. Sophie is just being silly." Dani began to say something, but Frankie firmly said, "Danielle."

Dani and Tyler jumped out of the Jeep. Dani went to sit on the porch swing to sulk while Tyler found Jake's dog Earl. She watched as the old dog chased after Tyler as he ran towards the tire swing. Frankie followed Sophie to the barn.

"What's up, little brother?"

"Hey Frankie!"

"Okay big brother, she's here. What's the big news?" Sophie asked.

"Geez, Sophie. Chill," Jake said.

Frankie stifled a laugh. Everyone thought *she* was the impatient one, "C'mon little brother. Don't keep us waiting."

"Fine. I'm going to ask Ann Marie…"

Sophie interrupted, "To marry you? See, I told you she's knocked up."

"What? No, to move in with me. What the hell, Soph – are you crazy? She's definitely not knocked up."

"She's got a point, little brother, why not ask her to marry you?"

"Because I'm not ready to buy a ring, and I need to make sure she's willing to live down here. Heaven knows I'm not moving to the city."

Frankie and Sophie said in unison, "No, you're not."

Before either could ask any more questions, Jake said, "Cool it, here she comes."

Frankie watched as Ann Marie drove up in her little car. The closer she got to the barn, the bigger Jake's smile got. Ann Marie pulled the car in next to Jake's truck and before she could turn it off, two towheaded boys tumbled out of the backseat. It was obvious they had been there before because the first place they went was to the tire swing.

Frankie knew Tyler would introduce himself and all would be well in the lives of the three little boys.

CHAPTER
SIXTY-NINE

"FRANK-EE!" The sound of Jake's best friend, Bill, echoed through the barn. "Where's your FBI friend?"

"Hey bud!" Frankie returned Bill's side hug. "He's probably working or breaking hearts this weekend."

"Well shucks, I was hoping he would be here," Bill quickly turned his attention to Sophie and Ann Marie. "Ladies, how are you two tonight?"

Frankie used the opportunity to slip out of the barn to find Dani, who was sitting on the porch swing with a scowl on her face.

"Mind if I sit down?" Frankie asked as she sat on the bench. "Looks like the boys are having fun."

"Glad someone is."

"What's wrong, Angel-girl?"

"I told you; I want to go to dad's house. The girls are there, and there's a big event at the church tomorrow. I'm missing everything."

Frankie sat quietly, watching the boys run around the field, undoubtedly playing a game they had made up. What she wanted to say was, *you are missing everything. Your grandparents, your aunt and uncle, time with me and your brother.* But Frankie knew there was nothing she could say that would change what Dani was feeling, so she said nothing.

The mother and daughter sat in silence for several minutes before

Frankie slapped Dani on the leg and said, "Let's go help Uncle Jake and Aunt Sophie."

With a barely disguised huff, Dani said, "Okay."

As they walked back to the barn, Frankie put her arm around Dani's shoulders and said, "Know how much I love you?"

Dani did not even try to hide her irritation but answered, "More than all the sand and water in the sea."

"Yep, even when you are grumpy." Frankie squeezed Dani's shoulder then let her hand drop. "Hey dad!"

Frankie's heart was full as she watched her father, Frank, stop at the truck door and wait for her to reach him. It had been months since the heart attack almost took his life and he seemed to be doing really well.

Frank ruffled Dani's hair and asked, "How are you?"

"Hey grandpa. I'm okay."

"Are you playing ball this spring?"

"If I make the team."

"I'm sure you will. Have your mother send me the schedule so I can come see a few games."

Dani nodded and walked away.

"What's wrong with her?" Frank asked.

Frankie filled her dad in on the latest.

"She'll come around. You just have to give her a little time."

"I know, dad. It's just hard. And they are not making it any easier."

"They're not going to. Her dad is going to do what he can to make her want to live with him. He knows you can't compete," Frank paused and added, "Not that you should be trying."

"You're right, dad."

Frank ruffled his daughter's short hair and laughed, "Aren't I always?"

Frankie nodded, ran her fingers through her mussed hair, and said, "Yep. Somehow you always are dad. Let's go see how long until we eat."

CHAPTER
SEVENTY

THE BONFIRE WAS REDUCED to smoldering embers when Frankie loaded up the kids to head home.

"Are you sure you don't want to stay the night?" Jake asked.

"I would little brother, but I have a mentoring event tomorrow at Macken Park and have a bunch to do in the morning."

"Alright, be careful driving home. You too, Soph."

"Who says I'm going home?" Sophie asked, winking at Frankie.

Jake held up his hand and said, "Honestly, I don't want to know."

Sophie leaned over and whispered, "See you in a bit!"

Frankie and Sophie spent the rest of the evening at her house, talking like sisters do. Dani stayed up with them for a little while but eventually fell asleep on the sofa. Frankie watched as the teenager slept peacefully, marveling at how the sweet girl sleeping could be so harsh when she was awake.

"Are you going to let her join the Bible Quiz team with those girls?"

Frankie sighed, "I take it she told you about that. Honestly, Sophie, I don't see how I can. At least not with her *sisters*. I offered to help her find a place near the house, but she snubbed her nose at that. She said it wouldn't be the same. There's no way I can drive her back and forth and I wouldn't ask anyone else to either."

"Did she tell you the girls told her she should move in with them?"

"What?" Frankie's voice rose slightly, enough to make Dani groan and move. Lowering her voice she asked, "Sorry, what? When did that happen?"

"I don't know exactly when they told her that. She just said something to me tonight. She asked me what I thought about it."

"What did you tell her?" Frankie's stomach was in her throat. She knew things had been rough, but she didn't want Dani to move out.

"I told her I thought it would be a mistake. What did you think I'd say?"

Tears welled in Frankie's eyes. She didn't trust herself to speak.

"But Frankie, I kind of see her point…"

Frankie interrupted, "What do you mean, you see kind of see her point?"

"The girls are her age, and they are all active in something so she could…"

"… be involved in normal kid stuff. You think I haven't thought of that? I know my schedule makes it hard…"

Sophie laid her hand on Frankie's arm, "Sis, you are a good - no, a great mom. You would move heaven and earth for these kids, but you are only one person and there are two of them down there. Right now, she's only seeing the weekends. The fun. The activity. Maybe you should let her stay for the summer and see what it is like to live there every day. I'm betting she will change her mind when it's not all fun and games every day; when she realizes she will have to go to school, do chores, and get disciplined there too."

Frankie thought about what Sophie said. Summer was just a couple months away, and Dani may not want to stay down there by then.

"I'll wait and see if she brings it up to me. Maybe it would help her to see first-hand that the grass isn't always greener on the other side."

CHAPTER
SEVENTY-ONE

SUNDAY'S WEATHER was a repeat of Saturday. Frankie took advantage of Sophie sleeping on the sofa and went for a quick run in the neighborhood. As she ran, she made a mental checklist of all the things she needed to load into the Jeep for the picnic. When Frankie got home, she could tell that Dani woke up even more surly than the day before.

"Danielle, you need to lose the attitude before we go to the park."

"Why, so those kids can think you are a perfect parent with perfect children?"

"Seriously, Dani, what the hell?" Sophie exclaimed.

"What? You know I'm right. She wants everyone to think she is so perfect, but really, she is a mess."

"Danielle, you know that is not true. Get ready to go," Frankie said.

"Whatever, you can't even remember to pay our lunch accounts."

Frankie stared in disbelief as Dani left the room. To Sophie she said, "Today, should be fun."

"Why don't you let me take her to church and then we will come to the park and help clean up. Maybe a little dose of the Holy Spirit will adjust her attitude."

"You'd do that?"

"Of course," Sophie answered, giving her sister a hug. "Tyler too."

With Sophie and the kids gone, Frankie loaded the Jeep and headed to the park. She was surprised to see Carl, one of the kids from VISION, was already there with Craven.

"Hey guys, are you early or am I late?"

"I think we are all on time," Craven said. "Carl told me he hopped the bus to come up here. I told him I'd take him home for you."

Frankie nodded a thank you to Craven and said, "Why don't we get things set up. Carl, do you think you can start the grill?"

A smile filled the boy's face as he nodded and grabbed the charcoal and lighter from the Jeep.

The laughter and chatter of the children she mentored almost made Frankie forget about Danielle's attitude that morning. The parents who were able to show up to the picnic chatted amongst themselves until it was time to start cleaning up the remnants of lunch.

"Frankie, when do you want us to start collecting hygiene items for our project?" Carl asked.

Frankie smiled at the enthusiasm of the young man eager to start planning for their volunteer project. The kids had voted to make hygiene bags for the unhoused, sex workers, and domestic violence shelters. It was intended to be an all-year project.

"Let me draft a letter, and maybe over the next couple of weeks, we can visit a few dentists and hotels to get donations. I also have a few ideas on how to either get bags donated or make our own."

The kids and their parents talked over one another with ideas on content for the bags, storage, and how they planned to distribute them. Frankie's heart was full. They had just about finished cleaning up when Frankie saw Danielle and Tyler walking towards her. Dani was smiling, and the moment Tyler saw Carl, he took off at a run towards the boy.

"Sophie said to tell you she had to go take care of something, but she'd call you later," Dani said.

"Okay. How was church?"

"I like the church my sisters got to more, but this one was okay."

Frankie just smiled and handed Dani a bag to put into the Jeep.

THE PHONE WAS RINGING when Frankie walked into the squad room. She tossed her work bag on the chair next to her desk and grabbed the phone, "Sex Crimes Detective Thomas."

A muffled voice pleaded, "I need your help."

"Who is this? Where are you?"

"It's Heather. I'm in a closet, and I'm scared."

"Where are you? Is there anyone there with you?"

"They're trying to get into my apartment."

"Where is your apartment, Heather? Did you leave the shelter?"

Frankie heard a door breaking and a woman screaming.

"Heather?!"

The phone line went dead.

Frantically Frankie dug Heather's file out of the desk and located the phone number for the caseworker at the domestic violence shelter. Frankie dialed the number but got no answer. Mia walked into the office as Frankie scanned the file, searching through her notes for anything that might help her locate Heather.

"Mia, will you please call the main number of Rose Brooks and see if they will give you Heather Whitaker's new address? Somebody's breaking in. We need to get a radio car there as soon as possible."

"Sure," the word not completely out of her mouth before Mia started dialing the number.

Frankie tried Heather's number again. One ring. Two rings. Three rings.

"You have reached Heather. You know what to do."

Frankie tried the number again with the same results. She tried a third time and was about to try a fourth when she heard Mia say, "8802 East 87th Street # 201. Okay. Thank you."

"Hey Laura, I need you to get a radio car out to 8802 East 87th Street #201 on a nature unknown."

"What's going on, Frankie?"

"I got a call about five minutes ago from a victim in one of my cases. Her name is Heather Whitaker. She was hiding in a closet and said someone was breaking in. I heard the door break, followed by her screaming. Then the phone disconnected."

"Okay. Want the officers to call you when they get there?"

"Yeah. We are going to head that way from headquarters, but I'll have the phone." Frankie hung up and grabbed her vest and bag. Looking towards Mia, she asked, "Are you coming?"

"Of course."

The twenty-minute drive to the apartment felt much longer. Frankie and Mia listened to the radio traffic as they drove, waiting to hear if the officers found Heather. And if she was alive.

They were ten minutes from the complex when they heard the radio car, *"244. We're 10-23. Hold the air."*

Frankie recognized the voice of Bryan Shane telling the dispatcher they were on the scene. Frankie pulled into the apartment complex minutes later.

"244. You can clear the air. Start an ambulance and a sergeant."

CHAPTER
SEVENTY-THREE

FRANKIE ADVISED the dispatcher she and Mia were on the scene, grabbed a pair of gloves, and took the stairs two at a time. The flimsy door to the apartment was hanging from its hinges. Frankie stepped into the unfurnished living room, taking in the lack of furniture and the bare walls.

Shane called from the bedroom, "She's back here, Frankie. She's pretty banged up."

Frankie made her way to the bedroom, careful not to touch anything in her path. Frankie caught her breath at the sight of the girl sitting on the floor, leaning against the frameless mattress. Patches of long curly hair lay between the closet and the bed.

Heather tried to speak, but the words gurgled in her throat. Blood ran down the side of her face from a gaping wound on the side of her head. Red tears drained from her right eye; her left was swollen shut. If Frankie had not known who she was, she wouldn't have recognized her.

Frankie knelt next to the girl and softly said, "Don't try to speak Heather. An ambulance is on the way."

Heather's head fell forward, and she began to sob. Her left arm hung from her body at an unnatural angle. Frankie reached over and put her hand on Heather's opposite shoulder, speaking softly.

"They ra…" Heather's voice cracked. "He rap…"

"Did they rape you, Heather?"

Heather nodded her head slightly.

"Do you know who did this to you?"

Heather nodded.

Before Frankie could ask any additional questions, the paramedics walked into the room.

"Hey sweety. Can you tell us your name?" asked the paramedic.

Heather tried to speak, but only a gurgle could be heard.

"Heather Whitaker," Frankie said.

"Okay, Heather. Let's get you onto the gurney and get you to the hospital. We're going to take good care of you."

To the paramedics Frankie said, "Tell the ER to call the forensic nurse on duty. Heather, I'll come see you at the hospital before the end of my shift."

The paramedics got Heather onto the gurney and were just about to leave when she motioned to Frankie.

"What is it, Heather?"

Heather motioned for Frankie to give her the notepad she had been writing on. Frankie handed the pad and a pen to Heather who scribbled something on it and handed it back to Frankie.

Frankie looked at the name Heather had scribbled and asked, "Are you sure?"

Heather nodded.

CHAPTER
SEVENTY-FOUR

FRANKIE LOOKED at the names scribbled on the notepad. Corey and Tubby. They had found her. Why hadn't Heather told her she moved? She needed to go somewhere where she would be safe. Somewhere Corey and Tubby couldn't find her.

"Frankie, do you want me to call Crime Scene?" Mia asked.

Frankie nodded.

"Do we need to call the Assault Squad?" Shane asked.

"No, we'll handle it. The men that physically assaulted her raped her as well. They are the same men from the other case we're working on her." Frankie looked around the room and loudly said, "Dammit!"

Intellectually Frankie knew there was nothing she could have done to protect Heather, but it was still frustrating. She grabbed her notepad and began taking notes of the scene, her back to Mia and the officers so they couldn't see the emotion overtaking her face.

"Crime Scene is en route," Mia said. Sensing Frankie needed a moment she added, "We'll go do an area canvas while you sketch the scene."

Frankie nodded in understanding. When she was sure they were gone, she reached up and wiped tears of frustration from her eyes.

She was just finishing up with her notes and sketch when Frankie heard a cheerful, "Hey girl, where are you at?"

"Back here Erin!" Frankie looked up just in time to see the crime scene tech's infectious smile.

"What's going on? Why are you all out on this? I heard 244 ask for a report number, and he said it was for an assault. Did you get more information after he called?"

"Yeah. When the paramedics were taking her away, she disclosed a rape. You remember that case where the girl was loaded into the trunk of her car in Kansas and brought over here?"

"Yeah."

"This is the same girl and the suspects in this assault are the same guys from the other case. They beat her up bad, Erin. Honestly, I'm surprised they let her live."

Mia walked in just as Frankie was finishing her sentence.

"I don't think that was their plan, Frankie."

"Did you find something on the canvas?"

"Yeah. We talked to two different neighbors who heard them kicking her door in. The first guy said he thought the apartment was empty, so he called the apartment complex instead of the police. The office told them they would send over the off-duty deputy who lives on-site. The second guy said he saw Heather move in yesterday. Apparently, he knows the off-duty deputy and called his cell, but no one answered. He walked out of his apartment at the same time as the first dude. They went down and started yelling in the apartment door but didn't go inside. Both said they heard the girl screaming and were about to go inside when two men ran out past them. One of them turned back and lifted his shirt to show a gun. He said they stood there trying to decide what to do when they heard the sirens. The neighbors figured since the police were coming, they didn't need to go inside the apartment."

Frankie shook her head in disbelief and asked, "Why didn't *they* call 9-1-1? Did they get a good look at them? Do you think they could pick Corey and Lamont out of a lineup?"

"Probably, but I don't know that they will. Both seem pretty shaken up."

"I guess all we can do is try. We'll run up to Metro and make some line-ups before we go see Heather. We need to find a safe place for this girl to go when she is released from the hospital too."

Mia pulled her cellphone out and said, "I'm on it. I'll call MOCSA and make sure they have someone going to sit with Heather at the hospital. They may also be able to make contact at one of the shelters for her."

"Good call, Mia," Frankie said. As an afterthought, she added, "Have security sit by Heather's door. These guys are out there and she's a sitting duck in the hospital."

FRANKIE LAID the folder on the table in front of Solomon Kendrick, one of Heather's new neighbors. She explained what she needed Solomon to do, then opened the folder.

Solomon looked at each photograph carefully before returning to the third one. He picked the piece of paper up and looked at it thoughtfully, careful not to make an error in identifying the man he saw. After a long pause, he said, "This is the man who lifted his shirt to show me the gun."

Frankie noted that Solomon identified Corey Simpson. "Thank you. Can you please do the same with the next set of photographs?"

"Mmhmm." Solomon repeated the same process, carefully looking at each photograph before making a choice. Pointing at the photograph of Lamont Foster, he said, "Here. That's the other guy."

"Thank you. Did you happen to see what kind of car they left in?"

"That's the thing, I don't think they had a car. I never heard one start up or leave. I don't know how they got out of here without the cops seeing them."

"Okay. Thanks. Do you know if the apartment complex has cameras covering the parking lots?"

"I don't think so."

Frankie thanked Solomon for his time and walked across the hall to the other neighbor who had seen the men leave. She explained the process to Benjamin Connor the same way she had to Solomon.

Benjamin looked at the stack of photographs carefully, stopping on the photo of Corey.

"That's the boy who showed us a gun."

"Okay, thank you. Can you please do the same with the other set of photographs?"

Benjamin looked at all the photographs, pausing on the photo of Lamont, without saying anything. After a few moments he tapped the photo and said, "That's the other boy."

"Did you happen to see or hear anything after they left? A car or anything?" Frankie asked.

"No. I don't think they had one. If they did, I didn't hear anything."

"Why didn't you all call 9-1-1 or go inside the apartment and try to help the girl you heard screaming?"

"We heard the sirens. We knew help was coming."

"You told Detective Boden you called the off-duty deputy that lives here. Can you give us their name?"

"Sure. It's Victor Nelson. Give me a second, and I'll get you his phone number."

SEVENTY-SIX

FRANKIE AND MIA walked into the Emergency Department amid a flurry of activity. Nurses were running to get medical equipment and additional medications. Doctors were running towards the trauma room, shouting commands at the interns and nurses. Frankie peeked into the room and sighed with relief.

"It's not her," Frankie said aloud.

"Good. Let's see if we can find her and determine exactly what happened tonight."

Frankie and Mia walked through the Emergency Department, glancing in each room as they passed. They were about to check in with the charge nurse when Alex called out to them.

"Hey Alex. I'm glad you were able to come out. Did they tell you what room she's in?"

Alex nodded as she said, "ED 12. What's the story?"

Frankie told Alex about the phone call and how officers had found her. "Witnesses put two of the suspects from her other case in the apartment."

"Are you serious? Poor girl."

Frankie and Mia nodded. Frankie heard Alex suck in her breath at the sight of Heather lying on the hospital bed. Mia touched Alex on the shoulder and nodded. The three spoke softly while walking closer to the broken woman.

"Hi Heather," Alex whispered.

"He..." Heather began to cough, a red tear seeping from her eye. "He..."

"It's okay. You're safe now," Alex assured, standing next to Heather's head. Alex reached down and gently placed her hand over Heather's.

Frankie walked to the opposite side of the bed. "Heather, I need to show you some photographs and see if you can identify the men that did this to you."

Heather nodded slightly.

Frankie held each photograph up in front of Heather for ten seconds. When she got to the photograph of Corey, Heather began to whimper. She lifted her unbroken arm and pointed to his face.

"Do you recognize the man in this photograph?"

"Ye...us," Heather coughed.

"Is this one of the men who assaulted you?"

"Ye...us."

Frankie handed Heather a pen and waited while she scribbled her name on the photograph.

Frankie took out the second set of photographs and started the process again. When she got to the photograph of Lamont, Heather raised her finger and tapped the paper.

"Do you recognize the man in this photograph?"

"Ye...us"

Frankie handed Heather the pen and waited for her to scribble her name across the photograph.

"Heather, do you think you can tell us what happened today?"

Heather tried to clear her throat, then began to cough. She motioned to the sink.

"Do you want a drink of water?" Alex asked.

Heather nodded. They waited while Alex got a cup of water and a straw. Heather struggled to sip the water, coughing, and sputtering. After she caught her breath, she said, "I... I just... moved...there. I don't... know how... they found... me.

Frankie asked, "What day did you move to your apartment?"

"On… Saturday."

"Did you tell Audrey where you were moving?"

Heather shook her head slightly. "I didn't tell… anyone where… I was… moving. My caseworker… and I… are the only ones… who had the… address."

"Have you been back to the shelter since you moved?"

Heather nodded. "This… this morning. I had to… go see my… counselor and caseworker. They helped me fill… out some papers… so I could get some… furniture."

"Did you notice anyone behind you when you left?"

Heather shook her head and began to cough. Frankie and Mia waited while Heather took another drink of water.

"What happened next?" Frankie asked.

"I got to my apartment and was talking to my neighbor. I… I was looking around the parking lot, and I thought… I thought I saw Corey. I told my neighbor I was going inside because I was scared. I locked my door, but I heard Corey and Tubby… they were running up the stairs and yelling at my neighbor. I went into my closet and called you."

Tears poured from Heather's swollen eyes. She coughed and sputtered as she tried to explain. Frankie waited patiently, careful not to push.

"I heard the door break, and it was just… it was just a few seconds later when they… when they found me. Corey drug me out of the closet by my hair. Tubby started kicking me. At first, it was in my legs and side. I tried to block him from kicking me but…Corey was pounding me on my face, and I… I couldn't protect myself. I don't even know how many times he hit me. I tried to fight back but… but nothing I did seemed to matter. Finally, I gave up… and just laid there. Corey said he was going to… he said he was going to get some before he killed me. Tubby watched him… watched Corey rape me. When he was done Tubb… he said he wanted his. When they were both finished, they started hitting me again. I started going in and out of consciousness but I'm pretty sure I heard Tubby say they needed to go. He told Corey… he told Corey… I was dead so they could leave me there."

CHAPTER
SEVENTY-SEVEN

FRANKIE GAVE Heather a moment before asking, "What happened next?"

Heather looked to Alex and asked, "Can I have a tissue, please?"

Alex nodded. She refilled Heather's cup of water and brought her a box of tissue.

"I laid on the floor and didn't move. I... I don't know how long I laid there... but the next thing I knew... the cops were standing over me. And then you were there."

"Heather, do you remember what Corey and Tubby were wearing?"

"I don't know. It all happened so fast."

"It's okay. Do you remember anything else? Anything they said or did?"

Heather gave the question some thought. Frankie was about to tell her she would be in touch when Heather started to make sounds as though she were trying to say something.

Heather took a sip of water and said, "Corey told me he should have killed me when he had a chance. Right before they left, he... he pulled his gun out. He...he pointed it at my... face. I laid there with my eyes closed and I held my breath so they would think I was dead. That's when Tubby said I was dead, and they should just leave."

"What did the gun look like?"

"It was black. It looked like yours."

Frankie nodded, "That's good, Heather. Is there anything else you remember or want to add?"

Heather tried to shake her head but began to wince in pain.

Frankie placed her hand gently on Heather's shoulder and explained she and Mia were going to try to locate Corey and Tubby.

"Do you know… do you know where they are?"

"No, but we have a few leads. The hospital knows if anyone calls or comes to see you, they cannot confirm you are here or give out your room number. Hospital security is going to guard your room too. Alex will let me know what room number they assign you when you are admitted. I'll come back and check on you tomorrow, okay?"

Heather nodded.

"Keep your call button close. If you see any of the men that hurt you, I want you to hit the button, okay?"

Heather nodded.

Frankie looked at the frail, broken woman lying on the bed. Silently she said a prayer. Aloud she said, "Alex, thank you for being here with Heather. We'll be in touch."

As they walked to the parking garage, Mia asked, "Do you think they know she's alive?"

"Playing dead probably saved her life. They did a number on her. I hope she agrees to stay in a shelter outside the city once they release her from the hospital."

"Yeah," agreed Mia. "Where do you want to start?"

"I think we send radio cars out to their momma's houses, and we roll through the neighborhoods and see if we can catch them standing on the corner."

"Swoop in and snatch 'em up?" Mia asked.

Frankie smiled at the image Mia conjured up in her mind.

Sitting in the parking garage of the hospital, Frankie called dispatch and requested they send radio cars out to the addresses Mia had found for Corey and Tubby. Mia used the in-car computer to see if she could figure out, based on previous arrests, where they like to hang out.

When Frankie disconnected the call, Mia said, "Looks like these guys have been the subjects in a few field interviews. Every single one was between 67th and 69th Streets on Askew. I'm betting if they're out, that's where they are."

"And if they aren't, the boys hanging out there will know where they are."

SEVENTY-EIGHT

THE SUN WAS STARTING to set over the City of Fountains and the streetlamps illuminated one by one as Frankie drove south towards 67th Street. Traffic was getting denser the closer they got to their exit. Frankie made the turn onto Gregory Blvd and could feel the anticipation building in her chest. Something was going to happen; she could feel it.

"You think we should call for a radio car?" Mia asked.

Mia must have the same feeling, Frankie thought.

"Text Mac and see if he'll come into the area."

Frankie knew Mia was right to want a radio car in the area. Even if they didn't encounter Corey or Tubby, the block they were heading to was always hot. Drugs and guns were staples with most of the young men they would encounter.

"Mac's off tonight. He said he'd get one of the other guys to head to the area."

Frankie nodded, slowing down as she turned north on Cleveland towards 67th Street. Frankie and Mia scanned the area for Corey and Tubby, hoping they would catch them together.

"Brings back memories," Frankie said. "Mac and I used to roll up and down these blocks looking to get into something. I remember one night..."

"Frankie, make a left, I think I see Tubby."

Frankie turned, resisting the urge to speed up. If they played their cards right, they would be close enough to snatch him before he realized they were the police. Mia released her seatbelt and got ready to jump out. Frankie followed suit, silently hoping they wouldn't have to chase him.

Frankie grabbed her mic, *"1061 and 1064 on Metro, copy a ped check."*

"Go ahead 1061."

"67 and Askew. Black male. White shirt. Khaki pants."

"1061 and 1064 on a pedestrian check.1905."

Mia started to open the door, and the man began to run. Mia bolted from the car, giving chase.

"1061, hold the air. He's running west through the houses. I'm circling the block. 1064 is behind him."

"242, we're almost 10-23."

Frankie gunned the engine as she circled the block to cut the man off at the pass. Mia didn't have a radio, so Frankie was hoping they went straight through. The sound of sirens was getting louder as radio cars came their way to help set up a perimeter. Frankie parked the car and jumped out just in time to hear Mia yelling.

Frankie ran towards the sound, not stopping until she found them.

SEVENTY-NINE

"YOU STUPID SON OF A BITCH!"

Frankie rounded the corner to see Mia wiping blood from her mouth with one hand and pinning Tubby's hand with the other, her knee resting on his back.

Frankie grabbed her handcuffs and grabbed Tubby's wrist. Once he was secured in handcuffs, Mia stood up and backed away. Frankie rolled the young man onto his side, searching him as she rolled.

"Why'd you run, Lamont? Or would you prefer I call you Tubby?"

"Fuck you, bitch."

"Now, now that's no way to talk to a lady."

Looking towards Mia, Tubby said, "That bitch hit me in my junk."

"Guess you should've bobbed instead of weaved. I mean, I can't believe I hit it. It's an awfully small target," Mia said.

Frankie shot Mia a sideways look, trying not to laugh at her partner's quick wit. She reached into his pockets, "Well, what do we have here?"

"That shit ain't mine."

Frankie took the plastic bag of a white, rock-like substance and held it up for Mia to see.

"1061, can you start us a wagon and a Sergeant with a test kit for crack?"

"240's almost 10-23."

"240 out with 1061 at 1915."

Frankie rolled Tubby over to check his other pocket then sat him up.

"Can you walk?" Frankie asked.

"What do you mean, *can I walk?* Did you not hear me? She. Hit. Me. In. My. Dick."

"I'll take that as a no." Frankie looked over at Mia. Her face was red, and her eyes snapped with anger. "Are you okay?"

Mia nodded. She tilted her head to the side and said, "It's over there."

Frankie looked in the direction of Mia's nod and saw what she meant. Laying on the grass, not two feet from where Lamont sat, was a black, semi-automatic handgun. She was just about to say something when a booming voice sounded behind her.

"Well, if it isn't the dynamic duo. What are you two doing down here tonight? Besides making more work for me?"

Frankie smiled. Without turning around, she knew it was Sergeant Seever. She had worked for him when she was in the field. Seever knew how to take care of business but having spent time undercover and with the tactical response team, he also knew how and when to cut up.

Seever looked down at the young man seated on the ground and, with a straight face, said, "You're looking a little gray."

Lamont looked up and started to say something then stopped. Seever, an imposing man by anyone's standards, hulked over the boy.

Seever turned to Frankie and asked, "What do you have for me?"

"He has a pick-up for kidnapping, sodomy, and aggravated assault. He ran when he saw us. Mia chased him down and they scuffled a bit and I found this in his pants."

Frankie handed Seever the baggie.

"Man, I'm telling you, that ain't mines. These aren't even…"

"Let me guess, those aren't your pants," Seever crossed his arms and looked at Tubby.

"Naw, man. I mean, that's right. You know how it is. These ain't my pants."

"How did you end up in another man's pants? I mean, I've had some crazy nights, but I don't think I've ever ended up in another man's pants."

Frankie and Mia both shook their heads and said, "Me either," in unison.

"What about that over there?" Seever asked, nodding towards the gun.

"I, uh…" Tubby stopped.

"I TOLD you them drugs ain't mine," Tubby shouted.

"Fine, if they aren't yours, then whose are they?" Mia asked.

"How many ways do I have to say it? I. Don't. Know!"

"I suppose as many ways as it takes for you to tell me the truth."

Frankie walked in with a manila folder full of paper and sat it on the table. She casually asked, "Do you guys want some water or something?"

"I could use a diet Dr. Pepper," Mia said.

Tubby hesitated then asked, "Can I get a Coke?"

Frankie left the room to grab the drinks then waited at the door, listening to Tubby talk about the drugs and gun, continuing to insist they weren't his. After a couple of minutes, she opened the door, cold drinks in hand.

"Thanks," Mia said.

"Yeah, thanks."

Frankie pulled up a chair, inching it closer to Tubby than Mia who grabbed her notebook and pen, ready to take notes. Frankie laid a photograph in front of Tubby and asked, "Do you know this girl?"

Tubby glanced at the photo then said, "I think she's a friend of my girlfriend's."

"When did you meet her?"

Tubby told a slightly different version of how he met Heather.

"She drove us to a party at my cousin's apartment, hooked up with my boy, and then left."

"Did she come back to the party?"

"The next day. She was our ride, so she came back and took us home."

"Did anything happen when she came back?"

"Naw. I don't know. She and my boy may have gotten into it, but that's it."

Frankie and Mia let Tubby spin his tale then began to poke holes in his version of events. Eventually, Tubby began to change his story.

"Yeah, Corey was pissed he finally convinced her to come back."

"What did he do when she came back?" Frankie asked. "Did he hit her or anything?

"He may have smacked her a little, but that's it."

Frankie and Mia continued to challenge Tubby's account. Eventually Tubby's narrative resembled William's. When asked about the assault at Big Bruce's house Tubby admitted to oral sex but, like William, said Heather wanted to do it.

"Mia, will you hand me that photo?"

The folder contained several photographs, but Mia knew which one Frankie wanted. She kept it facedown as she handed it to Frankie. Frankie began to shake her head, then flipped it over and placed it in front of Tubby.

Tubby looked at the girl with the broken face but did not say anything. After a moment, he grabbed the photograph and turned it facedown.

Frankie flipped it back over and said, "Tell me how this happened."

Tubby stared at the photograph then took his finger and touched her face. Under his breath, he said, "Damn."

"Here's the deal Tubby, we have already talked to William. You can either tell us your side of the story, or we can ask Corey. What do you think he's going to say?"

"He ain't putting this shit on me."

"So, why don't you tell us what *really* happened."

Tubby did not immediately respond. Frankie was about to say something when Tubby asked, "What kind of deal are you offering?"

EIGHTY-ONE

"WE AREN'T AUTHORIZED to make any deals, but we *will* talk to the prosecutor and make sure they know your side of things."

Tubby let that sit for a moment. Frankie looked at her watch. They had been at this for over four hours, and she was beginning to lose her patience.

"Mia, let's give Tubby a minute to think."

Frankie and Mia stood up and left the room. Once the door was secured, Frankie walked into the squad room and stretched while watching Tubby on the monitor.

"Check him out," Mia said. They watched with amusement as Tubby held his stomach and began rocking in his chair.

"Turn the volume up," Frankie said.

Mia increased the video's volume. The sound was faint, but they could hear Tubby mumbling.

"Corey is going to kill me. She was supposed to be dead."

Frankie and Mia listened to Tubby mumble and repeat himself for a few minutes, then watched as he grabbed a trash can and began to dry heave. When he sat back up and took a drink of his Coke, they went back into the room.

"You've had a few minutes to think things over. Are you ready to talk, or shall we take you back upstairs to the jail?" Frankie asked.

Tubby did not immediately respond. Frankie started to stand up to escort him to the jail when he said, "Wait."

Frankie sat back down on the hard chair.

"I'll talk, but you have to tell the prosecutor the truth."

Frankie nodded and said, "We will."

Tubby took a deep breath, sat up a little straighter in his chair and said, "We went over there to talk to her, but things may have gotten a little out of hand."

"*A little out of hand*," Frankie thought. Aloud she said, "Heather almost died."

"She wouldn't answer the door, so Corey pushed his way in. He had a little talk with her and then we left. I don't know how she ended up like that."

Frankie wanted to yank Tubby from the chair and beat him like he beat Heather but she needed some answers first.

"How did you know where she was living?"

Tubby smirked and said, "My girl told me that bitch got her car back and was moving out of the shelter. We waited until she left and followed her. She's not too bright, you know. I live in the same complex she moved to."

So that's why no one heard a car leave.

"Did you all knock on the door?"

"Corey banged on it a few times, but she wouldn't let us in."

Frankie didn't tell Tubby she could hear them breaking the door down through the telephone.

"Tell us who pulled her out of the closet?"

"Pulled her out…what? No one pulled her anywhere. She was sitting on her bed when we walked in."

Frankie stood up and said, "We're done here. If all you're going to do is lie, then I've got better things to do with my time."

"Wait! Alright. Corey found her in the closet and pulled her out. He was yelling at her for ratting us out."

"She didn't get those injuries from being yelled at," Mia said.

Tubby looked over at Mia and suddenly, his face fell. It was as if he realized he wasn't getting out of this as easily as he had planned.

EIGHTY-TWO

"SO, Corey yanked Heather out of the closet by her hair. And to hear Tubby tell it, Corey beat the hell out of Heather. Tubby held her down while Corey punched and kicked her. After a while, Tubby told Corey Heather was dead, so they left," Frankie said. "He denied kicking her or raping her and said Corey didn't rape her this time either."

"Do we have any DNA or anything that connects them to the scene?"

Frankie was glad the phone was on speaker as she looked at Mia and rolled her eyes. Jessica Moon was the on-call prosecutor, and as usual, she was fighting Frankie on everything.

"We have fingerprints on the duct tape used during the kidnapping. We have two eyewitnesses who saw them running from the apartment, and the victim identified them. This just happened today. You know as well as we do that it could be months before DNA comes back. These guys were stalking her and thought they murdered her."

"Do we know where Corey is?"

"We have a couple of flophouses he hangs at, and officers are looking for him, but according to Tubby, he could be just about anywhere."

"What time is he due out?"

"1900, um I mean 7:00 PM. Tomorrow."

"Okay, good. Have the dayshift bring a copy of the completed file over first thing. I'll staff it, then let them know what to do with him."

Frankie couldn't believe what she was hearing. In her mind, it was a no-brainer.

"Okay." Frankie made sure the phone disconnected before she said, "What the hell else does she want?"

Mia sat there, speechless.

"We have three people who put them there. Unbelievable injuries. A history with fingerprints at a previous scene." Frankie paced the floor and continued ranting for several minutes before collapsing into her desk chair.

"Face it, she's just a bitch who's afraid to do her damn job," Mia said.

"Why doesn't she just go do something else?"

Frankie felt her phone vibrate in her pocket.

You still up?

Still at work. Are you okay?

Frankie waited for an answer that didn't come.

"I'll be right back," Frankie said.

"Is everything okay?"

"I don't know. Derek texted but then didn't respond when I asked if he was okay. I'm going to give him a quick call."

"Okay, I'll start working on my reports and making copies of Tubby's interview."

Frankie felt a pit in her stomach. The last time Derek texted her late and then didn't answer, it was because he'd been shot. She was certain he was okay, but he'd been acting strange lately. Derek was having nightmares again and Frankie knew she wouldn't be able to concentrate if she didn't call him and hear him say he was fine.

The phone rang several times before Derek answered.

"Hey pretty girl, what are you wearing?"

Frankie smiled. He was fine. Instead of answering his question, she asked, "Are you okay?"

"I just needed to hear your voice."

Frankie's smile fell as Derek slurred his words.

"Another nightmare?"

"Yeah. This one was a doozy but, hey, I'll be okay. Do you want to help me forget about it?"

"I wish I could babe, but I'm trying to put a case together for an in-custody. Maybe tomorrow? Sophie is staying with the kids and Isabelle tomorrow night."

"That would be great. I'm going to go lay down now."

Frankie said good night and stared at the picture of Derek on her phone, wondering if he'd be able to sleep. Derek's face looked back at hers with soulful eyes. Frankie couldn't put her finger on it, but something was wrong. Very wrong.

CHAPTER
EIGHTY-THREE

FRANKIE WALKED into an empty squad room after a fitful morning of sleep. She and Mia had worked until 6:00 AM getting everything written and put together for the prosecutor's office. By the time she got home, Frankie was wired and couldn't shake the feeling that something was wrong with Derek. She had woken feeling anxious and on edge.

A note was on Frankie's desk when she got to work. Tubby was charged with aggravated assault and drug possession. His bond was set at $75,000. A sigh of relief washed over Frankie. She grabbed her phone and texted Mia.

75k!

Woo hoo! Are you going to go tell H?

Yeah, I'll go by there tonight.

Cool. Stay safe, and don't scare anything up without me!

You got it – enjoy your day off with Erik!

Frankie went to the hospital to tell Heather at least one of her assailants was locked up. She was visibly relieved and peppered Frankie with questions. When was he going to get out? When would the other two be arrested and charged? When would the case go to trial? Would she have to testify? The list went on and on. Frankie patiently answered as many of the questions as she could then returned to the office.

Frankie spent the balance of the evening in the quiet office working on reports and making notes to follow-up on other cases. She wanted Corey arrested on his pick-up but secretly hoped they did not get him tonight. Frankie was looking forward to some time with Derek, and an arrest would change that. The ringing phone jolted Frankie from her thoughts.

"Dammit!" Frankie said aloud. Picking up the receiver, she said, "Sex Crimes, Thomas."

"Got any sex?" the news reporter asked.

Frankie laughed out loud.

"Killer, you have no idea how glad I am it is you calling! We don't have anything for you today."

Frankie could have given him the information on Tubby being charged, but she didn't want Corey to see it and go deeper underground. She'd wait until she got all three of them, then let Killer know so he could air it.

FRANKIE WAS LOST in thought as she walked out the basement door of Police Headquarters. She was grateful her shift ended on time, and since the kids were at Sophie's she was planning to call Derek. A smile lifted the corners of her lips when she saw Derek leaning against her Jeep in the parking lot.

Reaching up to give him a kiss, she said, "Hey counselor, I was just about to call and see if you were still up for a visit."

Derek reached out and brushed the hair from Frankie's face. He stared, memorizing every detail of her smile. Taking a deep breath, he said, "We need to talk."

Frankie's smile fell at the intensity of his voice. She felt a weight in her stomach. She knew something was wrong the night before but had hoped it was her imagination.

"I...I..." He choked on his words. He had gone over everything he was going to say a dozen times, but seeing her in front of him, he found himself unable to speak.

Frankie dropped her bag next to the Jeep. A chill went down her spine. She asked, "Are you seeing someone else?"

"No! Frankie... It's just..." He hesitated before saying, "I'm leaving. Tonight."

Frankie felt the air leave her body. She opened her mouth to speak, but nothing came out.

"This last year has been a tough one. So much has happened…"

"And not just to you…" Frankie interrupted, suddenly defensive.

"I know. I just, I feel like I can't catch my breath. And the nightmares…"

Quietly Frankie said, "They're getting worse."

Derek nodded and said, "I am surrounded by violence and death at work. Then when I sleep, I dream about death. I'm always on guard, and right now, I just need a break from it all."

"Why do you have to leave *me* to take a break. Why can't you go to a different unit or take a sabbatical here? Or go work for a law firm or corporation? Things were just starting to…We were finally starting…I was finally going to ask if you wanted to meet my kids."

Derek reached out to take Frankie's hand, but she jerked it away, unwilling to allow the slightest comfort. He needed her to understand his leaving wasn't about her. He wanted to explain why he was going, but he wasn't sure he could. Derek wasn't completely sure he understood himself, he just knew he had to go, and he wasn't sure when, or if, he'd be back. Derek knew he wouldn't, no couldn't, ask her to wait on him.

"I know it doesn't make any sense. Even to me. I never wanted to hurt you, but I can't stay here, and I know you can't leave."

"Where are you going to go?"

"I've been asking myself that very question, and to be honest, I'm not sure. I'm going to start driving and figure it out along the way."

Frankie looked down and quietly asked, "When will you be back?"

Derek gently touched Frankie's chin, tilting it up, then reached out and took Frankie's hands in his. This time she didn't pull away. His eyes bore into hers as he softly said, "I'm not sure I will be back."

"What about your job?"

"I resigned. Jessica is leaving the sex crimes unit and taking over my cases. They brought in an attorney from Pennsylvania to take Jessica's place in SVU. The new girl seems like a real heavy hitter."

Frankie looked at her feet and sighed, "How long have you known you were going to leave?"

"A couple of weeks."

"You've known a couple of *weeks*, and you are just now telling me? What the…"

Derek's voice caught as tears filled his eyes.

"Frankie, I didn't know how to say good-bye to you. I still don't…"

Frankie slowly lifted her head as Derek let his hand caress her face. Leaning in, Derek gently kissed Frankie on the mouth then pulled her body into an embrace, resting his head on hers. After he was certain he had memorized her smell and the feel of her body, Derek pulled away. He kissed the top of her head and held her hands in his.

Derek's eyes spilled tears as he softly said, "I love you Frankie, but I've got to go."

With those words, he felt her hands leave his and fall to her sides.

Frankie knew he was gone, even before he walked away. She watched Derek slip into the shadows and felt a physical pang of loss. In her gut, she knew it had been a long time coming but she still couldn't believe he was leaving. Frankie wanted to run after him, beg him not to go. Instead, she sunk to the ground, her knees buckling beneath her, and began to sob. When she finally looked up, Derek was gone.

Frankie wasn't sure how long she sat crumpled on the ground in the police parking lot. One minute. Five. All she knew was the air had changed, and suddenly the life she knew was different. The buzz of her phone jolted her back to reality.

See you in a few.

Frankie started her Jeep as soon as she hit send.

WITHIN THIRTY MINUTES, Frankie was standing at her sister's door with a six-pack of beer, Doritos, and chewy chocolate chip cookies. Sophie gave Frankie a hug and without saying a word, the sisters settled onto the sofa with a favorite chick flick on the television.

After the first beer was emptied, Sophie asked, "What's up buttercup? Are you ready to talk?"

Frankie opened the second beer and laid out the conversation she had with Derek, still struggling to believe it was real. Absentmindedly she checked her phone in hopes there would be a message telling her he didn't mean it. He wasn't leaving – or at least not for good. A message asking her to come to him. They could make it work. But no messages came through.

Sophie listened in silence, letting Frankie get it all out. When she finished, Sophie said all the things a sister should say, "He's a jerk. What an idiot. He doesn't know what he's doing. His loss." But her words were hollow. Sophie had never met Derek but had seen the roller coaster he kept Frankie on and didn't like it.

Frankie's phone buzzed, causing both girls to jump in surprise.

Want to grab a beer?

"Is it him?" Sophie asked.

"Craven."

"Hmm."

"It's not like that. We're just friends."

"Okay," Sophie said in a tone that said she didn't believe it for a moment.

At Sophie's for some sister-time. Raincheck?

Do you even have to ask?

Run tomorrow?

8:45. Riverfront Park.

See you there.

"Thanks, Sophie."

"For what, sis?"

"For not saying 'I told you so' or a thousand other things you could say."

Sophie put her arm around Frankie and pulled her into her side, resting her cheek atop Frankie's head.

"I love you, little-big sister."

"Love you too, kid," a lone tear escaped Frankie's eye, but she didn't even try to brush it away.

FRANKIE WOKE UP TO TYLER, sitting on her feet asking Sophie why his mother was sleeping on the couch.

"She missed you guys and decided to crash here instead of going home to an empty house."

Sophie yawned and wiped her eyes. She wasn't used to staying up so late during the week.

"I'll get them to school, Soph."

Frankie pulled her feet out from under Tyler and urged him to get ready for school. Tyler shuffled off to the bedroom to get dressed and brush his teeth.

"Thanks for letting me crash here last night. I appreciate you; you know that?"

"You'd do the same for me, sis," Sophie said then added, "And have."

"Yes, I would. Now I guess I better get moving, or these kids are going to be late."

Frankie corralled Tyler, Danielle, and the dog. She dropped the kids off at their respective schools then hurried home to change into her running gear. She had almost forgotten she was meeting Craven.

Frankie spent the ten extra minutes at the park before Craven arrived stretching. Frankie had taken the top off the Jeep after dropping the kids at their schools and Isabelle sat in the front seat watching and waiting.

"Topless is a good look for you," was Craven's way of saying good morning.

Frankie laughed as she grabbed Isabelle's leash.

"Are you ready?"

Craven knelt to pet Isabelle and then said, "Let's go, girl."

The pair started off at a slow, steady pace, quickly finding a matching rhythm. They made small talk about the weather and Craven told her about a case he was working on. Frankie upped the pace the last half mile, preventing both from carrying on a conversation. When they finished, they were breathing heavier but smiling.

"Damn, that felt good," Frankie said. "But something tells me I'll pay for it later."

"It's always good to take it up a little every once in a while!" agreed Craven. "Is everything okay?"

Frankie wiped her face and filled a little bowl of water for Isabelle.

"Sure, why do you ask?"

"Just checking. You seem…well, off today."

"I'm good, just a little tired. Sophie and I stayed up a little too late drinking beer and watching *The Heat*. We probably shouldn't have sister nights on a school day." Frankie chuckled half-heartedly. She wasn't sure why she didn't tell Craven about Derek leaving. Maybe she just wasn't ready to say it out loud yet.

"Okay," Craven said, not convinced. "Do you want some pancakes?"

Frankie looked at her watch. 9:30 AM.

"Sure, why not? We'll have to sit outside with Iz, though."

Craven ruffled the fur on Isabelle's head.

"Sounds good to me. Maybe I'll even sneak her a piece of bacon."

Frankie laughed.

CHAPTER
EIGHTY-SEVEN

FRANKIE STEPPED ONTO THE ELEVATOR, checking out the people who beat her into the car. An older man with a woman one could only assume was his mother. A young man nervously tapping his foot. A young girl with water-filled eyes. Frankie was about to hit "4" when a woman pushed her way through the crowd. Frankie admired the petite woman. She was about her age and wore a well-fitting suit and three-inch heels. Her straight, dark hair fell to the middle of her back, and her smile was contagious.

Looking directly at Frankie she said, "Good, we are going to the same floor."

Frankie smiled and nodded. She had been summoned to the prosecutor's office to meet with Jessica Moon's replacement.

When they exited the elevator at the fourth floor, Frankie followed the woman to the secured door which led to the private offices. The woman stopped and asked Frankie who she was there to see.

"A new prosecutor, Samantha…"

"That's me, but please call me Sam," the raven-haired woman held her hand out for Frankie to shake. "You must be Detective Thomas."

Frankie couldn't help but smile as she said, "You can call me Frankie." She took it as a good omen – they were both girls with a boy's name.

"Come on in Frankie. I'm afraid I don't have any fresh coffee made. But I do have a cold diet Coke."

It was at that moment Frankie knew she and this woman were going to be fast friends.

"Thanks, that would be perfect."

"Make yourself comfortable. Don't mind the clutter, I'm still getting settled in. I looked over the case file you prepared on Heather Whitaker, and I think we can do something. Why don't you tell me what you think and maybe we can lock up some bad guys together? What do you say?"

"I say, where have you been all my life?"

Their smiles simultaneously dissolved into laughter.

Frankie and Sam spent the next two hours discussing Heather's case in depth.

"So, Corey hasn't been arrested yet?"

"No, he's in the wind. I have a few guys who are leaning on associates, but this guy is hardcore. Everyone seems to be afraid of him. William is still out there too. Your predecessor wanted to wait on DNA to charge him," barely disguised contempt fell from Frankie's mouth.

"I would have charged him," Sam said. As an afterthought she added, "But that's neither here nor there."

Frankie smiled. She and Sam were going to get along famously.

"We have fingerprints now. How far behind is the lab with DNA?" Sam asked.

"They are averaging six to nine months unless there is a rush or a trial pending."

"Okay, we can work with that. I'm going to write a warrant for William today so you can take it to the judge with Tubby, I mean Lamont's. As for Corey, have you all gone up on his phone?"

"The phone number we had was a burner, and he's already tossed it. No one is coming off with the new number. I've done some internet searches and had PIC..."

"What's PIC?" Sam interrupted.

"Oh, sorry. Perpetrator Information Center. I had them run an Accurint, Lexus Nexus, and a couple of other deep searches but came up with very little. We have his known associates, which is who my guys are leaning on."

"Okay, sounds good. I'll get you the warrants to walk through for Tubby and William and wait to hear from you regarding Corey."

Frankie stood to leave.

"Wait, are you the one working on Alexandre Kristof?" Sam asked.

"Yes, my partner and I have been working on it," Frankie said.

"What's your gut feeling on that one?"

EIGHTY-EIGHT

FRANKIE SAT BACK DOWN and decided she'd see what this prosecutor was made of. She explained to Sam how she and Mia first learned of Kristof, then explained the details of the search warrant, photographs, and videos. She saved the underage girls for last.

"Julia had started dancing at the Shady Lady but had not started doing private parties and they hadn't initiated Emma yet. I'm pretty sure Kristof is connected to a series of homicides involving young women who all have a rose tattoo on their wrist."

"Similar to Heather and Julia?"

Sam had been listening.

"Yes. Julia only had a rose stem, but according to Tessa, it's because she

had not been fully turned out. The rosebud comes later."

"Tessa is the one in jail, right?"

"Yes."

"Okay, I'm going to go through the file again. I feel like it may have been under-charged. Did anything come back on the liquid in the rum bottle?"

It dawned on Frankie she had not seen the results yet.

"I don't know. I'll email the lab tonight. If it's not GHB, I'll be surprised."

"That's what I was thinking too, but it's possible GHB wasn't what he used. I worked on a case in Philly where the guy was using liquid Benadryl, like what you'd carry on an ambulance. He drugged over twenty women before he was apprehended in Idaho."

"Really? Did he get prosecuted?"

"Yep. He will be in prison for the rest of his life."

"Nice," Frankie didn't hide her admiration. "Do you have the photographs from Kristof's case file?"

Sam grabbed a binder and flipped it open to a section labeled "Photographs" and asked, "What are you looking for?"

"I'm not sure, but I'll know it when I see it. There's a nagging in the back of my memory. Something I saw but did not realize at the time was important," Frankie scanned the photographs. "Wait, there it is."

Frankie pointed at vials in the small refrigerator by the pool. Frankie had seen the same vials in the refrigerator in the kitchen.

"Please tell me you recovered these," Sam stated.

"I'm pretty sure we took everything from the bar fridge, but we did not take the ones from the kitchen. I guess we assumed he was diabetic, and that was his insulin."

"Is he diabetic?"

"I'm not sure. I can check with the jail. They should know."

"Is anyone staying in his house?" Sam asked.

"Not that I'm aware of," Frankie said. "Are you thinking what I'm thinking?"

"If you are thinking of a piggy-back warrant, then yes."

Frankie was impressed. It had been a long time since she had worked with an aggressive prosecutor.

"Okay and see if you can get Keeley back in for an interview. She would know if he was diabetic. If he isn't then let's work up a second search warrant for the house. Does she have long or short hair?" hair?"

"It's pretty long."

"Good. Maybe we can get her to submit to a hair follicle test. How soon do you think you can set up an interview with her?" Sam asked and added, "I'd like to sit in."

Frankie wasn't sure she'd ever had a prosecutor want to sit in on an interview. This was new territory for her. It was obvious this woman wanted to work as a team.

"Let me call her now. When's good for you?"

"Is tonight too soon?"

"Not for me. We have a full squad working, so we should be good to go."

"Good. Let's see if she can come down tonight."

CHAPTER
EIGHTY-NINE

"KEELEY, my name is Samantha Ryan. I'm the prosecutor assigned to your case. Thank you for agreeing to meet with us tonight."

"Sure. I don't understand. I mean, Alexandre has been charged, right? Is he still in jail? Why did you need to talk to me again?"

Frankie sensed Keeley was nervous, but before she could say anything, Sam said, "You are correct. He's been charged and he's still in jail, but I think there is more that we can do. Would you mind answering a few more questions for us?"

"Sure."

"What can you tell us about Alexandre's health?" Sam asked.

With a puzzled expression, Keeley asked, "What do you mean?"

"Were you aware of him taking any medications or having a chronic illness?" Frankie asked.

"Not that I know of. He seemed to be in good shape. We've been dating for a while, and I don't even remember him going to the doctor."

"Did he ever mention having any allergies?" Sam asked.

Frankie noticed Sam asked questions that did not immediately give away the reason she was asking. She could have asked if Alexandre required insulin or took Benadryl, but instead, she left the questions open.

"I think he was allergic to cats. Or at least that was the excuse he gave for not coming to my house. I don't think he took any allergy medication, though."

"Did he ever tell you he needed insulin or that he ever took Benadryl?" Frankie asked.

"No and I would have remembered the insulin for sure. Why are you asking?"

Frankie pulled out the photo of the outdoor refrigerator and laid it on the table in front of Keeley. She pointed at the bottles in the door and asked, "Do you have any idea what these bottles might contain?"

Keeley shook her head.

Sam softened her voice and asked, "Have you ever heard of a hair follicle test for drugs?"

"I'm not sure."

"Basically, we would have a lab technician collect hair samples from you and have it tested for drugs."

"I don't use drugs."

"We weren't thinking you were using drugs, but it is possible drugs were used on you." Sam explained.

Sam and Frankie waited while the information sunk in.

Keeley exhaled loudly and said, "What do you need me to do?"

Frankie provided directions to Keeley than, almost as an afterthought asked, "Were you at the 4th of July party last summer?"

"Yeah, why?"

"Do you remember a girl named Candi being there? Or being in a hot tub with her?"

Keeley gave the question some thought before shrugging her shoulders.

"Do you remember being in the hot tub after everyone else left?

"I don't remember much. After everyone left, Alexandre handed me a glass of a new red blend he was trying out. We got into the hot tub alone. I don't remember anything else until the next morning. I guess I had more to drink than I realized."

CHAPTER
NINETY

FRANKIE, Mia, and Sam sat in the squad room after Keeley left. They discussed the case and what would happen next. They would write a search warrant specifically for the vials and try and execute it later in the week. Frankie looked at the clock only to find it was after 10 PM. She was about to ask if Sam and Mia wanted to grab a beer when the phone rang.

"It's probably just Killer," Mia said.

"Killer?" Sam asked.

Frankie could hear Mia explaining the reporter and his nickname as she answered the phone.

"Okay. Yeah, come to 4, and I'll give you a May-I." Frankie disconnected the call and said, "Guess who they are bringing in?"

"No way," Mia said.

"Yep. Mac and Payne found Corey on 69th and Askew. Apparently, he was hiding out at his grandmother's house. Of course, grandma had no idea he was there."

"Of course not."

Frankie looked to Mia and said, "Do you want to stay? I can handle this if you want to go home and spend time with Erik."

"And miss this? No way. He's the final piece to the puzzle."

"Good, you know I appreciate...."

"Mind if I stick around and watch?" Sam interrupted.

"Unless he invokes, we'll probably be in there 3 or 4 hours."

"I don't mind if you don't," Sam said with a smile.

Frankie nodded.

Thirty minutes later, she and Mia were inside the interview room asking Corey basic biographical questions, attempting to build a rapport. Frankie was treading lightly at first, not wanting him to invoke his right to an attorney before giving them something they could work with.

Once the small talk had run dry, Frankie pulled out a photograph of Heather and asked Corey if he recognized the girl.

"I think she might have been at a party I was at."

The questions and answers were benign at first. Do you know her? When was the last time you saw her? I saw her at a party. The day after the party. No, I didn't have sex with her. No, I never laid a hand on her. She drove us back to the block and that was it.

It never ceased to amaze Frankie that criminals could be so stupid. Did Corey really think she didn't have the answers to the questions she asked? Frankie let him lock himself into his lies. That would do nothing but work in their favor.

Once Frankie had him locked into this story, she brought out the photograph of Heather after the kidnapping.

"Corey, how did this happen?"

Corey's legs, which were stretched out in front of his body, began to bounce lightly. He tapped his hands on his knees and said, "How the hell do I know?"

Frankie and Mia questioned Corey further, challenging his answers until he finally admitted to slapping her with an open hand.

"Corey, those black eyes didn't come from an open hand. Why did you hit her in the face? I mean, what could she have done that pissed you off so much?"

Corey pulled his body up into a full, seated position. His face contorted in anger. The slight bounce in his leg became more fervent. Finally, Corey slammed his hand onto the table and said, "The bitch had it coming."

FRANKIE JUMPED SLIGHTLY, hoping Corey didn't notice. She wasn't expecting Corey's sudden outburst of anger. Her eyes stayed fixed on his face. Her expression was unwavering.

"That girl told us she'd take us back to the block after the party. Bitch didn't keep her word, so when she finally showed back up, I was mad. I had stuffs to do, and she messed it up."

Frankie wanted to know what he had to do that was so important and made him so mad but waited. Somehow, she knew if she just let him talk, he'd take them there. Frankie let silence fall over the room, and eventually, Corey began to talk again.

"That girl came to the door like she ain't done nothin' wrong. She sure was surprised to see me though. That look on her face," Corey smirked. "I wiped it right off. She didn't know what was coming. She started begging me. Said she'd do whatever I wanted. Told me she was sorry for not coming back."

"Did you take her into the bedroom?"

Corey laughed, "Naw man, she took me into the bedroom. Like I said, she told me she'd do whatever I wanted. She was begging me for it. Guess she didn't get enough the night before."

"So, you are saying there was physical contact the night before?" Frankie asked.

"What you mean, physical contact? We had sex if that's what you mean," Corey explained then added, "And it was with her content."

"Her content?" Mia asked.

"Yeah, you know, she agreed to it."

"Okay. So, she took you into the bedroom. What happened next?"

"Man, I told you, I gave her what she wanted."

"What did she want?" Frankie asked.

Corey looked at Frankie like she had two heads, gestured towards his lap, and said, "My dick."

Frankie and Mia did not react to his gesture. Frankie asked, "Did you hit her in the bedroom?"

"Man, I never laid a hand on that girl."

"What happened after you gave her what she wanted?"

"I went out to see where Tubby was. I told you I had stuffs to do, and I was already late."

"But you had time to rape her?" Mia asked.

Corey shot Mia a look. She just cocked her head as if to say, "Well?"

"It wasn't no rape. We had sex. Bitch had already made me late, so I gave her what *she* wanted."

"Did she follow you out of the bedroom?" Frankie asked.

"I don't think so. William went in and got him some, then we all left together."

"You were already late, but you had time to let William get some?" Mia asked.

Corey glared at Mia as he said, "We was waiting on Tubby to get back."

"What happened when Tubby and Audrey got back?" Frankie asked.

"We got in the car and came back to the city."

Frankie began asking details about who was driving and who was sitting where. Corey's version was like Tubby's, except he said Heather willingly got into the trunk.

"We had the middle seat down, and she laid there with her head out."

Frankie and Mia looked at one another.

"Tell us about going to Big Bruce's house."

"Ain't nothin' to tell. We went to his house. Girl said we could use her car, and she'd hang out with Bruce. I guess she got tired of waiting 'cause when we went back to get her, she was gone."

"Do you know if Tubby was ever alone with her?"

"I don't know, maybe. Yeah, I think he was. That girl, I think she's a nymphomaniac or something."

"Why do you say that?"

"I went into the living room to tell him we was leaving, and that girl was sucking his dick."

"Is it possible she was being forced to do that?" Frankie asked.

"Looked to me like she was enjoying it," Corey said.

"Did anyone use any drugs at Big Bruce's house?"

"Naw man, ain't none of us use drugs."

Frankie fought back laughter. She was pretty certain if they screened his urine, it would tell a different story.

"Did anyone ever put duct tape on her?" Mia asked.

"No, nobody needed to put no duct tape on her."

"Why did she have duct tape on her when she got to the hospital?"

"Man, I don't know. Maybe Big Bruce put it on her."

Frankie pulled out a lab report and asked, "Says here that your fingerprints were on the duct tape that was taken from her body. DNA should be back soon as well. Any reason why your DNA will be there?"

NINETY-TWO

COREY'S STORY SUDDENLY CHANGED. Tubby put duct tape on her, but she got into the trunk on her own. He did put the seat down and gave her a drink of soda, and a few drags from his cigarette when they stopped at the gas station. When they got to Big Bruce's house, he helped her get out of the trunk and that must be how his fingerprints (and possibly DNA) got onto the tape.

"Did you stop by some trailers and threaten to put a shirt over her head?"

Corey appeared to give the question some thought before answering, "That bitch would not shut her mouth. She was driving me crazy."

Frankie saw an in, "She does talk a lot. I mean, there've been a few times I wouldn't have minded…."

"Yeah. She was on my nerves, so I told her I was going to put a shirt over her head. I didn't do it, though."

"Did you put your gun against her face and threaten to kill her? Maybe tell her you'd put her body in the Missouri River, and no one would find her?"

Corey smirked but did not answer.

Frankie retrieved a photograph from the second assault. She flipped it over and laid it on the table in front of Corey.

Corey stared at the photo. His face growing ashen. Corey picked the photograph up and turned face down then pushed it towards Frankie.

"What happened that day?"

Corey mumbled to himself.

"Why did you go to her apartment?" Frankie asked.

Corey mumbled something under his breath.

"What was that? We couldn't quite hear you."

"I wasn't at her apartment."

"So, we won't find your DNA on her body or your fingerprints in her apartment?"

"Naw, I don't think so."

"Did you beat and rape that girl again?" Frankie asked.

"I ain't been at her apartment."

"We talked to Tubby. We have his version of events, and now we need yours."

"Man, I said I wasn't there. Now, I'm done talking. You can take me upstairs."

"Okay. We can take you back upstairs, but I have one more question for you. What did you miss the day after the party that was so important you hurt that girl?"

"Man, I told you I. Had. Stuffs. To. Do. I had abortions to get taken care of. I needed to take my girl for an appointment and 'cause that bitch didn't come back she missed it. Now…" Corey stopped.

"Now what?"

"Now I'm gonna be put on child support and man, I ain't got no time for that."

"How far along is she?"

"I don't know, we ain't cool no more. She says she's going to put me on child support, though. I don't even think the kid's mine. I'm gonna make her have a fraternity test or something."

"Do you mean *paternity* test?" Mia asked.

"Yeah, that test that says if you're the dad. That one."

Frankie stood up and asked, "You ready to go?"

NINETY-THREE

FRANKIE LOOKED at the clock when they returned to the squad room. 2:00 AM. And Sam was still there. To herself, Frankie thought, *"This girl either has no life or she's hardcore."*

"I need to check the state statutes, but he is definitely getting charged. I'm going to ask for a $500,000 bond." Sam was standing by the monitor with her designer bag slung over her shoulder. "Thank you for letting me watch. That guy is an idiot and a creep. I'm glad he gave you enough for me to charge him. Make sure you include the abortion piece in the probable cause statement. Also, don't forget to include the lab results. Were his fingerprints really on the duct tape?"

"Yes. We're hoping for DNA too, but it will probably be a few months before it comes back."

"Well, all that can do is help. Alright, I'm out. I have an 8:30 meeting, and it looks like a warrant to type. Have a good night, ladies!"

After she was certain she had left the floor, Mia asked, "Is she for real?"

"I think so. I did a little internet search on her, and her background is impressive. She's spent her entire career prosecuting sexual assault and domestic violence cases. She's from Pennsylvania but has published articles and done training workshops all over the country. I have no idea why she came to Kansas City, but I sure as hell hope she stays. She's a badass."

Mia laughed and said, "I think the tide is going to turn for victims in Kansas City."

Frankie smiled and said, "It looks that way."

The sky was beginning to lighten when the pair finally walked out of police headquarters. Frankie yawned and stretched as they walked.

"Have you heard from him?"

Frankie didn't immediately answer. She stopped at her Jeep and after throwing her bag inside said, "No."

"Do you know where he was going?"

"No. He said he didn't even know," Frankie's eyes welled with tears. She looked across the street at the Federal Building and blinked.

Mia touched Frankie on the shoulder and started walking towards her car.

"Mia?"

Mia turned around and said, "Yeah?"

"Thanks."

Mia nodded, got into her car, and pulled away.

Frankie rested her head on the steering wheel of the Jeep and sighed. Her head knew leaving was something Derek had to do, but her heart had not caught up yet. Frankie pulled out of the parking lot but instead of turning right to go home, she made a left. She had one more thing to do before she called it a night.

CHAPTER
NINETY-FOUR

"SHE HAD to undergo emergency surgery. She's out now, but we've got her on some strong pain meds. I don't know how lucid she'll be."

"If you don't mind, I'd still like to try and talk to her. I think she'll be happy to hear the news," Frankie smiled at the ICU nurse, hoping she would bend the rules and let her into the room.

"Don't stay too long. Heather needs her rest." The nurse nodded towards the door and said, "Looks like you could use some yourself, detective."

Frankie gave the nurse a half-smile and nodded.

The hospital bed was slightly elevated. Heather was covered in bandages. Frankie looked at the IV tubes coming out of Heather's arm. The other was sheathed in a cast. Oxygen cannulas laid in her nose, surprising Frankie who made a mental note to ask the nurse why they were there. Heather's hair lay in sharp contrast of the white pillow. The room was quiet, sans the steady beeping of the machines. Frankie gently touched the hand not encased in a cast, and whispered Heather's name.

Heather blinked lightly and moaned.

"Shh, you don't have to say anything. I just wanted to tell you; you are safe. We got Corey. He's locked up and isn't going anywhere. We have a new prosecutor, and she is going to set his bond at $500,000. The only one left is William and I have officers looking for him now."

A tear escaped Heather's non-bandaged eye.

"Get some rest now. I'll be in touch," Frankie lifted her hand from Heather's and started to walk away.

Heather reached out, touched Frankie, and said, "Detective... Thomas..."

Frankie turned back around.

"Thank...you...for...believing...me."

Frankie felt a lump in her throat. Softly she said, "You are welcome, Heather."

KEELEY EMPTIED the contents of her pockets into her purse before placing it into the trunk of her car. She collected her car keys, driver's license, and the envelope she found on her front door when she got home the day before. As she closed the trunk, Keeley played back the conversation she had with Sam and Frankie before leaving police headquarters.

"We need to have the lab collect a few samples of your hair," Frankie said.

"I have a contact at the FBI who will do some tests to try and determine what, if anything, was used to incapacitate you," Sam explained.

"How long before you get the results back?"

Sam explained it could be as little as a few weeks or as long as a few months.

Keeley agreed to go the next day after work, but tonight she needed to figure out what this letter meant. She took a deep breath and walked inside the entrance of the jail.

"Put everything from your pockets into this bowl, then walk through the scanner."

Keeley laid the keys, driver's license, and envelope into the bowl. As a second thought, she patted her pockets then walked through the scanner. Once she was cleared, the deputy escorted Keeley to the visiting room where a partition made of Plexiglas was all that separated her from Alexandre.

Keeley picked up the phone and said, "Alexandre."

"Hello, Keeley. How are you?"

Keeley did not answer. She was surprised by his cavalier greeting.

"It's very nice to see you Keeley, but I must admit I'm a bit surprised."

Keeley pressed the envelope against the Plexiglas, "Really? You are *surprised* to see me after *this*?"

"What is that?" Alexandre asked.

"Look, don't play stupid with me. I know you had a part in this. Who did you send to my house?" Keeley's voice began to shake, "And why?"

"Keeley, I didn't send anyone. I wouldn't do that to you. You must believe me," pled Alexandre.

And for some reason Keeley did not quite understand, she wanted to believe him.

"What does the letter say?" asked Alexandre.

Keeley glared at Alexandre, who had suddenly lost the allure and sophistication she had once thought him to have. She hung up the phone and signaled to the guard she was ready to go. Keeley walked away without looking back.

When she got to her car, Keeley began to shake. If Alexandre was telling the truth and didn't have someone put the letter on her door, who did? It was not lost on Keeley that Alexandre could be lying. At that moment, she did not know who to believe but she did know who to trust. Keeley's hands were trembling as she dialed Frankie's number.

"Sex Crimes Thomas."

"Detective Thomas, this is Keeley. Are you in your office?"

"I will be in about fifteen minutes. What's up?"

"I found something in my door when I got home yesterday. I think you need to see it."

"I'll see you in fifteen. Meet me at the garage entrance of police headquarters. Where you came in last time."

Keeley hung up the phone, but instead of relief, she felt a growing sense of dread. Alexandre wasn't able to hurt her, but he had friends in low places. Suddenly fifteen minutes felt like an eternity to wait.

CHAPTER
NINETY-SIX

"ALRIGHT ANGEL-GIRL, I need to get off here. I have a victim waiting by the door for me."

Frankie smiled as Danielle continued to talk. It was a pleasant change after the past few weeks. She parked the car on the corner of 12th Street and Locust, grabbed her bag, and was about to cross the street when the sound of screeching tires caused her to stop. The culprit rounded the corner, and Frankie saw the barrel of a gun extend through a lowered window. The sounds of gunshots and screams filled the dead air.

"Mom! Mom!" Danielle yelled frantically.

"It's okay Dani. I'm fine, but I've got to go. I love you," Frankie disconnected the call and unholstered her weapon as she ran. Frankie stopped in the middle of the street and fired shots at the SUV as it sped eastward towards the highway.

Frankie yelled to the patrol officer standing at the door to put the shooting out over the air, "Broadcast the partial license. Missouri license, Boy Adam 7 8. It just turned south on Holmes. Looks like the car is heading towards 71 Highway."

Keeley was conscious but struggling to breathe. Frankie holstered her weapon and applied pressure to the wound, listening to the sounds of sirens as they got closer. She silently prayed they would make it in time. Keeley thrust the envelope at Frankie and tried to speak.

"Shh, it's okay, Keeley. You're going to be fine. Medics are on the way. Hang on. Just hang on."

"Take. This. It's…" Keeley's eyes closed.

"Come on, Keeley. Hang on. Keeley. Keeley," urgency punctuated each word.

"What do we have detective? Frankie?"

"Bruce. Thank God," Frankie released the pressure and moved out of the way of Bruce and his partner. She explained what she had seen and what type of weapon she thought had fired the shots. "Is she going to make it?"

"We'll do everything we can, Frankie," to his partner he said, "Let's get her to County."

Frankie stepped out of their way and watched as they loaded Keeley into the back of the ambulance. She stood there in shock as they drove away with lights and sirens activated. Frankie didn't even realize she still had the envelope in her hands until, out of nowhere, she heard a familiar voice asking what was in her hands.

CHAPTER
NINETY-SEVEN

FRANKIE TURNED to find Craven and Fitzmeyer standing behind her. She tried to remain stoic, not wanting them to see the overwhelming sense of responsibility she felt. Craven didn't say a word, just placed his hand on her shoulder.

"Let's go inside, Frankie," Fitzmeyer said.

"I need to…"

"The patrol officers have this," Fitzmeyer said.

The tunnel vision Frankie had been experiencing widened, and she realized there were officers blocking off the crime scene and taking charge of the area. She nodded and followed Fitzmeyer through the door that led into the basement of police headquarters. Craven kept his hand on Frankie's shoulder while they walked to the elevator.

She used her badge to open the elevator and once inside, Frankie felt her knees buckle and quickly righted herself, hoping they didn't see her stumble. She quickly hit the button for the 4th floor out of reflex.

"We're going to 2, Frankie," Fitzmeyer said.

Frankie nodded. The assault squad and homicide unit were on the 2nd floor. It made sense they would need to go there.

The elevator doors opened to an empty foyer. Fitzmeyer led Frankie to an interview room where the three sat and waited. Fitz texted the floor supervisor that they were there. Not trusting her voice to be calm, Frankie sent Danielle a text message to reassure her she was fine. Frankie laid her cellphone on the table, looked down and, for the first time, realized she was covered in blood. Keeley's blood. And she was still holding the envelope Keeley had thrust at her before the paramedics took her away.

Sergeant Scott Millsap entered the room just as Frankie was about to ask for something to lay the envelope on while they waited. She wanted to open it but had the forethought to realize it was likely evidence, and she needed to follow protocol.

Frankie was glad Millsap was going to interview her. She had worked for him when she was on patrol and felt a sense of ease with him. It was at that moment that she realized she was a witness and would be questioned like the witnesses she questioned daily. It was surreal to be filling that role.

"Damn Frankie, you can't even go to Quick Trip without stirring up trouble," Millsap said, trying to lighten the mood.

Frankie smiled and wondered how he knew that's where she had been. Even though it had been less than twenty minutes, it seemed like a lifetime since she had left the store. She wasn't even sure what had happened to her diet Coke.

"I just got off the phone with the hospital, and it looks like the woman you helped is going to pull through."

"Keeley. Her name is Keeley LaCorte."

"Did you know her?"

"Yeah. She was coming to headquarters to meet me. Remember that guy, Alexandre Kristof? She was the one that blew the whistle on him. She gave me that," Frankie pointed towards the envelope she had laid on a piece of plain white paper.

"What is it?"

"I don't know. I think that's why she wanted to meet. To bring it to me. She called me about fifteen minutes before this all happened and said she found something on her door when she got home last night."

Millsap left the room and returned with gloves and a camera After he carefully photographed the envelope from all angled, he opened it.

Millsap unfolded the white piece of paper to reveal a carefully printed note.

Frankie leaned in to read what was printed in black ink. She read the document twice before leaning back in her seat and saying, "Son of a bitch."

NINETY-EIGHT

THE NOTE WAS HANDWRITTEN in neat, block letters. The message was simple and to the point.

DROP THE CHARGES OR PLAN YOUR FUNERAL.

"Any idea who might have left this for her?" Millsap asked.

"Alexandre Kristof? He's over at County Jail, but he's not in solitary. I don't get it. How did they know she wasn't meeting me to withdraw her participation or to recant?"

"Maybe they are listening to her calls somehow?"

"Maybe. It could also be one of Marzullo and Midori's cronies. Kristof, her former boyfriend, is in county lockup because of a report she made. He's tied to the Marzullo family, and we are pretty sure they are trafficking women and using the Shady Lady as a cover."

"Any chance Kristof will talk to you again?" Scott asked.

"He lawyered up when we were talking to him about the open case," Frankie looked at Craven and Fitzmeyer and said, "But I think I know someone who might be willing to talk."

With the help of Craven and Fitzmeyer, Frankie explained the latest case to Sergeant Millsap and the connection between Kristof and Tessa Kemp.

"You mean that girl from Thanksgiving is connected to all this?"

"Indirectly, yes."

"Do you think she'll talk to you?"

"I don't know. But it's worth a shot, don't you think?"

Millsap rubbed the stubble forming on his chin. He looked at his watch then back to the letter.

"Who's the prosecutor on Tessa's case?"

"It was Jessica Moon but a new prosecutor, Samantha Ryan, is taking it. Want me to call her? She and I met with Keeley earlier this week to discuss the case."

"Yeah, I think you need to give her a call and get her take on things before you try to talk to Tessa again. I want to make sure we can use anything she gives you." Millsap hesitated and then said, "We are going to need your clothes and gun for evidence Frankie."

Reluctantly, Frankie said, "I know. I have a pair of jeans and a t-shirt in my locker. Can I change there?"

Millsap started to say something then thought better of it.

"I know the drill, Sarge. I'll stand on paper and package everything separately. Is it safe to say you only need my blouse and pants?"

"That will work."

Frankie grabbed her cellphone and said, "I'll call Sam while I change."

FRANKIE STOOD in the empty locker room and stared at her phone. She pulled up Derek's contact in her phone and gazed at his photo. Frankie wanted to call him, wanted to hear his voice, and let him distract her from the million thoughts racing through her mind. She wanted to tell him about Keeley getting shot and how she felt that it was somehow *her* fault. She dialed Sam's number, put it on speakerphone, and laid it on the bench.

Frankie took a piece of white butcher paper and laid it on the floor in the empty locker room. She was grateful Sergeant Millsap allowed her to do this unobserved. It would have been humiliating to undress in front of another detective or crime scene tech. Frankie opened three paper bags and sat them on the floor next to the white paper. As the phone rang, she removed her blouse and placed it inside the first sack. She closed the bag and wrote, "blouse" on the outside.

"Don't you ever go home, Frankie?"

"Keeley's been shot."

"What?! When? What happened? Where?"

Frankie described what happened to Sam as she finished packaging and labeling her clothing.

"Are *you* okay," Sam asked.

"Yeah, but I need to talk to Tessa. I want to do it tonight, but she has counsel, and I don't want anything she gives us getting thrown out. We have officers posted with Keeley but…."

"I have her attorney's info. Give me five, and I'll call you back."

Frankie finished changing her clothes, grabbed the bags, then walked back to the interrogation room where she had been interviewed by Millsap. The room was empty but before Frankie could walk to the space, they called the "Murder Room," her phone rang.

"Thomas."

"Frankie, it's Sam. I'm on my way to the jail. Can you meet me there?"

"Of course. Did her attorney give us permission to talk to her?"

"Something like that. It took a little convincing, but she agreed it was in her client's best interest to cooperate."

Frankie smiled. Derek was right, Sam is a real heavy hitter.

"Frankie?"

"Yeah, I'm here. We'll meet you down there."

ONE HUNDRED

FRANKIE, Fitzmeyer, and Craven decided to walk to the jail. It was only a couple of blocks and Frankie needed to burn off some nervous energy. She carried a file folder that contained a photo of the letter and a photo of Keeley taken by an officer at the hospital.

"You think she'll talk to you, Frankie?" Craven asked.

"If she knows what's good for her, she will. *And* she'll tell me what I need to know."

Frankie started to say something more when Sam yelled, "Wait up!"

The trio stopped about a block from the jail entrance. Frankie felt frumpy next to Sam, who wore a tailored suit and heeled boots.

"Sam, this is special agent Jim Craven and Detective Scott Fitzmeyer. They worked with me on the original case with Tessa and are working on the homicides we think may be connected by the tattoos."

After the pleasantries were exchanged, Sam asked, "Frankie, what's your play?"

"I want to see if they will let us listen to Tessa and Alexandre's jail calls. There may be something there we can use. Then, if she doesn't volunteer the information, I want to go hard. This bitch has been lying to me for months, and I've had enough."

"Okay. Her attorney may or may not be there. I will not be able to ask questions, but I will sit in with you, so she knows how serious this is.

Gentlemen, as much as I'm sure she would like the scenery, I think you'll need to watch from the camera room."

Craven started to say something when his phone began buzzing. He looked down at the message on his phone in alarm.

"Is everything okay?" Frankie asked.

Craven flipped the phone around.

"HELP – they got me."

"Is that…"

"Yeah. How did they know she talked to us?"

"They have eyes everywhere," Frankie answered.

"Fitz, we should…"

"Go to her house. Call and see if we can get up on her phone. Sorry, Frankie."

As the men turned to jog back to their SUVs Frankie said, "Be safe and let me know what happens!"

Both men nodded and waved.

"I appreciate the shorthand, but can you fill me in on what just happened?" Sam asked.

"Sorry. The text was from a girl named Candi. Looks like Alexandre may have gotten to her too."

"I thought Alexandre was in here."

"He is, but his reach is farther than we realized."

Frankie went on to explain about his parties and his connections to all the other women.

"Based on what you are telling me, there is a good chance Candi may already be dead."

"Yes."

ONE HUNDRED ONE

"YOU SHOULDN'T HAVE CALLED me. If you keep your mouth shut, they can't connect us to the business."

"That detective is sniffing around."

"Send her a different direction or play dumb. Either way, don't say anything."

"Where are the new girls?"

"Safe."

"What does that mean Alexandre? Have they figured out the deal yet?" Tessa asked.

"They are in the safehouse. We're going through the routine with them," Alexandre laughed. "They all think they are going to be models or dancers or movie stars. Stupid girls."

"How long before they are broken in and ready to go?"

"Not long. This group has been pretty easy."

Tessa and Alexandre discussed the enterprise they had built and, in code who was handling business while they were inside.

"What are you going to do about the problems?" Tessa asked, referring to the women who had spoken to police.

"It's being handled. And if that detective doesn't stop snooping around, she'll be handled too."

Tessa began to laugh.

Frankie and Sam told the guards they had heard enough. Frankie was surprised, although she wasn't sure why. Tessa and Alexandre had both called the same person who merged the calls together. The third party did not speak but Frankie suspected when they got the jail phone records, they would learn that it was Luka Petrov.

ONE HUNDRED TWO

"I'VE ALREADY TOLD you all that I know," Tessa said. "I was locked up in here. How in the hell do you think I still know what's going on out there?"

Frankie resisted the urge to immediately ask where Candi was or who might have her. She had dealt with Tessa enough to know if she went too hard up-front Tessa would shut down, and she wouldn't get all the information she needed.

"Tessa, do you realize all your jail calls are recorded? Do you realize the only ones we cannot legally listen to are the ones where you are speaking with your attorney?"

Frankie let the information sink in.

"Before we pulled you out of your cell, we listened to your and Alexandre's phone calls. It seems the two of you have quite the enterprise going. We've put together most of the puzzle, but I'd recommend you fill in the missing pieces."

Tessa leaned back in her chair; her face had gone pale. She appeared to be sizing Frankie up as she considered her options. Stay silent and take the heat for everything or talk and likely end up dead. Midori's reach was long, and once his trust was broken it was almost a guaranteed death sentence.

"I want full immunity and to be put into witness protection program."

Sam, who had been listening quietly, said, "I can't offer full immunity or WITSEC without any basis. What I can offer is consideration for both."

"This goes much deeper than you can imagine. The people involved are not going to go down easily, and even if you get some of them, you won't get them all. And their reach is far. Just talking to you will put my life in danger. Even inside here, I'll be a sitting duck."

Tessa's voice trembled as she talked. Frankie would feel sorry for her if she didn't know all this woman had done.

Sam said, "Tell us what you know, and we'll see what we can do to help you."

Tessa looked at Frankie and asked, "Are you recording this?"

Frankie nodded.

"As you know, I work at The Shady Lady. I've been there for a long time. That place was a dump when I got there. I met Alexandre there, and together we grew a solid team. I started recruiting good talent and built a following. I earned the Boss' trust quickly. I would find the girls and Alexandre would break them in. By the time the girls were going on dates or doing parties we owned them."

"What do you mean you *owned* them?" Frankie asked.

Tessa didn't initially respond. She seemed to be mulling over her response. When Sam opened her mouth to say something, Tessa let out a sigh.

"Some of them have a little cocaine addiction while the undocumented are dependent on our silence to stay in the country. A few are just afraid of what we will do to them if they try to leave.

"Eventually, I convinced the Boss if he tattooed the girls, it would promote loyalty. We sold it to the girls by making it sound like an incentive. Getting a tattoo signified they are part of a special club. And they are. The girls we found all want to be part of a family; be part of something bigger than themselves. All the girls get the stem tattoo when they start working at the club. As they build up regulars and venture into private parties, they have the potential to earn the rosebud. The girls don't realize we are marking them as our property. Most of them aren't exactly smart. Most of them. They all know the boundaries too."

Frankie noted Tessa's language was present not past tense. She didn't think it was a mistake.

"What are the boundaries?"

"Stay away from the DiCapoli family, turn in all your earnings, only use what you are given, and don't talk to the police. Kat was the first one to mess up. She skimmed a little off the top here and there and got a little extra blow on the side from time to time. Then I heard she was talking to Jeremy DiCapoli. I knew she'd be in trouble but was surprised she ended up in the trunk of that car."

"Why were you surprised?"

"She was one of Alexandre's favorites; he had a real soft spot for her. He and Luka thought of her as family. They were all from the same small village and bonded over that. When Midori found out she was skimming cash and getting extra blow Alexandre protected her. I really don't think Alexandre knew about the hit, or he would have stopped Midori."

"Do you know what she and DiCapoli were doing? Were they dating, or was it more of a business arrangement?" Frankie asked.

"It started off as business. He was offering her more money for less work, but I think eventually they started hooking up. Andi and Nicki started following Kat's example. I warned Andi after Kat disappeared, but she didn't want to hear it. She told me something bad had happened to Nicki at Alexandre's. She told me she would do whatever she had to do to protect her. Andi was fierce when it came to that girl. If I didn't know better, I'd think they were sisters." Tessa paused then added, "Or lovers."

"Did Andi tell you what happened to Nicki?" Frankie asked.

"She didn't give a lot of details but said she found some cameras. I didn't ask anymore. I knew about the cameras. It was all part of the business expansion."

"Business expansion?"

Tessa smiled and said, "Detective, surely you don't think private parties offer the diversity and longevity to make any *real* money?"

Frankie did not answer but instead waited for Tessa to expound.

Frankie was stunned at how callous Tessa sounded as she discussed growing a business built on the buying and selling of human beings.

"Video streaming and adult films is where the money is. It doesn't take a lot of money to make a film these days. The patrons of what we create are not interested in CGI or HD. It's more about content.

"Actually, it all started as an accident. As you know, Alexandre has cameras set up in various places throughout his house. I stumbled upon them, shall we say, accidentally. The footage I found was hot and I told him we could make some real money if he edited them together. Alexandre was the one that came up with the idea of putting some of the clips online. He has some video editing software for his marketing business, so it was a no-cost experiment. He played around with it, took out the less desirable footage, and loaded a few samples onto the website he created.

"When we started recruiting new talent, Alexandre suggested we put cameras in the rooms of the loft. At first, I thought it was odd, but we have a couple of guys that break the girls in, so it ended up being an added safety measure. Luka gets a little rough, so he needs to be watched. I think Alexandre watches the young girls' rooms pretty carefully."

"What did Alexandre use to help facilitate the filming at his house?" Frankie asked.

"What exactly do you mean, detective?"

"Did he ever use drugs to facilitate the sexual encounters?"

Tessa smirked as she said, "He may have used a little Liquid X on occasion."

Frankie had a million questions but kept it simple.

"Do the girls know they are being taped or put online?"

"The ones who are filmed in the studio do. Did you find the studio detective?"

ONE HUNDRED THREE

FRANKIE LOOKED at Sam before asking Tessa, "Is the studio in the building where ARK is located?"

"It is well-disguised, but yes."

"How is the building laid out?

"The first floor is strictly business. The remaining floors are secured, and only a

limited number of people are allowed onto them. Midori runs the third floor, and we keep the girls on the fourth."

"So, the studio must be on the second."

"Very good detective," Frankie noted an air of superiority in Tessa's tone. "As I mentioned, we do some filming in the loft but that is mostly with the younger girls. Of course, the profits there are significant."

Frankie felt bile rise in her throat at the thought of the images that were creating "profit."

Tessa continued, "On the second floor, we have a formal film studio with props and lights. You'd be surprised at what people want to see… but I digress. There is also a large party room. We often get some good footage from there."

"Tell me more about the filming that occurs in the loft."

Frankie wasn't sure she really wanted to know, but the details would help with the search warrant.

"As I said, we initially started filming in there to monitor Luka. Some of these girls needed to be broken in slowly, and well, Luka does not have a lot of patience. Alexandre is the one who said we could make a lot of money by adding those films to the site. He decided it would be profitable to put a separate subscription for the live feed in the room where the youngest stay. It is our most profitable subscription."

Frankie felt her stomach churn. Emma was only 10 years old and had already been through so much. God only knew what else they were going to find. She looked at her watch and wondered if Emma was still at Synergy and if it was too late to talk to her again.

"How old is the youngest girl you have brought to the loft?" asked Sam, who up until that moment had been listening in silence.

"I think Emma might have been the youngest. What is she, 9 or 10? We carefully vetted the girls before we brought them here. Trust me when I tell you we were saving them from worse situations."

Frankie looked at Tessa incredulously. Did Tess actually believe the repeated abuse the children were experiencing was better than the lives they were pulled from?

"Previously, you said you didn't really know them. Are you now telling us that you do?" Sam asked.

Tessa smirked and said, "We did a little background on them before we brought them here. We met most of the girls at the mall or a similar location. Rarely did we take the girls the same night. We would arrange for them to meet us the following day and then follow them to see where they went. There were a few girls we did not accept after we saw where they came from."

"What do you mean?" Frankie asked.

"Well, there were a couple of girls in Illinois who lived in nicer neighborhoods, and one who's parent was a cop. Those were girls who would be missed, and people would look for. Therefore, those weren't the girls we wanted. We tried to rescue girls from homes full of poverty and abuse."

Frankie thought to herself, *"Oh yeah, you rescued them, alright."*

FRANKIE LAID the photograph of the letter in front of Tessa.

Tessa leaned forward in her chair and rested her hands on the table. She scanned the document then leaned back in the chair.

"What is this detective?"

"I was hoping you could tell me."

Tessa did not immediately answer. When she did speak, she asked, "Who received this note?"

Frankie laid a photograph of Keeley in front of Tessa and asked, "Do you know this woman?"

"That's Alexandre's teacher-girlfriend. Keeley-something. Did she find the note?"

"Who would be doing Alexandre's footwork on the outside? Luka?"

Tessa laughed, "Luka is too much of a coward to do anything to a woman. Detective, he might be a little rough with the young girls during their break-in period, but he would back down the second an adult woman raised her voice."

"Then who?"

"I'd probably look at Craig Midori. If you recall, he rather enjoys intimidating women."

Frankie grabbed her phone and texted Craven.

Craig Midori

Frankie looked back to Tessa and asked, "Where would they keep someone they snatched?"

Tessa began picking at the strings on her jail-issued pants.

"Who do you think was kidnapped Detective?"

Irritation, exhaustion, and frustration were setting in, and Frankie's patience was wearing thin. Tessa was playing with them, and she'd enough.

"We believe Candi may be in harm's way."

Tessa seemed to be giving her response serious thought.

"Tessa…"

"How much of the loft did you actually search Detective?"

Suddenly it made sense. Katarina and the two men were found in the trunk of a car in the west bottoms. The car was the dumpsite, but they had not located where they were murdered. The loft was close and offered privacy. Frankie realized they needed to get a warrant for the entire building unless they could articulate exigent circumstances.

"Is that where he would take Candi?"

"Honestly, I'm surprised it has taken them this long to snatch her. She always seemed like a weak link to me."

Frankie gathered some additional information from Tessa. As she was preparing to leave, Frankie asked, "How many other girls are we going to find there?"

Tessa looked at Sam, then back at Frankie, "Dead or alive?"

ONCE FRANKIE GOT outside the jail, she took long, deep breaths. She had already sent Craven a text telling him to meet her and Sam in the parking lot adjacent to the loft.

"You sure you want to ride along? It's likely to be an all-nighter."

"Are you kidding? I want to be there when you find these girls," Sam said.

Frankie grabbed her cell phone and called Sergeant Baker, followed by dispatch. They needed a supervisor on the scene and a couple of cars to help them clear the building.

"Send canine, too if they're working."

The walk back to police headquarters was quick. Frankie and Sam went to the squad room, grabbed vests, radios, and Frankie's go-bag.

"I'm glad Mia's vest was at her desk. Put it on," instructed Frankie as she thrust it towards Sam.

Frankie demonstrated by putting her own vest over her t-shirt. She threw the radio in the bag after explaining to Sam how to use it in the case of an emergency.

"And you are sure we shouldn't be typing up a warrant?" Frankie asked.

"We have exigent circumstances to go into the space to locate the missing woman and possible children based on Tessa's statement and the text Craven received from Candi. You can search anywhere a person is capable of hiding, and if you find any contraband, it is able to be seized. However, you cannot search anywhere a person cannot be hidden. For that, we will need to get a warrant," Sam explained.

"How many girls do you think we will find?" Frankie asked.

"She was pretty cagey on that question, wasn't she?"

"Jared said he'd continue monitoring the calls and text me if he hears anything that will help." Frankie threw her bag in the backseat of the car, looked at Sam, and said, "Let's go get these girls!"

En route to the meeting spot, Frankie called Mia and updated her on the case.

"Are you sure you don't want me to come in? I can be there in 30," Mia said.

"No, you enjoy your night off. I'll text you with updates when I can."

"You two are pretty close," Sam observed.

"Yeah. Mia is one of the first detectives I trained. We have been through hell together. She's more than a friend or partner. She's family."

Sam nodded but didn't say anything more. She seemed intent on listening to the traffic on the radio, occasionally asking Frankie questions during the brief ride.

"My father was a cop until he died. My brother is on the job now."

"Really?" Frankie asked. "Where at?"

"A small town in Pennsylvania."

"Was it hard to leave and move here?"

"Yes and no," Sam said. "I still talk to my mom twice a day, and I video chat with my nieces and nephews every weekend. It's not ideal but the opportunity was too good to pass up."

Just as Frankie began to say something her phone rang.

"Where are you at Frankie?" Craven asked.

"About 2 blocks away. Everything okay?"

"Yeah. There's a light on the second floor, but we haven't seen anyone pass by the window."

CHAPTER
ONE HUNDRED SIX

FRANKIE FOUND the blacked-out SUVs with ease and pulled in right behind them. With only one light illuminated, the building had a dark, ominous feel to it. The air was damp, and there was no breeze to cool the unseasonably warm evening. Frankie and Sam joined the team assembling between the cars. Frankie introduced the new prosecutor to Sergeant Baker and all the officers gathered. Frankie was relieved to look around the group and see the familiar faces of officers she had worked with and a few from the Tactical Response Team.

Frankie began the debrief, "We are searching under exigent circumstances so we can only search in places where a person can hide. If you find any contraband in a place a person can hide, you can seize it. Otherwise, we will get a piggyback warrant later." Frankie took a drink of water and waited to see if anyone had questions. Hearing none, she continued, "We think a woman is being held against her will in this building. This man has murdered at least one other woman and two of her associates. We have no reason to believe he will spare her. My source said there are also an unknown number of young girls being held here. We have already rescued a 10 and 12-year-old but it appears the others are being held in a secret space. We do not know for sure what condition the girls are in, but you can expect them to fear the police. We suspect the young girls are on the 2nd floor and Candi is being held on the 3rd. That does not mean they couldn't be on the 1st or 4th. Kristof likes to disguise doors in the wall so search each space meticulously. There may be two men holding these girls. One is Luka Petrov and the other is Craig Midori. Both should be considered armed and dangerous. Any questions?"

The officers grunted their understanding and began putting their gear in place. Frankie turned to Sam and said, "Stay here. I'll let you know when it's safe to make entry."

Sam nodded in understanding.

Frankie led the officers towards the building. At the entrance, officers peeled off and went to the back of the building. The main door was unlocked, making initial entry easy. The layout of the lobby had not changed since the last time Frankie was there but somehow, knowing what she now knew, the entire space had changed. The energy was darker, and she felt an urgency she had not felt before. She scanned the entryway looking for any anything she may have previously missed.

The team systematically cleared the office space housing the ARK Marketing firm. They were about to give the all-clear when Frankie noticed something out of the corner of her eye.

"What's that?"

Craven stopped, turned, and said, "We're about to find out."

Frankie pulled what looked like a piece of wall but was actually a door. She held her breath, wondering what she would find.

With their guns directed toward the opening the team lined up, leaving Frankie room to step back once the door was open.

"What the he…"

ONE HUNDRED SEVEN

THE WALL of the closet-sized room held two giant screens with a live-feed. The first screen broadcast a small room with young women and girls asleep on makeshift beds. The second screen looked like a horror movie playing out in front of them.

Frankie turned towards Craven, "Doesn't that look like the fourth floor?"

"I think so. Let's go!"

Frankie followed Craven and Fitz to the elevator. The adrenaline increased with the rising of the elevator. When the doors opened, they each rushed out and stacked two on one side and one on the other side of the door. Frankie reached down and tried the handle of the door, surprised to find it unlocked. With deft precision, they entered the room and began clearing the area. A muffled scream cut through the silence. Their deliberate steps increased in speed.

Frankie was the first to see Candi. She was perched on a wooden chair, duct tape holding her upright. Dried blood matted her once-blonde hair to her head. A strip of duct tape covered her mouth. Her exposed skin was bruised and bloody. Luka stood behind her, his back to Frankie. Candi saw them and started to moan but Frankie motioned for her to be quiet. Fitz peeled off and started to circle around to the right while Frankie moved to the left with Craven close behind.

"Luka Petrov put your hands where I can see them," Frankie yelled.

Luka spun around in surprise.

Frankie yelled a second time with more emphasis, "Show. Me. Your. Hands!"

Luke lifted his right hand, and the light caught the reflection of the blade on the knife he was holding.

Frankie, Craven, and Fitz yelled in unison, "Drop the knife!"

Luka's mouth lifted in a demented smile just as he lunged towards Candi with the knife. The sound of gunshots filled the room as Luka's body jerked from side to side with the impact of the bullets ripping through his body. Later Frankie would say although it happened fast, the way Luka's body fell, it appeared as if everything was moving in slow motion.

Once Luka's body was still, Frankie moved towards Candi and Craven moved towards Luka. Frankie took a knife from her pocket and carefully cut the duct tape holding Candi to the chair. When the tape released Candi's body slumped forward. Her body convulsed in sobs.

Frankie keyed her radio, *"1061 on Center Zone air. Start an ambulance to my location."*

"1061 copy. Ambulance en route. 2325."

"Candi, you're going to be okay. Can you sit here?"

Candi nodded.

"Jim, we need to clear the rest of the floor. We need to find those girls."

Frankie barely heard Candi's voice, "They…they…they're in the hidden room on three."

Frankie turned, "Is there anyone else up here?"

"I… don't… think… so. Watch…watch…" Candi began to cough. "Watch for tr…tra…traps."

"What kind of traps?"

"I'm not su…sure. They just said if…if…I tr…tried to leave, I… would… get hurt."

CHAPTER
ONE HUNDRED EIGHT

FRANKIE DID NOT TRY to hide her surprise as she looked at the changes Luka had made to his bedroom. One corner of the room appeared to be dedicated to different types of restraints. There were various cameras clearly visible, and Frankie suspected a few that were not. Lubricant, condoms, and sex toys littered the bedside table and bookcase near the restraints. A swing hung from the ceiling.

"Check the walls," Frankie directed.

Craven and Frankie carefully examined the wall but found no false or hidden doors.

Sirens were getting closer.

"Let's get Candi downstairs and help search the rest of the floors."

Craven said, "Frankie, why don't you take Candi...."

"1061, I need two uniforms on 4."

Frankie shot Craven a look that said, *"Don't mess with me."*

When the uniformed officers got to the 4th floor, they quickly directed them to get Candi to the paramedics.

Once the uniformed officers had Candi, Frankie followed Craven down the hall of the loft apartment. It had only been a few days since they had been in the space, but she noted the changes. The room where Julia and Emma slept had different bedding and the dollhouse was gone.

A television, video game system, and two gamer chairs stood in its place. Frankie grabbed her radio.

"1061 to 1060 on private."

"Go ahead, Frankie."

"They either have little boys hidden somewhere, or they are planning to grab some."

"Copy."

Frankie was about to push the button for the elevator when something made her look to the right. She dashed to the wall and pushed.

"What are you…"

"There's a door," Frankie explained as she tested the wall to see if it was meant to be pushed or pulled. When the doorway finally gave way, she said, "Give me something to prop it open. I don't know where this is going to lead and sure as hell don't want to get trapped in here."

Craven scanned the foyer and found a potted plant heavy enough to hold the steel door open. Before Craven released the pot, Frankie was on the move. She made it less than twenty feet when she stopped. Craven started to say something, but Frankie motioned for him to be quiet. Frankie began to move quietly down the hall, the sound of crying becoming more prominent the closer she got.

Frankie paused briefly at the end of the hall and looked down a short staircase. She moved quickly towards the landing. Frankie looked quickly to the left then to the right.

"Move right?" Frankie asked.

"Yeah. I'll hold the hall."

Frankie saw a door about three-quarters of the way down the hall, but something told her to stop. Frankie scanned the area, starting on the right side of her vision and moving to the left, deliberately slowing down.

"Stop! Get back to the stairs! Don't touch your radio!"

Frankie and Craven hurried back to the stairs, taking them two by two, not stopping until they reached the top.

ONE HUNDRED NINE

"EVERYONE OUT! Do not key your radios or use your cellphones. Get out of this building now!"

Frankie and Craven led everyone off the floor onto the elevator. They rode the elevator down a floor, getting off quickly as the doors opened. Fitzmeyer got off the elevator with Frankie and Craven. Before the doors closed, Frankie instructed the officers to go a block away and call for the bomb squad, fire department, and another ambulance.

"Dammit, I wish Mia were here. Let's find the teams and get them the hell out of here. Who knows how many other explosives are in this building."

Fitzmeyer took the lead, Frankie followed close behind, and Craven brought up the tail. The team moved quickly, only pausing to look in open doorways. They were no longer on a rescue mission, but a search to make sure none of their own got left behind.

Frankie scanned the halls, walls, and doors for explosives. Fitz passed a closed door but suddenly, Frankie stopped and said, "Wait. Do you hear that?"

Craven laid his ear against the door and said, "There's someone in there."

"We can't leave anyone inside," Frankie said.

"We have to get our guys out, Frankie. We'll come back with the bomb dogs," Fitz said.

"He's right, Frankie," Craven said.

"You guys go ahead and look for Baker and the others. I'm going to get these people out."

"We aren't leaving you here alone, Frankie. Come on, let's at least finish the floor and come back."

Frankie knew Craven and Fitz were right, but she also knew she couldn't leave anyone behind even if it meant she was at risk.

Craven looked at Fitz and said, "Hold on. Let's see if we can get the door open and get these people out. Then we can clear the rest of the floor."

Fitz shot Craven a look that said, "you're an idiot," but didn't move. Frankie and Fitz stood back, guns drawn, as Craven pushed the door open. A loud pop and cloud of smoke exploded in their faces.

ONE HUNDRED TEN

FRANKIE'S VISION WAS MUDDLED, and there was a ringing in her ears. She blinked her eyes and tried to clear the noise filling her head. Once the immediate shock wore off, she realized the loud popping and poof of smoke was not an explosion but instead a flashbang grenade, like what the tactical response team used in search warrant entries.

"Are you okay, Frankie?" Craven yelled.

Frankie nodded and said, "You? Fitz?"

"Good."

"Good," Fitz added.

Frankie led the way through the smoke and haze. The room was dark, the only light coming from the brief flashes of Fitz's flashlight. The room was narrow and long and smelled of human feces combined with stale urine. The ringing in Frankie's ears dissipated just as Fitz flashed on the faces of four young boys huddled in the corner.

"It's okay," Fitz said. "We're here to help you. To take you home."

The boys cowered and clung to one another.

"We've got to go," Frankie urgently said.

The boys looked at the two men, then at Frankie. Seemingly convinced the three were there to help them, the tallest boy nodded at the other three to get up.

Franke smiled at the boys and directed them out of the room. She asked, "Is there anyone else here?"

The boys shrugged their shoulders as they walked out of the room. Frankie put them on the elevator, and just as she was about to continue the search, she saw Sergeant Baker walking towards her with two young girls close behind.

"Just in time. Let's get out of here. Hopefully the bomb squad is on the way," Frankie said.

Sergeant Baker started to ask Frankie what she was talking about, then thought better of it. Instead, he said, "No one key up their radio or mess with their phone."

Everyone hurried towards the doors. Frankie thought they were in the clear when out of the corner of her eye she saw a sudden movement by one of the women that had followed Sergeant Baker out of the building. The woman put her hand in her pocket and pulled out a solid black object.

Frankie turned and yelled, "Sarge!"

Sergeant Baker turned in time to see the woman raise the object above her head. He lunged towards her, knocking the cylinder from her hand. It rolled away from the crowd, and a cloud of smoke filled the air, but once again there was no explosion. Baker and Frankie wrestled with the woman and brought her to her knees and quickly secured her with handcuffs.

Baker said, "Cuff the rest of the woman. Put each woman in a different car and make sure you thoroughly search them. Do not leave them alone."

ONE HUNDRED ELEVEN

FRANKIE EXITED the building in time to see the radio car with "K-9" emblazoned on its rear quarter panel. The bomb squad followed close behind. As Frankie walked to the lot where the cars were assembling, she felt as if her legs were full of lead. She looked to her left then to her right; Craven and Fitzmeyer were walking in step.

"Hey Jordan," Frankie said.

Jordan Franklin was one of the specially trained officers assigned to the K-9 Unit. Her dog Ero sat next to her when she stopped.

"Girl, somehow I knew you had to be involved," laughed Jordan. "What do we have?"

Frankie gave a brief synopsis of the case, explaining the connection to Midori and the Shady Lady.

"You mean those guys from Thanksgiving are involved in this too?"

"We think…no, yes, they *are* involved. We found four boys hidden in a room and two women who may or may not be victims as well. We also found another girl being tortured on the fourth floor. When we went into the hidden passageway…"

Jordan interrupted, "Hidden what?"

Frankie described the hidden door and the device she found in the hall. She shared the warning of traps and the flash bang grenade that was attached to the door where the boys were hidden.

"So basically, what you are saying is there could be proverbial land mines anywhere we go."

"I'm afraid so. Is there anything…"

Before Frankie could finish her questions Detectives Haggerty and Paridis from the Bomb Squad Unit made their presence known.

Haggerty said, "We can send the robot in. Based on what you are telling us, that seems like the safest plan. Is there anyone else in the building?"

"I don't think…I did hear crying from a room down the hidden passageway, but I'm not so sure it wasn't a trap. The sounds came from behind the door that had a device on it."

"Okay, we'll start there. It sounds like these guys are more interested in preventing people from trying to escape than they are in blowing up their building. We'll check the room where you think there may be people and then systematically clear the building from there."

Frankie nodded and walked away. When she was certain she was at a safe distance from the building she made a phone call. She was going to need some help after all.

ONE HUNDRED TWELVE

FRANKIE DIDN'T KNOW what time it was and was afraid to look at her watch. She, Sam, Fitzmeyer, and Craven had left the scene while Haggerty and Paridis cleared the building. Baker had called her on the way back to headquarters to tell her they had taken two confirmed and two possible explosives from the building. Frankie's gut had been right; if she had tried to open the door it would have ended badly. And for nothing. The only thing in the room was a video feed of the room the boys were in. No one else was found in the building.

Fitzmeyer and Craven interviewed the boys while Frankie and Mia teamed up to interview the women that had been found. What they learned was enlightening.

The boys had been taken much in the same way as the girls had been taken but with slightly different tactics. Instead of modeling or dancing, they had been lured to the city with promises of freedom, money, and drugs. The boys ranged in ages from 13-15 but seemed, somehow younger and older at the same time. When Frankie watched them on the videos, their eyes seemed sad and empty. They reminded her of a couple of the kids she worked with in VISION who had been on the streets just a little too long.

Frankie and Mia discovered the two women Sergeant Baker brought out were part of the new recruitment team, but in their own way, they were victims too. Both girls had rose tattoos but neither had the symbol Tessa had on hers. The girls had been locked in a room but did not seem to understand that it was a crime. Their captors, Luka and Alexandre, had told them to set off a diversion device and run if anyone tried to remove them from the loft. The women told Frankie and Mia they thought Sergeant Baker and the team were part of the DiCapoli family. That seemed illogical to Frankie, but then again, nothing about the case was *logical*.

In between interviews, Frankie learned Candi had been admitted to the hospital. She had a few injuries, but none were life-threatening. She was going to be okay.

When the last interview was completed, Frankie and Mia collapsed in their chairs. Frankie closed her eyes and images of Candi, and the flash-bang filled her mind causing her to open them with a start. Without a word, she grabbed her bag and started towards the door. Mia, Sam, Fitzmeyer, Craven, and Baker followed close behind.

ONE HUNDRED THIRTEEN

THE CREW SAT AROUND A TABLE, in an otherwise empty bar, with cold beers in front of them. It wasn't quite eleven, so the lunch crowd had not made it to the pub. None of them were ready to go home after the stories they had heard. Instead of taking it home, they were going to sit in the bar and decompress.

"I think I could sleep for a week," Sam said with a laugh.

"Can I be honest?" Frankie asked.

"Of course."

"I'm surprised you hung with us all night. I don't think a prosecutor has ever done that. At least not since I've been in the unit."

"I like seeing things through," Sam said. "Besides, I can't let you have *all* the fun!"

"We are duly impressed," Mia said.

Baker raised his bottle and said, "Here's to a successful all-nighter. May we not have another one for a long time!"

"Here, here," the crew said in unison as the bottlenecks clicked.

Frankie looked over at Fitz and said, "Hey man, I'm sorry. You were right. I put us all at risk by insisting we go in that door."

"You did, but you were also right. I don't think I could have lived with myself if we had left those boys behind, and something had happened."

"Are we good?" Frankie asked.

"Better than good kid. Better than good," Fitzmeyer said as he ruffled Frankie's hair.

Frankie turned to Craven and asked, "How was Candi?"

Craven had stopped at the hospital on the way to the pub.

"She was doped up, but I think she'll be okay. Physically at least. I'm going to try to get her to leave the city when she gets released. There's nothing but trouble for her here," Craven said.

"Sadly, I think you are right."

The group finished their beers, and one by one, left the bar. Frankie looked at her watch and realized her dad should be on his lunch break. Taking the chance, she dialed his number and chatted with him all the way home. Frankie barely remembered lying down on her bed and or closing her eyes.

The next thing, Frankie knew the smell of bacon was waking her up. Breakfast for dinner was one of their favorite meals. She could hear the faint sounds of music coming from Dani's room and the chatter of Tyler talking to Sophie about the renovations she and Frankie were planning for the space over the garage. Tyler was trying to convince her to build him a treehouse in their yard instead. Frankie laid there listening to the happy sounds of her house before wiping the sleep from her eyes and joining them in the kitchen to help with dinner.

ONE HUNDRED FOURTEEN

THE FOLLOWING couple of weeks were busy. In between new cases, Frankie and Mia executed a second search warrant on the warehouse and on Alexandre's house. They recovered four vials of a clear liquid from the house, but it could be several weeks before they knew what the contents held. The search of the warehouse yielded similar vials and a myriad of other drugs.

Along with drafting reports, Frankie and Mia met with Sam about the upcoming grand jury. They would both be called to testify, and the result could be the difference between Alexandre answering to additional charges, or potentially making bail. None of them wanted to see him released. They had restricted his and Tessa's phone calls in the hope it would prevent them from rebuilding their business from the inside.

They were finally on their last night of second shift, and then they would both be off for a couple of days. Frankie was holding her breath, hoping for a quiet night but at 9:00 PM her cellphone rang. Assuming it was her children calling to say good night, Frankie did not stop typing or look at the caller-id before answering, "Hello!"

Frankie stopped typing and grabbed a pen. The color drained from her face as she jotted information onto her notepad. Before hanging up, she told the caller she would meet her at the hospital in fifteen minutes.

"What's going on, Frankie?" Baker asked. "Rick and Brett can handle whatever it is. You and Mia need to finish up your reports."

"It's Heather Whitaker. Apparently, William found her. I don't have all the information, but it looks like he raped her. Again."

"Do you know where it happened? We can go out and do the scene," Rick offered.

"No. She's down at County with Alex. Let me go meet with her, and then I'll call you with the details," Frankie said as she walked to the door. "This son of a bitch needs to be taken into custody. If Jessica Moon hadn't let him go in the first place, this wouldn't have happened."

Baker nodded towards Mia.

"I'm on my way, Sarge."

At the stairwell, Frankie turned to Mia and said, "You don't have to go with me. I can handle getting her statement on my own. You have just as many reports to finish as I do."

"I know, but I want to see this through with you."

Frankie nodded as they exited the garage. They both shuddered as the brisk, Midwest air hit them in the face.

CHAPTER
ONE HUNDRED FIFTEEN

HEATHER AND ALEX were waiting in the forensic examination room when Frankie and Mia arrived. Heather still wore a cast and had stitches across her face and the bruises from the beating had begun to change colors. Heather forced a smile when Frankie and Mia entered the room, but the tears made the smile hollow.

"Is she going to charge him now, Frankie," Alex demanded.

"There's a new prosecutor on the case, Samantha Ryan. She's already issued a warrant for William's arrest in the other case. I haven't called her about this one yet. I wanted to have all the details first. Heather, do you feel up to telling Detective Boden and me what happened?"

Heather nodded but didn't immediately speak. Alex began to say something, but Frankie shot her a look that told her to give Heather a minute.

"I went to see my therapist, and when I got to the parking lot, he was there waiting for me. He had a knife and told me to get into my car. There were a lot of cars in the parking lot, so he said to drive. I was scared Detective…."

Heather began to sob. Frankie looked at Mia, then quickly looked away. Tears of anger filled Frankie's eyes. Rationally she knew the only person to blame was William, but her current mind blamed Jessica Moon.

When Heather had collected herself, she said, "He made me drive to the park, back by the pool. He forced me to get into the backseat and take my clothes off. He raped me, and when he finished, he said, 'that was for Corey' then he got out of the car and started walking. I called Alex and she told me to come here."

"Where is your therapist's office, Heather?"

"Right there off Blue Parkway and Cleveland, by Brush Creek. I talked to a counselor at the hospital, and she told me to go there. This was my first appointment since I got released."

"What time did this happen?" Frankie asked.

"My appointment was at 4:00 PM. It was right afterward."

Daylight, Frankie thought. Aloud she said, "Do you know the name of the man that did this to you?"

"William. I don't know his last name, but he's friends with Corey and Tubby," Heather said.

"What park did he take you to?"

"Swope Park. Not at the zoo, though. He made me drive down by the pool since it's still closed."

"Where's your car?" Mia asked.

"It's here. In the garage," Heather said.

Frankie got Heather to sign a release waiver while Mia went and called Crime Scene and the office. They were going to ask the boys to process the car while they went to find William.

By the time Mia returned, Frankie was finishing up with Heather's statement. Heather told Frankie she thought she saw William get into a black Chevy Capris. She did not see the license plate number but said it had something hanging from the rearview mirror. Heather did not know where he went but Frankie and Mia had a pretty good idea, and it was time for this to end.

ONE HUNDRED SIXTEEN

MIA DROVE while Frankie pulled up the addresses associated with William and his mother. She was pretty sure he wasn't there, but she had a patrol car sit nearby and watch, just in case. Frankie and Mia had talked to Sergeant Baker and decided they would try to hit all the addresses at the same time, or at least close to the same time. They did not want this guy in the wind again.

Mia's husband Erik was working and responded to the area to assist with the search. Erik and his partner went to one of the addresses not far from where Mia and Frankie were going. Frankie had called Craven. He and Fitzmeyer went to one of the houses on the list while Mac and Payne went to a fourth. In all, they had four houses covered and a patrol car roaming the streets in case he was on foot.

The officers had switched their radios to the TAC channel temporarily so they could send the message to approach the houses. Mia and Frankie had their handheld radios with them but kept them on the same station as the dispatcher. Just in case.

Frankie keyed up the car radio and said, "1061 to all cars. Let's do this."

All four teams made contact at the house they were sent to at the same time. Erik and his partner were at William's mother's house. Laronda had no idea where her son was. She told Erik she had not seen him in over a week. She allowed them to search the house, but the only thing they found was an unmade bed and a duffle bag with a few pieces of clothes inside.

Erik sent Mia a text message, *"He's not here. He left a duffle bag with clothes on his bed. He was either just here or is planning to come back."*

"Okay. Maybe sit up on the house and see if he comes back."

"Read my mind."

Fitzmeyer and Craven went to the house of one of William's cousins. They talked to William's cousin, who also said he had no idea where William was or where he might be. It took a little convincing, but he eventually let Fitzmeyer and Craven search the house.

Fitz sent Frankie a text message, *"No luck. Any other possible addresses?"*

"No. Keep an eye out for a black Chevy Capris. He may be rolling in that."

"Copy."

Mac and Payne went to the house of one of William's associates. They attempted contact at the front and back door, but no one answered. The mailbox was overflowing with mail, and the doors were secure.

Mac sent Frankie a text message, *"House looks vacant. We'll sit up and watch it for a few minutes."*

"Copy."

Frankie and Mia were at the house of William's girlfriend. They approached the house from an angle and noticed a black Chevy Capris parked in the driveway, half-hidden behind the house.

Frankie knocked on the door with force. The door was answered by a statuesque, African American woman with an attitude.

"What the hell do you want?"

"William Kennedy."

"He's not here," and with that slammed the door in Frankie's face.

ONE HUNDRED SEVENTEEN

FRANKIE KNOCKED AGAIN, resisting the urge to mule-kick the door. She realized she did not have exigent circumstances, and quite frankly couldn't prove he was there.

Reluctantly Frankie and Mia returned to their car. Frankie announced over the radio they had struck out at the residence but asked officers in the area to be on the lookout for William, who might be on foot.

"What do you want to do now?" Mia asked.

"Kick that door in and make her tell us where that son of a bitch is." Frankie gave a half-laugh and added, "But I guess we drive around then maybe sit up on the house for a few minutes."

Mia laughed and said, "I like your first idea, but guess we should do the second."

The pair drove the streets slowly, looking for William Kennedy or anyone he may have associated with. They were about to give up when Mac announced he had spotted Kennedy near the church on Gregory and Agnes.

"Which way was he going, Mac?" Frankie asked.

"He just crossed Gregory, heading south on Agnes."

"En route."

"242 copy a ped check.... he's running southeast through the houses. Hold the air."

Frankie and Mia were one block east.

"1061 and 1064 are 10-23 at Gregory and Bellefontaine."

Sirens could be heard as additional cars made their way to the area. Mia was mid-block when they saw Kennedy run out from between the houses. Frankie jumped out of the car before it was in park and began to run. She reached Kennedy just as Mac tackled him to the ground.

Mac pulled Kennedy's arms out from under his body while Frankie secured him in a leg lock. Once he was secure, Frankie released his leg, and Mac rolled Kennedy over and searched him. Satisfied he did not have drugs or weapons on him, Mac stood Kennedy up and walked him over to the patrol wagon.

Frankie waited until Kennedy was secured in the wagon before saying anything. Just as the door was closing, she leaned in and said, "It's over, William."

William hung his head and didn't say a word.

THE NEXT SIX weeks went by in a flurry of activity. Frankie and Mia worked endless hours, putting case files together for the new prosecutor who was intent on reviewing the ones Jessica Moon had previously declined. Frankie was tying up loose ends on the Kristof and Whitaker cases while counting down the days until school was out so she and the kids could start planning their summer vacation.

Frankie was finishing up a report when her cellphone began to ring. She looked down and was shocked to see her ex-husband's phone number on the screen. Frankie got up from her desk and went into the empty interview room.

"Hey Chris. What's up?"

"I think we need to talk about Danielle," Chris began. "She told me she wants to come live with…"

"Wait, what?"

"Danielle wants to live with us. She wants to go to church and school with the girls. I thought I'd talk to you and see if we could come up with a reasonable solution before getting an attorney involved."

"Attorney? You know what, never mind, Chris. I'm at work and can't talk about this now. Why the heck would you bother me when I'm at work?"

Chris let out an exasperated, "When aren't you at work? That's the whole point, Frankie."

Frankie took a deep breath and composed herself before saying, "Chris, can I call you when I get home? I should be leaving here soon."

"Call me back when you get home." Chris added, "You know it's the right thing for Danielle, Frankie."

Frankie hung up the phone and collapsed in the chair. Her mind was racing while her heart was breaking. Things had been going better between her and Danielle and this call left her blindsided. The idea of her daughter living anywhere but with her in their house was unfathomable. Frankie didn't understand how this was happening or why Chris was doing this. He had promised her when they divorced that he would never try to take Danielle from her. A light knock on the door jolted Frankie from her thoughts.

Frankie wiped her eyes and cleared her throat, "Yeah?"

Mia opened the door and asked, "Are you okay, Frankie? You've been in here for a while. I thought I'd check on you before I left."

Frankie wiped the tears from her face and looked at her watch. 2:50 PM. Time for the dayshift to end.

"Give me a second to shut down my computer, and I'll walk out with you. Did the other squad already get the phones?"

"Yep. Sarge and the boys left, so it's just you and me here."

Frankie shut her computer down, grabbed her bag, and followed Mia down the stairs.

"You want to talk about it?"

"Not yet, but thanks."

Frankie wasn't sure where to begin. Maybe Chris was wrong. Maybe he had misunderstood Danielle. After all, she hadn't said a thing to Frankie. Sophie hadn't said a word since the night they were all at the farm, and that was two months earlier. Surely someone would have said something before now.

ONE HUNDRED NINETEEN

FRANKIE WALKED INTO A QUIET HOUSE. She had about fifteen minutes before the kids would be home from school. Fifteen minutes to figure out what she was going to say to Danielle. Her drive home had yielded nothing.

Frankie was still at a loss when Danielle walked through the front door.

"Hey mom! I'm surprised you're home already," Danielle said.

"Why don't you sit down for a minute. We need to talk."

Danielle gave Frankie a look of concern and asked, "Is everything okay? Did something happen to Grandpa?"

"No, but I did get a phone call from *your* dad today. Do you have any idea why he would call me at work?"

Dani began to fidget in her chair. She looked at her lap to avoid looking at Frankie.

"Danielle?"

"I, um, I, um," Danielle stuttered.

"Dan…"

Dani began to cry, "I just want to go to church and be on the Bible Quiz team with my sisters. You aren't ever here, and I want to go live with my dad."

Frankie felt like someone had stabbed her in the stomach. She wanted to lash out and tell her daughter what a fool she was. She wanted to get her ex-husband on the phone and call him every name under the sun. Instead, Frankie sat there and fought the bile that was rising in her throat.

Dani continued to ramble, but Frankie could not process what the child was saying. Tyler came through the door and sensing something was wrong, he sat next to Frankie and reached for her hand. Dani started to tell Tyler to go to his bedroom, but Frankie stopped her.

"No. You don't get to tell him to leave. This impacts *him* too."

"What's going on, mom?" Tyler asked.

"Tell him, Danielle."

"I'm going to go live with my dad."

"I have not told you that you can go, Danielle." Frankie looked down at Tyler and said, "I believe she meant to say she has asked to go live with her dad."

"But why would you want to live there? You wouldn't get to see us every day. Who would be here when I get home from school? Who will play games with me and watch movies and…" Tyler began to cry and let go of Frankie's hand. He grabbed his cat, Koda, ran to his room, and slammed the door shut behind him.

Danielle glared at Frankie.

"You don't get to look at me that way, Danielle Elizabeth. This isn't just about you. This impacts that little boy too."

Dani wisely stayed quiet. Frankie did not fight the tears that filled her eyes and ran down her red cheeks. The pair sat in silence for what seemed like hours but was just minutes. Frankie stared at the photograph of the three of them at the beach that hung above the television. A happy memory of their first family vacation.

Taking a deep breath, Frankie said, "School is out in a week. I will let you stay the summer, but you *will* come back here in August so we can go on vacation as a family. And you *will* go to school *here* in the fall. That's the only compromise I'm willing to give at this time."

"But…"

"Don't push me, Danielle or you won't go for the summer. Do you understand?"

Danielle nodded her head as she got up and left the room.

CHAPTER
ONE HUNDRED TWENTY

OUT OF THE corner of her eyes, Frankie saw something fall to the floor when she dropped her work bag onto the sofa table as Tyler ran to the kitchen for a snack before running out the back door to check the progress on the garage apartment. A few weeks after Dani moved out, Frankie decided it was time to renovate the space above her garage. It was something she and Ty's father had planned to do, but never got around to. With the help of her sister, brother, and dad, the apartment started to take shape. Sophie used her skills as a master carpenter to add charm and function to the space. The distraction was also helping Frankie and Tyler adjust to Dani's absence.

Frankie initially planned to use the apartment as an income property but when it was all finished her little sister surprised her.

"The lease on my apartmetn is up at the end of the month. What if I move in? It will make it easier to help with Ty when you have to work late," Sophie said. "Plus, when we have sister-nights, I won't have far to go."

Frankie laughed and said, "I was hoping you would suggest that."

At the sound of the back door slamming, Frankie remembered seeing something fall. She bent down and absentmindedly picked up the post-card, assuming it was junk mail, but something about the card caught her eye. The cover of the postcard was a bicycle leaning against a sand dune. The quote read, "Life is a beautiful ride. Ocracoke NC." Frankie's hand began to tremble as she flipped the card over. There, scrawled on the back next to her name and address, was a message. *Miss you and wish you were here.*

There was no name at the bottom, but Frankie knew who it was from. The pain of Derek leaving was still there but slowly beginning to fade. Frankie took the card and put it on the refrigerator next to Tyler's painting and Danielle's permission slip to play soccer in the fall.

Frankie placed her hand on the card as she pressed it into the refrigerator and whispered, "Miss you too."

Frankie let her hand drop and went into her bedroom to change her clothes so she could head to the garage. She sat on her bed and thought of all the changes she and her kids had experienced over the past twelve months. Frankie was starting to wonder if she should consider leaving SVU or possibly even the job. A part of her feared Danielle would refuse to come back in the fall, and she wasn't sure what she would do if she did. The day she left was crystal clear in her mind. Tyler had sat on his bed with his guinea pig and refused to come out and say good-bye to Danielle.

"I'm glad you agreed to this, Frankie. I really didn't want to have to get an attorney," Chris said.

Frankie resisted the urge to curse Chris out. Or punch him in the face. She refused to look at the man she had been married to but instead focused on her daughter.

"Danielle, do you have your bathing suit and allergy medication?"

"I have a bathing suit at dad's house. He bought all of us new suits for our trip next month," Danielle said.

"I'll come and get you on my next day off, okay?"

"We have Bible Quiz meets and church on the weekend but if you want to come during the week and take me to dinner, I'm sure dad won't mind."

Frankie didn't respond but instead grabbed her daughter and gave her a hug.

"I love you, Angel-girl. Remember that okay?"

"I know mom. I love you too."

With that, her daughter climbed into her father's SUV. Frankie stood on the porch with a lump in her throat as she watched a piece of her heart drive away.

Chapter One

FINLEY THREW her backpack over her shoulder as she walked out the front door. Rubbing her cheek, she vowed this was the last time she would be hit. Finley's foster mom looked the other way when her boyfriend got mad and knocked the kids around. With only one year of school left, Finley thought she could put up with the punches, but the night before her foster mom's boyfriend had come into her room after everyone was asleep. Finley, asleep on her side, heard him step into the room and felt him sit on the bed. She did not move when he ran his hand along her hip and up her body, grazing her breast. She gripped the knife she kept under her pillow, prepared to plunge it into his body if he tried anything. Just when he lifted the blanket, the baby began to cry, and he was gone. That was the moment she knew she had to leave.

Her foster mom thought she was walking to school, but Finley had other plans. Instead of textbooks, her backpack held her journal, a couple changes of clothes, and money she had saved from babysitting the neighbor kids. She told her foster mom she had a field trip with her summer school class and would be late getting home. If everything went well, she would be on a bus far away before anyone even knew she was gone. Her boyfriend said a ticket would be waiting for her at the bus depot. Twenty minutes after walking out the door, Finley was on the Greyhound bus heading north to Kansas City.

At the first stop a woman sat down next to Finley and said, "I'm going to see my daughter in Omaha."

As the woman spent the next ten minutes talking about her daughter, her daughter's "lowlife" husband, and her grandchild, Finley let her mind wander. She could hardly believe she was on a bus, and she was finally going to meet Wes face to face. After months of talking and exchanging photographs, they would be in the same room. It seemed surreal to her.

"It's been almost a year since I've seen them. I really hope my grandbaby remembers me." The woman stopped to take a breath and then asked, "Where are you heading to?

"Kansas City," Finley pause and then added, "To meet my boyfriend."

"How sweet. How did you meet?"

Finley thought about her answer, wondering what the woman would think. Finally, she said, "He started messaging me on Instagram."

CHAPTER 2

WHEN SHE GOT off the bus, Finley looked around the busy station. She did not see the boy she had been talking to online but about the time she began to panic, a man approached.

"Are you Finley?" the stranger asked.

"Who are you?"

"I'm Hudson. My boy, Wes asked me to pick you up. He had to work today and asked me to take you to see him. He wasn't kidding, you really are pretty."

The hair on the back of Finley's neck prickled, but she looked at the old man, shook off her concerns and said, "Okay."

Finley followed Hudson to his truck and climbed in with her backpack securely on her lap. She looked out the window and watched the people walking on the broken sidewalks. After a short drive, Hudson pulled into the driveway of a house that looked to be abandoned.

"Where are we?"

Hudson evaded the question and said, "Wes works here part-time taking care of an old man. Come on inside with me."

Finley hesitated. Wes hadn't told her he took care of an old man, but Hudson said it was part-time, so maybe Wes had forgotten to mention it. Hudson was on the porch by the time Finley got out of the truck. He looked back and motioned for her to come inside.

"Here, let me get the door," Hudson said.

Finley walked in and heard the distinct sound of a lock click behind her. She turned back towards the door, but Hudson grabbed her and pushed her into a dark room. A hand covered her mouth when Finley started to scream.

"No one will hear," Hudson said. "And even if they did, they wouldn't help you."

Hudson began to grab at Finley's clothes, but he wasn't prepared as she struggled under his hands. Her backpack had fallen to the ground, and Finley knew if she could get to it, she could get away. She kicked and pushed Hudson's hands away, doing everything she could to keep him from getting under her clothing. Tiring of the fight, Hudson put his hands around her neck and squeezed.

"I didn't want it to be like this."

Finley barely heard the words as she faded into the darkness. She did not know how long she had been in the house when she regained consciousness. Finley grabbed at her body, noticing the rips in her shirt and bare skin below her waist. Finley's body ached from the struggle and the violation. She moved quickly and quietly, feeling around in the dark for her bag and jeans, careful not to wake the sleeping man beside her. With her bag and jeans in her hands, she tiptoed from the room, unlocked the front door, and began to run.

ACKNOWLEDGMENTS

To all my family and friends who continue to believe in, support, and encourage me on this writing journey, thank you. This past year has not been an easy one, but you kept me moving forward even when it sometimes seemed easier to just stop.

To my friend and editor Kimberly Hanson. Thank you for the time, effort, and skill you put into this manuscript – especially when you have such a full and busy life! I value your time, insight, guidance, contribution, and friendship! This novel is the polished piece it is because of you.

To my cover artist, Jaycee, at Sweet N' Spicy Designs. You continue to amaze me with your talent and ability to make my rough vision an unbelievable reality!

And finally, an enormous thank you to my readers. Thank you for taking a chance on these books and being so patient for this one to be released. I hope you find as much joy in reading this story as I did in writing it! And in case you were wondering, I have already started book 4!

For more information on how to respond to victims of sexual assault please visit www.startbybelieving.org.

ABOUT THE AUTHOR

CJ Johnson was born and raised in the mid-west and spent over ten years working for a major metropolitan police department with the last six spent as a detective in the Sex Crimes Section of the Special Victims Unit. Passionate about her work, she fought hard for justice for every victim – especially those others often overlooked.

In 2012, she left the high-stress, fast paced career of law enforcement investigations to spend more time with her family. As a nationally recognized subject matter expert on sexual assault investigations, she focused on developing and executing training curriculum focusing on sex crime investigations to law enforcement agencies and their officers for the state of North Carolina.

She continues to play an active role in her mission to end interpersonal violence through training, volunteerism, and leading a team of investigators for an organization with an aligned mission while working on the *City of Fountains* series.

BOOKS BY C.J. JOHNSON

FEATURING FRANKIE THOMAS

Thorns of Deceit

No Stone Unturned

Across State Lines

Moonglow Road

Visit:

https://www.cjjohnsonbooks.com

9 7 9 8 9 8 9 9 9 9 6 4 4